Oyster Spat

A Sylvia Avery Mystery

BOOK FIVE

Jan Bono

Sandridge Publications
Long Beach, Washington

This is a work of fiction. Names, characters, places, and incidents are either the product of the author's imagination or are used fictitiously, and any resemblance to actual persons, living or dead, business establishments, events, or locales is entirely coincidental.

Copyright © 2020 by Jan Bono

All rights reserved. No part of the contents of this book may be reproduced, transmitted, or performed in any form, by any means, including recording or by any information storage and retrieval system, except for brief quotations embodied in critical articles or reviews, without written permission from the author.

First Printing, Summer, 2020

Printed in the United States of America
Gorham Printing, Centralia, WA 98531

Sandridge Publications
P.O. Box 278
Long Beach, WA 98631

http://www.JanBonoBooks.com

ISBN: 978-0-9906148-9-0

OYSTER SPAT

DEDICATED

to the men and women
who work in any and all of the sustainable
commercial fishery industries.
Thanks for dinner!

OTHER BOOKS BY JAN BONO

Sylvia Avery Mystery Series:
Book 1, Bottom Feeders
Book 2, Starfish
Book 3, Crab Bait
Book 4, Hook, Line, & Sinker

Health and Fitness:
Back from Obesity:
My 252-pound Weight-loss Journey

Collections of humorous personal experience:
Through My Looking Glass: View from the Beach
Through My Looking Glass: Volume II
It's Christmas!
Forty-three stories and three one-act plays
Just Joshin'
A Year in the Life of a Not-so-ordinary 4th Grade Kid

Fiction:
Romance 101:
Forty-two Sweet, Light, Delicious, G-Rated Short Stories

Poetry Chapbooks:
Bar Talk and *Chasing Rainbows*

A number of Jan's books are now available as eBooks at Smashwords.com. Find them at:

http://www.smashwords.com/profile/view/JanBonoBooks

OYSTER SPAT

NORTH BEACH PENINSULA

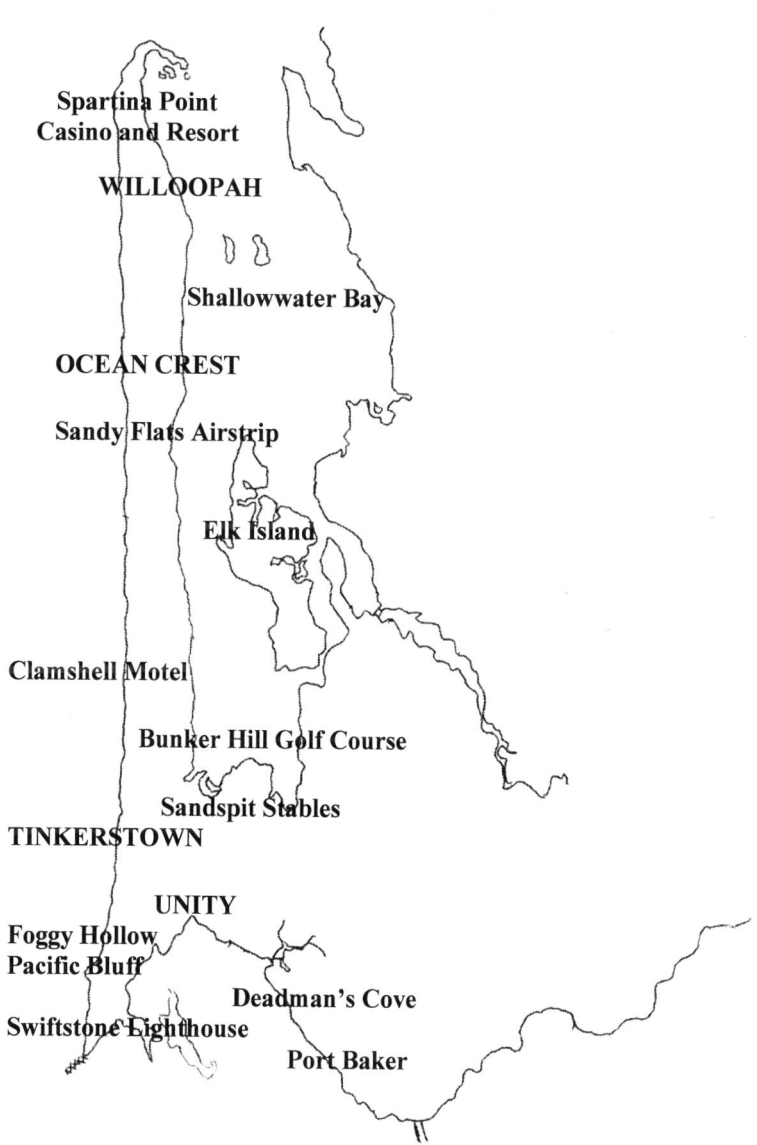

JAN BONO

OYSTER SPAT

OYSTER SPAT

CHAPTER 1

I peered out from behind the privacy curtain on the window separating the main congregational area from the small room provided for family and close friends. I felt like a peeping Tom, secretly spying on the unsuspecting mourners arriving for the memorial service. From my hidden viewpoint I could tell how well our departed friend had been loved in this community, and how much she'd be missed.

The church was tastefully decorated for Christmas—just a few weeks away—with evergreen boughs and well over a hundred bright red poinsettias. Somehow it seemed almost wrong to look forward to the Christmas festivities when there was someone no longer with us to celebrate.

I watched as a man in a long dark robe and satin sash set a beautiful ceramic urn on the altar. He arranged an 11"x20" photo and a few smaller things next to it, reverently displaying the honored items with care. "That must be Father Bishop," I said to no one in particular.

Orpha tugged insistently on my sleeve. "Make up your mind," she said. "Is he a father or is he a bishop? I don't think bishops are allowed to have kids, so if he's a bishop, then it's probably safe to say he's not a father."

I kept my sigh to myself and patiently explained. "His

name is Father Allan Bishop. He is the North Beach Peninsula's Catholic Priest."

"So now he's a priest?" asked Orpha. Her eyebrows shot up above her gold-rimmed glasses. She shook her over-permed, fuzzy gray hair adamantly. "So when did that happen?"

Thankfully, before our conversation could dissolve any further into another convoluted version of Abbott and Costello's "Who's on First?" comedy routine, Kanji stepped through the side entrance in a smartly tailored, dark blue suit.

"Ahhh! My loveliest of ladies! I have found you!" He looked directly into my eyes he as spoke, but he bowed respectfully toward Orpha as if talking only to her.

Tall, dark, and indisputably handsome, Kanjirappally Kumera, one of our community's newest semi-retired residents, never missed an opportunity to display his most impeccable manners. And since Orpha Starr, at 90, is the eldest member of The Veiled Rainbow, our local geriatric belly dancing troupe, he would naturally address her first.

He gallantly offered Orpha his elbow. "My dear Mrs. Starr, I would be so honored as to be allowed to be your escort into the nave today."

"Did you say there's a knave?" said Orpha, tucking her tiny, withered hand into the crook of Kanji's arm. "Which one is he? You'll have to point him out."

I smiled with unreserved gratitude at Kanji. The service was going to be pretty stressful on all of us, but bless his heart, he was doing what he could to make everything run more smoothly by stepping up to take a turn at "Orpha duty."

Riding herd on the ladies of the dancing troupe usually fell to me. My name is Sylvia Lee Avery, and since I'm a freshly retired Child Protective Services social worker, the troupe must think I'm the best suited to handle this type of job. As Meredith, the leader of this feisty gang of hip janglers often says, "If anything goes wrong, Sylvia's responsible."

I could probably take offense at that, but since Meredith is also my mother, I understand she might be onto something.

The church was filling up. I could see the first two rows had been corded off for those of us gathering in the family room, and I irrationally wished I didn't have any reason to be here. The five ladies of the Veiled Rainbow ranged in age from 68 to 90, so my rational mind knew that the odds were strong I'd be saying goodbye to at least three or four more of them before my own number was called, but funerals and memorials just aren't my idea of a very good time.

The ancient church organist started playing on the ancient church organ. It was a quiet hymn, and slightly familiar, but I couldn't recall the name of it, or any of the words. No surprise, as I wasn't exactly a frequent attender of any religious gathering, but it comforted me that at least I could hum along if I had to. Instinctively, I knew the hymn was simply background noise, an unspoken signal for everyone that it was time to take our seats.

An usher from the mortuary opened the door, looked at me, and nodded. I, in turn, looked at Goodie, the only one of us who was undeniably Catholic, and the only one among us who knew exactly how these things normally functioned.

Goodie Godwin stood up from her seat on one of the couches, cleared her throat, and determinedly pulled herself to her full and mighty height of 5'5", which really wasn't all that much, but bless her heart for attempting to take charge. I had a strong feeling I'd be doing a lot of heart blessing today, and was glad we could all surround ourselves with this unorthodox, but very special kind of support system.

"Well," Goodie addressed the group, "I guess it's time to

go in and say goodbye to our dear friend Deenie." She turned to Meredith, who was holding tight to Lester's arm. "You go first, okay?"

Merri nodded. "Of course, Goodie. That makes perfect sense. First red, then orange, then yellow, and then…" And then her voice cracked with emotion, and she abruptly stopped speaking, placing a hand over her mouth in grief.

"Blue and violet will follow behind yellow," said Lester.

I silently gave thanks for Lester's presence, and blessed his heart too for speaking right up. Only a few months ago, when several of the—uh, rather "mature" ladies—had decided to try online dating, Meredith had accidentally found, then reconnected with, Sylvester Woods, a.k.a. Lester, a.k.a. Les, a.k.a. my biological father, whom she hadn't seen since having a short relationship with him back in the days of what we now refer to as "free love."

They'd both been thrilled to find each other again, and I'd been in total shock. Now I was getting used to the idea of having a real live father around, and I liked it a lot.

Lester helped Meredith put her red chiffon dancing veil around her neck, draped tastefully as she would any scarf made of more traditional winter cloth, and they lined up first at the door.

Orpha, wearing a similar orange veil scarf and escorted by Kanji, stepped into the spot behind them, and I couldn't help but smile. "Orange is the color of rust," Orpha often said with pride, "and since I'm the oldest, it's only fitting."

Goodie looked around the room as if she'd lost her best friend, which in this case, she had. I quickly moved forward and took her hand in mine.

"May I walk with you, Sunshine?" I asked, affectionately using her belly dancing nickname. She nodded, wrapped her yellow silk scarf around her neck, and gratefully clung to me as we took up position number three to leave the room.

OYSTER SPAT

Next came Nova Johanssen, escorted by Rich Morgan. Blue was Nova's color; the color of the open sea. Nova is a Dungeness crab fisher, and Rich is a salmon and sturgeon charter boat captain, and although their match happened under extremely difficult circumstances, we all heartily approve of their union.

Seeing Nova and Rich together in clothes other than those they normally wear for work at the port docks gave me pause. Although I'd seen Nova in her belly dancing attire, I realized I'd never seen Rich without his Captain Morgan's Charters ball cap. I smiled, thinking that they both cleaned up well, and were apparently a good influence on each other.

Jimmy Noble, the manager of the Clamshell Motel, had recently been recruited to run the sound for the ladies when they performed, and lo and behold, he either didn't get the message about toning down his wardrobe for the service, or he just didn't care. Head to toe, he was fully decked out in shades of lavender and purple, including a turban and pointy-toed slippers.

I smiled and shook my head. Only our Jimmy could pull this look off at a memorial service, or anywhere else for that matter, and maybe he was just what the group needed most today—a bit of comic relief. I guess I should have been thankful he hadn't shown up in an embroidered poodle skirt. A parade of colorful poodle skirts had been one of the options the Rainbow Girls had considered wearing to honor Nadine's penchant for dressing in authentic 1950's attire.

The walk down the aisle seemed endless; my shoes felt like they'd been filled with cement. Each of the Rainbow Ladies solemnly nodded to many of those seated, or briefly squeezed their hands as we walked past. It surprised me how many faces I recognized myself, and I did my share of acknowledging many mourners with a nod or a small smile as well.

Lester, Kanji, Rich and I settled our colorful troupe into the row closest to the altar and slid in behind them in the second pew. I ended up on the end, next to Kanji. He reached down and gave my hand a gentle squeeze, then released it. To be honest, it would have been okay with me if he'd continued holding my hand, but I realized why he'd released it a few seconds later.

Deputy Frederick Morgan, Rich's son, and my much-younger, part-time maybe boyfriend, arrived in full uniform and attempted to slide into the pew next to me. We all wiggled tighter together in order to give him enough room, and I momentarily wondered if Father Bishop had rules about guns inside the church.

Freddy had obviously not left his service revolver secured in his car, and it pressed hard against my thigh. An irreverent thought almost gave me a bad case of the giggles as I scooted over, and I bit down hard on my lower lip to keep from saying something hopelessly inappropriate for the time and place.

It was rather awkward sitting between the two men on this planet I most loved and cherished, but it was also very comforting. I turned and gave Freddy a quick smile, then looked back over our shoulders at the packed church behind us.

Directly behind me sat Felicity Michaels, a good friend and high school history teacher, and her recently acquired English teacher boyfriend, Mark. Next to them were Bim and Geri, partners and co-owners of the Sandy Bottom Coffee Cup. After that, the sea of faces was a blur, and I turned back around, working hard to swallow the lump in my throat.

Father Bishop came into view again, followed by Nadine's much younger boyfriend, Patrick O'Leary. I smiled. When Patrick first came on the scene, it was through an online dating app. A little background check provided by

OYSTER SPAT

Sheriff Donaldson had revealed his birth name was Patrick Paulsen, but he had legally changed it to avoid any confusion with the Patrick Paulsen who had run for President back in the 80s, or maybe so he would sound more Irish, as if his graying red hair and beard weren't enough.

I couldn't fault Patrick for wanting to put his best foot forward. It must have been hard for him to appear desirable, or even respectable, given that back then he lived in his van and gave seances for a living. Nevertheless, Patrick had turned out to be one heckuva stand-up kind of guy, and just what 80-year-old Nadine had needed as she neared the end of her life.

Father Bishop sat to the left, waiting for the organist to finish, and Patrick took his place in the chair behind the lectern to our right. Patrick had a multi-shades-of-green scarf wrapped and knotted around his neck. He looked strangely relaxed. When our eyes met, he gave me a wink, a thumbs up, and a lopsided grin.

Kanji leaned over and spoke softly, but loud enough so that Freddy and I could both hear him, and I wouldn't have to repeat what he said. "I do believe Mr. O'Leary has appropriately medicated himself for the tribulations of his solemn responsibility."

"You mean he's stoned?" Freddy asked incredulously.

I stifled a small snort. I wouldn't have expected any less from the guy the gals had affectionately nicknamed Paranormal Patrick.

The organist finally completed the 8th or 9th repetition of the slowest hymn ever performed, and Father Bishop stood and welcomed us all. After a short prayer, he introduced Patrick as "Nadine's very special friend," and the person who would be giving the eulogy.

Patrick stood and adjusted his microphone. "Our beloved Nadine Larsen, our little green environmentalist, has gone to that big ecologically-friendly pasture in the sky, and she has tasked me with reading her eulogy, which she dictated to me in the weeks before her passing. So I ask you to please remember, these are Nadine's words, not mine." He self-consciously cleared his throat. "Don't blame me, I'm just the messenger."

A murmur of acknowledgement and appreciation went through the crowd.

Patrick took a big breath and began. "Nadine NMN Larsen, was born in Seattle, Washington, some 80 years ago." The crowd mumbled among itself. Patrick paused, and his brow wrinkled in deep thought. "Oh! I'm so sorry. NMN means No Middle Name." He frowned. "Nadine's parents never put a middle name on her birth certificate, and she didn't want anyone to think she was ashamed of some hideous moniker, so she insisted on being clear about that." He grinned again. "If there's anything else you don't understand, just raise your hand, and I'll straighten it right out. I've never done this before, so please be patient with me."

Chuckles rippled throughout the church.

As Patrick began reading a little about Nadine growing up in the north Seattle 'burbs, her accomplishments in science classes "even though she was a girl," and her earliest years, I kind of zoned out. But I quickly zoned back in when he mentioned her military service.

"Nadine was proud to have served in the Army Nurse Corps in Vietnam, although she believed it may have been what ultimately killed her, and she lived another 50 years before the disease took her, give or take."

Patrick didn't elaborate, so I made a note to ask him about it later. As far as I knew, Nadine had died of Non-Hodgkins Lymphoma, and I wondered if she had been one of those who were sprayed with Agent Orange, which was a supposed "harmless to humans" weed killer used to knock down the heavy jungle vegetation in Vietnam. Too late, it was discovered that Agent Orange had very nasty, sooner-or-later lethal, side effects for those who were accidentally covered with the toxic chemicals during their military service.

"Nadine returned to Seattle from Vietnam at loose ends, but she was just in time to get in on the ground floor of the Greenpeace movement," continued Patrick. "No, she wasn't lucky enough to be in the old fishing boat named The Greenpeace that opposed the U.S. underground nuclear testing at Amchitka Island in Alaska, but she joined up as a direct result of the efforts of those brave, original activists.

"Saving the environment became Nadine's passion." Patrick stopped again to smile his goofy smile. "It's why she chose the color green as her rainbow color, and why she drove a smart car, and why she liked to help out during the Grassroots Garbage Gang beach cleanups, and probably why she chose to forego artificial or chemical solutions to her cancer, choosing instead to smoke a quantity of natural weed to ease her pain." He looked fondly at the scarf around his neck. "Nadine was a woman who really walked the walk."

I was pretty sure I couldn't meet either Kanji's or Freddy's eyes at the moment without busting up laughing, so I just stared straight ahead at the beautiful urn, then at the photo of Nadine up on the altar. I thought of all her good deeds on this planet, and fully appreciated the depth of her commitment.

Patrick looked up from his notes. "As most of you know, Nadine chose not to do chemo, and not just because she hated being bombarded with manmade chemicals. Even when I told her she could be a real fashionista with a colorful assortment of wigs and hats, Nadine was just too vain to lose her hair."

Laughter erupted throughout the church. Orpha turned around, and in a voice loud enough for everyone to hear said, "How many times did I tell her that her driver's license should have come with a color wheel?"

As the laughter subsided, Patrick returned to the script. "Nadine has included a couple... uh... okay, there are three and a half, 'suggestions' that mention a few of you by name." While he waited for more twitters to subside, he took another deep breath. "Now remember, I'm just the messenger."

For some reason, his words made me start to squirm in my seat.

"Number One: Felicity should hang onto Mark. I don't know if they teach you in school how to recognize a good man, but this guy is a keeper."

I couldn't turn far enough around to see the looks on the faces of either Felicity or Mark sitting behind me, but I was pretty sure Felix had already come to that very same conclusion.

"Number Two: Merri, you need to make sure The Veiled Rainbow keeps dancing. It kept me in pretty good overall shape, and made me feel young enough to start dating again, and that turned out great—just great—being as how I found myself the best boyfriend ever in the process."

None of us could deny her words. Paranormal Patrick had been the most perfect companion for Deenie that any of us could ever have imagined. He'd steadfastly hung in there, even after he learned she had terminal cancer, kept her secret until it could no longer be hidden, and had taken wonderful care of her, morning, noon, and night.

"Number Two Point Five." Patrick looked a little embarrassed, but, bless his heart, he read it directly from the paper anyway: "Meredith, Patrick promised he would take over dancing in the green rainbow position if you want him

OYSTER SPAT

to."

Meredith was nodding and trying to smile and wiping her eyes all at the same time.

"And Number Three: Sylvia, would you make up your mind, already?!"

I wanted to crawl under my pew, but I was pretty sure it would turn out to be quite crowded under there, as both Kanji and Freddy had suddenly stiffened in their seats, and not in what I'd call a good way.

"Moving on," said Patrick. "As you all know, Nadine was cremated." He walked to the front of the altar and stood next to the urn. He put two fingers to his lips and lightly touched the side of the urn. "I'm doing the best I can, Deenie, honey."

Then he picked up a necklace that I hadn't been able to see from my seat in the second row of pews.

"Deenie had a small portion of her ashes mixed with flecks of colored glass and tiny clear prisms and put into five necklace pendants so they will refract a rainbow when a bright light is aimed at them."

He held up one of the necklaces for all to see. It was about two inches long, and one inch wide, and in the shape of a cross. Then he came out to the first row of pews and handed one each to Merri, Orpha, Goodie and Nova. The fifth one he put reverently around his own neck.

"Now she will always remain close to our hearts. The remainder of her ashes will be dispersed in Shallowwater Bay, an ecosystem she fought hard to protect, on a yet-to-be-determined future date. Nadine NMN Larsen desires to be 'at one' with nature."

I didn't have to look around to know there was not a dry eye in the front two rows, maybe not even in the whole church.

Father Bishop got up again, and led us in the 23rd Psalm.

It came as a pleasant surprise that I remembered almost all the words, and that both Kanji and Freddy were also familiar enough with the passage that they could keep up with the regular congregation. Then Father Bishop invited us to the church's reception room for "snacks and beverages."

At the mention of food and drink, Patrick suddenly jumped back up to the microphone and quickly added, "Wait! I almost forgot! Nadine made me pinky-swear promise not to put any, uh, you know, 'funny stuff' into the cookies, so I didn't."

Amid giggles, knowing smiles, and a few tears, we stood and departed row by row for the adjoining reception room.

OYSTER SPAT

CHAPTER 2

After Patrick's impromptu proclamation of pot-free cookies, we were all in a pretty good mood when we went through the double-wide doors into the reception hall. The conviviality of the gathering was added to by Mercedes, who had come down from the Spartina Point Casino and Resort at the north end of the peninsula to play the piano for the reception. She was decked out in every imaginable shade of green sequins, including the rims of her Elton John sunglasses, and was happily tinkling the ivories with gusto.

Mercedes is Sheriff Donaldson's main squeeze, and he had dropped her off a little earlier, electing to stay out and about, protecting the rest of the county so that Freddy could feel free to attend the service. The sheriff's department is small and spread out over a large area, but with a substantial cadre of volunteer deputies, our crime rate stays relatively low.

There was a bottleneck of people right inside the door where Patrick was installed as official greeter and one-man reception line. He dutifully shook each hand, thanked them for coming, and told them to please enjoy the refreshments.

"Oh thank goodness!" he said the moment he saw me. "I was beginning to think I was in the wrong room or something. I don't think I know a tenth of these people."

I smiled and shook his hand. "Nadine was well-loved in our community," I said. "And you did an especially fine job up there at the lectern. I've never had to do anything like that myself; it must have been pretty tough."

Patrick smiled ear to ear, leaned in close to me and whispered, "I promised Nadine no pot cookies at the reception, but I never promised I wouldn't make myself a memorial warm-up batch of the good kind."

I impulsively hugged him. "You earned them," I said, and I meant it. Then I moved on into the big reception room, caught Mercedes' eye, and waved. She tootled her fingers back at me, never missing a note on the keyboard. I don't know exactly how she manages that, but then again, the only thing I can play with any proficiency is the radio.

I picked up an oval paper plate and joined the food line. I'm not sure why I'd worked up such a crazy wild appetite just sitting and listening to the story of Nadine's life, but I was feeling hungry, with a capital H. In fact, I was so hungry I decided to skip the main dishes and loaded my plate only with those things that contained a large amount of sugar. I helped myself to several kinds of cookies, pie, and cake, then found a seat among a long group of tables where The Veiled Rainbow was apparently holding court.

"Did you ever see so many yummy goodies?" asked Meredith, staring at my plate as I pulled a chair up beside her. I gave her a stern warning look that clearly told her to keep her hands off my treats—*or else!*

"The Catholic ladies are famous for trying to outdo each other in the baking arena," I replied. "And any occasion, happy or sad, gives them a chance to show off their skills, while giving the community a chance to enjoy every last morsel." I dramatically took a big bite of a cinnamon-coated Snickerdoodle and licked my lips.

"Speaking of Goodie," said Orpha, from across the table, "I've been wondering where she's going to live now that Nadine has passed. It was Nadine's house, after all."

OYSTER SPAT

The hush that fell over the group was nearly deafening, and all eyes turned to look at Goodie, who, like everyone else in the room, had overheard Orpha's well-meaning, but poorly timed, question.

"I really don't know what's to become of me," Goodie began. "When I sold my own house to Kanji and moved in with Nadine, I thought I'd live out my life right there with Patrick and her."

Patrick's timing was unquestioningly better than Orpha's, and he arrived at the table just in time to catch the gist of the conversation. He went over and stood behind Goodie, squeezed her shoulders, and gave her a quick kiss on top of her head.

"Have no fear, my little Goodie-two-shoes, my ray of sunshine, my once hesitant but now fully committed to sharing the remote control roommate. Nadine provided well for both of us in her will."

"She did?" Goodie strained to look up over the top of her head at him.

"She did," replied Patrick. Then he walked to the head of the table so he could address everyone in our group at once. "I wasn't going to drop this little bombshell on anyone here today, but since it's a very happy kind of bombshell, I suppose now is as good a time as any."

I looked from face to face, wondering what kind of a bombshell we were in for next. Every eye of the Rainbow Girls and their escorts was glued to Patrick, and he'd attracted the attention of some of the other attendees at nearby tables as well. I know that I, for one, was holding my breath, wondering what was going to come out of his mouth that would justifiably qualify as a bombshell, good or bad.

Patrick took a deep gulp of air and grinned sheepishly. "Okay... Here goes..." Then he froze, second guessing himself. "Or maybe it would be better to talk about this when we have a little, uh," he looked around at all the ears at all the other tables leaning his way, "a little more privacy."

"You want us to have some privacy?" asked Orpha, eagerly looking to stir up some excitement. "Then meet me in the bathroom and we can do all our talking in there!"

Orpha's statement was a ridiculous idea, and even in Patrick's "medically enhanced" condition, he realized she was just pulling his leg.

"Okay, well, I'm not going to do that, Orpha, no offense or anything, so I guess I should stop stalling and just tell y'all that Deenie and I got married a couple weeks ago."

A big burst of "What?!" "What the hell?" "Oh my god!" and "What in tarnation's sake are you talking about, boy?" erupted simultaneously from everyone at the table, quickly followed by the ladies firing individual questions at Patrick, machine gun style.

"When?" asked Nova.

"Where?" asked Meredith.

"Why didn't she tell us?" asked Goodie.

"How come we all weren't invited?" asked Orpha.

I noticed the Rainbow Gals were all talking at once, while the men seemed to have been struck mute. Must be another one of those gender specific differences, I thought.

Patrick held up his hands for silence. "Nadine warned me that a few of you might be a little mad after I told you about this."

"Mad?" said Goodie, a bit indignantly, but wiping her eyes with a paper napkin. "No, I'm not mad, Patrick. I'm just sad she didn't even tell me, her roommate and alleged best friend, that she'd decided to take the marriage plunge again."

Meredith reached over and patted Goodie's hand. "I'm sure she had her reasons, hon."

Patrick nodded. "Deenie didn't want to make a big deal out of it. We got married so that there'd be no question of me inheriting the house. In Washington, spousal inheritance is a done deal, and—" He smiled directly at Goodie. "And I inherited the house on the contingency that you, and Stella, and Adolph, can live there with me for the rest of your lives, or as long as you all choose to live there."

At the mention of Stella, Nadine's special needs black and white Papillon, and Adolph, a German Shepherd that was more scaredy cat than guard dog until the moment it really mattered, Goodie's face crumpled and her shoulders shook with big, heaving sobs.

"I'm sorry, Goodie," said Patrick, and it was clear to everyone that he was truly sincere. "Deenie knew you'd all want to be there, and her health was fading so fast at that point she just wasn't up to more than a quick trip to the courthouse where we got the license and stood before the judge in his chambers. He was very accommodating, and waived the waiting period due to our 'special circumstances.' Please forgive her, Goodie—and forgive me, too."

"Well," said Orpha. "Good thing Nadine wasn't a Catholic, or you two would have had to attend pre-nuptial classes for months, and promise the Father Bishop Priest Nave guy that you'd raise your children Catholic, and eat the wafers and drink the kool-aid, and wear out your knees genuflecting when you come in or go out of the church and all that other froo-froo ritual stuff before allowing any marriage knot to be tied."

Even Goodie managed to smile at Orpha's messed up understanding of some of the tenets of the Catholic faith.

"Nadine was not a Catholic?" asked Kanji, speaking for the first time since Patrick shared his shocking news. "How is that so, since Nadine's most beautiful service was held here in this most welcoming and open arms friendly Catholic church?"

I shook my head. "Goodie is the only practicing Catholic

in the group. But Nadine attended catechism growing up, so Goodie insisted that the service be held here, and Patrick agreed." I smiled, then added, "And I think Father Bishop enjoyed seeing the pews filled to capacity today, no matter what the occasion."

Orpha heard what I said to Kanji and added that there are more recovering Catholics than practicing Catholics on the peninsula. "Really!" she concluded. "There ought to be a 12-step program for 'used to be' Catholics."

While the rest of us mulled that over, Orpha smiled and continued mischievously, "You know, that's a pretty good idea, if I do say so myself." She bobbed her tightly permed silver curls up and down again for emphasis. "Twelve steps—one for every apostle."

Sometimes I'm sure Orpha's gone around the bend and isn't coming back, and at other times I think she's the sharpest one of us all. This time it was definitely a combination of the two.

After successfully navigating the shock of Nadine and Patrick's secret marriage, the group started telling Nadine stories. Most I'd heard, but some were new to me, and I attentively listened to a life well lived with genuine awe and fondness. In the end, I found I knew next to nothing about her time in Vietnam; everything about her time in The Veiled Rainbow; and perhaps half of what was shared about her Greenpeace days.

Lester told the lion's share about "Deenie-bo-beanie's" time in Greenpeace. As it turned out, they'd both worked for the organization in Seattle shortly after Nadine returned from Vietnam. But they, too, had lost track of each other in the ensuing years, and only just reconnected when Les and Meredith found each other again, and Merrie had brought him to one of Kanji's exotic dinners over at the Clamshell Motel in October.

OYSTER SPAT

They say you can take the activist out of Greenpeace, but Greenpeace will always be inside the activist. At least it was sure that way with Nadine. There wasn't an environmental cause on the peninsula she didn't continue to champion throughout her so-called retirement. She wrote postcards to our government officials, stood at the grocery store exits gathering signatures for petitions, and sat on the street corner by the post office holding a large sign encouraging others to "Call Congress Today!"

While most reminisces were on the lighter side, a few of them were real tear jerkers, and Goodie soon had a pile of used tissues on the table in front of her.

"You know," said Orpha, repeatedly jabbing her finger across the table to point at the tissues, "more of us are going to be dying, Goodie, so you really should invest in a hanky. They're washable, which in this case is the same as recyclable, so I'm sure Nadine would approve."

Thankfully, Bim and Geri chose that moment to stop by the table to say goodbye, and no one had to respond to Orpha's suggestion that we have a stockpile of designated grieving hankies.

"Leaving?" I quickly asked Bim, quite unnecessarily.

"Yes," she replied. "The Sandy Bottom Coffee Cup can't stay closed all day, and we need to be getting back." She grinned. "And this afternoon, we've decided to finish out the workday in our tuxes." She spun around and flipped the tails as she did so. "Can't hurt to add a little class to the place now and then."

"I like it," I said, "but don't make a practice of it, or we'll all be too intimidated to hang out there in our t-shirts and jeans."

"We'll take that under consideration," said Bim. She lowered her voice. "But it wouldn't hurt your image any to put a dress on and glam it up every once in a while."

I had no comeback for that, and I didn't need one. It was a long-standing joke between us that I ought to let my more feminine side shine through now and then, and when that feeling struck, I had free access to any of her numerous wardrobe closets.

"What a beautiful funeral," said Geri, shaking Patrick's hand again.

"Technically," said Jimmy, joining us from another table just in time to put his two cents in, "a Funeral Service is a service held to memorialize a deceased person with their body present, and a Memorial Service is a service held to memorialize a deceased person with their body not present. So, since Nadine's cremation has already taken place, it's a memorial."

"Thank you, Mr. Encyclopedia," said Geri, rolling her eyes. "I stand corrected."

Bim's response was far less tactful. "Geez, Jiminy Cricket, give us a break, would you?"

Jimmy looked a tad uncomfortable and contritely bobbed his head. "Sorry, ladies," he mumbled. "I forget where I am sometimes."

"It's okay, Jimster." I put an arm around his shoulders. "We all know you mean well."

Jimmy was saved further embarrassment as the main crew from the Cinco Amigos Chinese Cuisine approached the table to pay their respects.

Juan, José, Fernando, Luis, and Julio are five guys who tired of the backbreaking labor out on the oyster flats on the north end of the peninsula and in the canneries on the southern end in Unity. So they got together and decided to pool their resources to open a centrally located ethnic restaurant in our community a few years ago.

The obvious choice would have been a Mexican eatery, but we have plenty of those here, so they opted to "wok their

OYSTER SPAT

way to culinary success" with a quality Chinese restaurant. Even in their wildest dreams, I don't know if they imagined how great that success would be, but good food always draws a crowd, and they're doing swell.

In the past few months, Jimmy and Julio had become special friends, and now Julio stepped forward and put his arms around Jimmy for a quick hug. "Nice outfit," he said, tongue-in-cheek.

Jimmy missed the tiny trace of sarcasm and beamed back at Julio. "I'm glad you like it."

Their touching sentimental moment was abruptly interrupted by a commotion in the back of the common room. Two male voices were shouting at each other loud enough to be heard above Mercedes' piano playing, despite the fact she was striking the keys more and more vigorously to mask their behavior.

When I looked over at Merc, she shrugged, threw up her hands, and abruptly stopped playing, since everyone's attention was already refocused on the brewing conflict.

Brent Booi and Tom Diamond, both oyster farmers who lived and worked in the tiny north end peninsula village of Willoopah, appeared close to duking it out.

I knew Brent and Tom had been classmates and friends 40 years ago, and had even joined the Navy together after graduation from Unity High. But since their return to the peninsula, the philosophical gaps between them had widened year by year. I'm sure they no longer considered themselves friends, but more like nemeses they were forced to tolerate.

"You got a helluva lot of nerve," said Brent, "showing up here today." He stood at one side of the table which had recently held the main dishes. He'd been folding up the tablecloth, getting ready to help put the tables and chairs away when Tom had approached him.

"Lorraine wouldn't think of not helping out in the church kitchen today," answered Tom, "I came along with her so we could both pay our respects, same as you." He stood with his hands in his pockets. He hadn't been coming over to lend a hand, but more than likely he'd deliberately seized an opportunity to push Brent's buttons.

Though on the surface, Tom's words sounded reasonable enough, the force at which he spit them at Brent underscored a much stronger, and less amicable, motivation. And quite possibly a little more than a snoot full of alcohol.

Brent scoffed. "As if you ever gave a damn about Nadine."

Tom's upper lip curled back, and he boisterously laughed in Brent's face. From the abrupt way Brent jerked his head back, it wasn't much of a stretch for me to confirm the smell of liquor on Tom's breath without actually smelling it myself.

"Well, you got me there! I came along because I wanted to see for myself that the little meddling Greenpeace gal is truly dead," said Tom. "Even you can't deny she caused all of us Shallowwater Bay oyster farmers enough grief for at least two lifetimes!"

While I sat like a deer in the headlights and watched as Brent's hands balled into fists, Freddy and Kanji had both leapt to their feet and were moving quickly to intercept the ruckus. Naturally, in his uniform and non-regulation cowboy boots, Deputy Frederick Morgan commanded Tom's attention, but it was Kanji, who worked part-time for Freddy as a hospitality specialist, bartender, and bouncer at the casino, who came at them from the side and pulled Tom away from Brent before the men could come to blows.

As if on cue, Tom's wife Lorraine came breezing through the door from the back room and took her husband by the elbow. "I need your help in the kitchen," she said, as if nothing was wrong. "We've got a lot of cleaning up and loading out to do." She deftly maneuvered herself between Tom and Brent and turned Tom toward the door she'd just come out.

Over her shoulder, Lorraine called back to The Veiled Rainbow, "I hope to see you all at the quilt show up at the casino next week." Then she turned to Freddy and said, "It was very generous of you to provide us with a display room for our crafters, Deputy Morgan."

Then Lorraine disappeared through the kitchen door and the breath I'd been subconsciously holding for about six hours came rushing out. I felt my shoulders slump with relief. The last thing any of us needed to make this day complete was a brawl between two oystermen inside the Catholic fellowship hall!

The ladies of the church were busy boxing up leftovers to be sent home with everyone who would take them. Naturally, there were plenty of cookies and brownies and pie for the taking. And among the most sought-after main dishes were the oyster casseroles that had been donated by Brent Booi, a most generous man. The Cinco Amigos had left trays of enchiladas, Bim and Geri had brought pastries from the coffee shop, and Lorraine Diamond had donated a lovely crab and cranberry salad and several blackberry pies.

The fracas at the back of the room effectively put an end to the reception, and we began gathering our coats, purses, and boxes of leftovers before moving toward the door.

Nova and Rich went back down to the port, Felicity and Mark returned Orpah to her assisted living apartment in Unity, and several of us made plans to head over to Jimmy's to "detox" from the memorial. In other words, I just wasn't ready to be alone with my thoughts and emotions today, and Jimmy's is always a good place to hang out.

"Can I hitch a ride to the Clamshell with you?" asked

Mercedes. "I just texted the sheriff and he said he can pick me up there later, so you don't need to drive me all the way back up to the north end."

I smiled at her. "I'd be happy to, Merc," I said. "Just as soon as I snag one of those apple turnovers from the Sandy Bottom Coffee Cup."

"Make it two!" said Mercedes as she boxed up her microphone. "And a few of those biscotti, if there are any left! The sheriff just loves biscotti with his morning coffee!"

It was far more information than I wanted, but I simply nodded that I'd heard her and headed for the kitchen without saying anything more.

OYSTER SPAT

CHAPTER 3

The Clamshell Motel manager's office was everyone's home away from home—if that particular place happened to be built of 1960's cinderblock construction and sported one main room divided by linoleum on one half the floor and an aging shag carpet on the other. But Jimmy, the manager of the derelict 6-unit complex, was an amicable host, and there was always plenty of coffee and diet soda handy when any of us gathered midway up the peninsula for a friendly rendezvous.

Over the past nine months, some configuration of family and friends had put our heads together around the red Formica table on the kitchen side of his apartment to figure out certain puzzling crimes and local mysteries. Like how illicit drugs were being smuggled up the peninsula, or who'd murdered two people on a television movie set, or what had happened to a missing crab boat fisherman, or which, if any, of the millionaire belly dancers had committed insurance fraud, and which, if any, dating profiles were "safe enough" for The Veiled Rainbow Gals to consider meeting the men who advertised for love online.

Jimmy got up from the table to get Mercedes a cup of coffee when we entered through the door leading from the tiny motel check-in lobby. He knew better than to offer me any coffee right then, as caffeine doesn't agree with me in the afternoon. Freddy, the cop with a cast iron stomach, was already seated at the table, enjoying a cup of joe, and Kanji was busy unloading a box of leftovers from the memorial service into the refrigerator.

Kanji's smile, always warm and inviting, penetrated deep inside my heart when he caught my eye over the top of the fridge door and slowly winked. His intimate greeting meant just for me, made me suddenly feel all fluttery and fuzzy.

"Would my dear Miss Sylvia care for a caffeine free diet cola?" he asked, turning from the fridge and holding up a can of my favorite brand of soda from Jimmy's ever-present stash.

Without waiting for my response, he graciously opened the can and set it on the table at what was traditionally accepted as "my spot" to sit. I plopped down into the chair and smiled my thanks up at him before lifting my can to the group in salute. "To Nadine."

"To Nadine," echoed Freddy, Kanji, Jimmy and Mercedes.

I took a big swig of soda, then sighed. "What an incredibly long day."

"And it's only 3:30," said Jimmy.

"Well, I'm sure glad I'm not going to be singing at the casino lounge tonight," said Mercedes, kicking off her strappy heels underneath the table. "I don't think I've got it in me anymore to perform all afternoon and then sing half the night away too."

"Be sure to thank your generous boss for the extra time off," said Freddy.

Mercedes barely kept from snorting coffee out her nose, but caught herself just in time. "Thank you, my most generous boss." She inclined her head and made a rolling motion in front of her with her hand as if she were bowing to some type of esteemed royalty.

OYSTER SPAT

Merc wasn't the only one still adjusting to the way Deputy Morgan had suddenly found himself the owner of the Spartina Point Casino and Resort. Even Freddy himself had been taken by surprise. But it turned out to be a very good thing for the community, the economy, the tourists, and even the county's law enforcement, for a man of his background and caliber of professionalism to be the one who took the reins after his shady uncle's untimely demise.

Kanji had broken down the large cardboard boxes and added them to Jimmy's recyclables in the motel lobby before joining us at the table. Now he slid into the seat next to me, and for the second time in one day, I found myself sitting between the two most eligible, and dare I say most attractive, men on the peninsula.

Kanjirappally Kumera, a former insurance fraud investigator now semi-retired at 60, was quite a catch all right—not only tall, dark, and handsome, with impeccable manners and a smooth, lyrical voice. I was sure I would never tire of listening to that voice. And in addition, he was a genuinely compassionate man who heard you with his whole heart, anticipated everyone's needs, and never failed to do and say exactly the right thing at exactly the right time.

On the other hand, Frederick Morgan was also quite easy on the eyes, not as tall, but with enough Native American blood to be just as dark and handsome at 45, with a quick wit, a bountiful spirit, and integrity in spades. Freddy had been born and raised on the peninsula, and was fully committed to the community's "progress," but not at the expense of its natural beauty and pristine ecology. He was generous beyond belief, and took most things in stride, even when it looked like those things weren't going the way he hoped they would.

I smiled to myself as I compared the men who vied for my affection. In truth, they were more alike than different, with the most obvious difference being in their ages. Kanji was close to five years my senior, and Freddy, somewhere around 12 years my junior, but I was the only one of us who seemed to find that a possible roadblock to our continued relationship. I sighed. Who knew that in my mid to late 50s I'd be lucky enough to have my choice of two such fine men?

"And speaking of my music this afternoon," said Mercedes, abruptly bringing me back from my reverie, "who were those two guys causing all the fuss at the reception? Were they purposely trying to drown me out?"

I chose only to respond to the first one of her questions. "The short answer is that Tom Diamond and Brent Booi are rival oystermen up in Willoopah."

"So what were they arguing about?" asked Merc.

"Who knows?" I shrugged. "I don't think they even need a reason anymore."

"Well it's a pity they had to be so rude at the reception," said Merc. "Churches are supposed to be holy places, not places to air your grudges and petty grievances."

I wanted to ask Mercedes when she'd suddenly gotten religion, but I held my tongue because I couldn't, and wouldn't, disagree with what she was saying.

"Those two should have just left their differences at the door," said Freddy. "The afternoon was about Nadine, not about whatever fire they wanted to fan."

"I agree, 100 percent," said Kanji. "It was most unpleasant to have to referee grown men in a church reception room. It made me very uncomfortable that they did not have more respect for either the dead or the living."

Jimmy took it upon himself to interrupt the thoughtful pause that followed by asking if anyone had tried either one of the oyster casseroles Brent had brought to the reception.

I tried not to meet his eyes, as I'd never made it back to the food tables after loading my first plate up with a plethora of desserts. "No, I guess I missed them."

"I never eat before, during, or directly after I'm working," Mercedes chimed in. "It's kind of a cardinal rule for musicians." She smiled. "I sure do love eating oysters, but I owe it to my fans to do everything I can to protect my pipes."

"I had a taste of one made with mushroom soup," said Freddy. "It was just like the one we always had at Christmas when I was a kid. I didn't know there was another kind."

Jimmy nodded. "One was the standard recipe with mushroom soup and saltine crackers and plenty of butter," he said. "And the other one had a few surprises in it. Things like red bell pepper, green onions, celery, panko bread crumbs and parmesan cheese. It made it taste like a totally different entrée."

"I believe there are several servings of both casseroles among the leftovers I stored in your refrigerator," said Kanji. He looked around the group. "In case anyone would like to sample them when we decide to eat a little later."

Jimmy nodded with appreciation. "Mmm-mm." Then he took the conversation in a totally new direction, and offered up some of his endless local trivia. "In 2014," he said, "Washington recognized the native Olympia, or Shoalwater Ostrea Lurida, as the state oyster."

"Wait." I held up my hand to halt Jimmy's encyclopedic data bank. "First off, I didn't know there was more than one kind of oyster, so I'll concede that point, but secondly, are you kidding me when you say that Washington has a state oyster?"

"I wouldn't kid you about something like that." Jimmy shook his head. "In the late 1800s in San Francisco they called the oysters they imported from our region 'Shoalies,' named after their source in Shallowwater Bay."

I could almost feel the furrows on my brow deepening

as I strained in thought. "A state oyster? No kidding? Do we have a state clam, too?"

"Yes, of course we do," said Jimmy, looking at me as if I'd lost a few too many marbles by even asking the question. "It's our very own Pacific razor clam, the siliqua patula." He bobbed his head rapidly up and down.

"But oysters were the first agricultural export of Washington state," Jimmy continued, "and Brent and Tom run the two farms that dominate production on the west side of Shallowwater Bay. There are bigger companies over in South Bend, but these two guys have a solid, continuous market for their quality mollusks."

"Please be so kind to explain," Kanji interjected. "What are these mollusks of which you speak, Mr. Jimmy? I am confused at the differentiation of types of seafood. I thought there were either fish or shellfish. Is that not so?"

Jimmy, always eager for an audience to his never-ending pool of knowledge, was only too happy to elaborate. "There's a lot more out there swimming in the sea than just fish and shellfish," he said. "But for the sake of brevity, let's say there are basically two subsets of shellfish," he said.

"First, there are the crustaceans, which include shrimp, crabs, and lobster. Then there are mollusks, which include clams, oysters, mussels and scallops. Bivalve mollusks have an external covering that is a two-part hinged shell protecting their soft bodies."

I am certain my mouth was hanging open in surprise as I listened to Jimmy expounding on the varieties of seafood found along our coast.

Mercedes was looking at me over the top of her coffee cup and grinning ear to ear. "How do you not know any of this, Miss Sylvia Smarty Pants? Weren't you raised here too?"

I shrugged. "No big deal. I guess I just never paid too much attention to anything about the oysters because I don't care to eat the slimy things."

"You don't like oysters?" Freddy asked incredulously.

I looked around the table for any sign of support. The only one who had not responded to Jimmy's earlier question about trying the oyster casseroles was Kanji.

"Kanji?" I asked tentatively. "Am I alone in not liking oysters?"

Kanji looked a little embarrassed. He cleared his throat. "No, my dear Sylvia, you are not alone." He lightly patted my hand. "But I am reticent and perhaps chagrined to admit that I have never been quite able to accept the unwelcome appearance of the green surprise when dining on several species of local seafood, predominantly oysters."

"The green surprise?" asked Merc. "Is that something like the green flash at the end of a sunset?"

Freddy chuckled. "I believe Kanji is referring to the seaweed stuff left intact inside the oyster's digestive tract."

"Eeewwwww!" said Merc. "That's just gross!"

"You're the one who asked," I replied, trying hard not to roll my eyes.

"If a change of subject would be appropriate at this time," said Kanji, looking at my face for approval, "I believe your mother and Lester just pulled around to the parking lot in the back."

"Appropriate, and timely!" I said, leaping to my feet. "You guys scoot over and I'll get a couple folding chairs from the closet."

Jimmy, ever the host, was ready with a cup of coffee for each of them as Meredith and Lester came through the interior door. We scrunched together to accommodate seven around the table, plus one more chair, which would be for Sheriff Donaldson, whenever he arrived.

"So," said Meredith, taking Lester's hand and giving it a squeeze. "Were you talking about us before we got here?"

That got a good chuckle from everyone.

"Sorry, Mother, not this time." I chose to back up a subject or two before I answered her question. "We were just talking about the unfortunate timing of the brouhaha between Brent and Tom over at the church."

"Wasn't that just awful?" said Meredith, wiggling out of her jacket and hanging it on the back of her chair. "I suspect all that testosterone in the oysters is primarily to blame."

"Actually," said Mercedes, barely beating Jimmy to the punch, "I don't think men would enjoy eating oysters nearly so much if they didn't believe they were some kind of magical aphrodisiac that helped them to be more... uh... let's just call it 'manly'."

"Agreed!" said Jimmy. "If men took a daily zinc tablet, they'd have no trouble at all."

This turn in the conversation had made the ever-so-polite Kanji a little squeamish in mixed company, but Freddy had no trouble joining right in. "It's no wonder the sheriff's department gets so many calls out on the bay side of the north end," he said. "Too bad the tiny burg of Willoopah doesn't have its own law enforcement. Those two have made a bad habit out of pulling our regular staff away from the county's real problems."

"Their feud goes back for decades," said Meredith. "Brent and Tom were in the same class in high school, just a year ahead of Sylvia." She nodded. "And as soon as the boys graduated, they lit out of here and joined the Navy. Another football playing friend of theirs, John Heikkinen, from Ocean Crest, enlisted with them, even though he was two years younger."

Meredith laughed. "In fact, John Heikkinen enlisted under the name of John Henry, because the guys in high school had called him that. He was big and strong as an ox. You know, like the legendary big guy in West Virginia that

OYSTER SPAT

worked building the railroad?" She looked from blank face to blank face. "Doesn't anybody remember? There was a folksong about him..."

Mercedes set down her coffee, drew a lung full of air, and rambunctiously belted out, "John Henry was a little baby, sitting on his papa's knee. He picked up a hammer and little piece of steel, said Hammer's gonna be the death of me, Lord, Lord. Hammer's gonna be the death of me..."

I held up my both hands. "Stop! Stop! Stop! We got it! Now please, can we get back a little closer to the point?"

Meredith chuckled. "Fine. Well, the Navy didn't care what John Heikkinen called himself as long as he signed on the dotted line, so it was John Henry, not John Heikkinen, who enrolled with Brent Booi and Tom Diamond."

"I guess things were a lot easier to lie about before the age of computers," said Lester.

I'd almost forgotten Lester was with us. As his early time on the peninsula was brief—only long enough to fall in love with my mother and conceive me—he'd had nothing to contribute to the conversation until now.

The momentary lull as we each stopped to ponder technological changes before and after the advent of computers gave Jimmy an opening to insert a little more of his vast knowledge of miscellaneous trivia. "Booi," he said to no one in particular. "Pronounced Boo-Eee. Spelled B-O-O-I."

Since no one moved to stop him, he continued. "Booi is a rare and interesting surname of Dutch origin. It means 'dweller by the small harbor, or little boats.' The derivation of the name is from the Dutch "bootje," little boat, and the English word buoy, B-U-O-Y, also contributes to the origin of the name.

"Topographical surnames were among the earliest created, since both natural and manmade features in the landscape provided easily recognizable distinguishing names in the small communities of the Middle Ages."

Jimmy pushed his glasses up with his middle finger and looked directly at me as he did so. "Enough?" he asked.

"Much more than enough, Jiminy Cricket," I replied with a heartfelt sigh.

Jimmy mimicked an exaggerated zipping of his lips, and got up to warm up the coffee in a few cups and pour a few kibbles into Priscilla's cat dish. I suspected he did those things to prove he could do something more useful than spout trivia, which, while vaguely entertaining, often came flying at us right out of left field.

"Yes," said Meredith. "Brent Booi's family had the rights to the oyster beds out in front of Willoopah for generations. And way back before either Brent or Tom were born, Tom's grandfather was given a portion of the tidelands by Brent's grandfather. So the Boois and the Diamonds have pretty much monopolized the industry out there for several generations."

"Please excuse my interruption," said Kanji, bowing his head slightly in Meredith's direction. "But are you saying that one family generously gave another family a portion of their oyster land to farm for themselves without compensation or any future financial strings attached?"

"That's what neighbors did back then," said Meredith. "They shared the wealth, so to speak, and I'm sure everyone thought the families would get along till the end of time."

"So what happened?" asked Freddy, who had lived most of his life on the south end of the peninsula, which pretty much made him oblivious to the history of the north end nearly a century ago. "Something monumental must have happened to turn best friends into the north ends' continually warring neighbors."

"For decades, it was a match made in heaven," said

Meredith. "The families coexisted side by side, sharing barges, skiffs, pickup trucks, dredging equipment, doing weed control, and so forth. They functioned like one company, but profited as two independent businesses. It was very congenial, and the families were the best of friends."

"So I'll ask again," prodded Freddy. "What happened?"

"Brent, Tom, and John returned from their military service about the same time," said Meredith. "Brent was an only child, and he immediately took over the oyster business for his folks. They must have been counting the minutes until his return. Faster than you can say, 'Adios amigos,' they packed up and retired to Florida and lived out their remaining years in a condo.

"Tom, on the other hand, never really wanted anything to do with the family business, but since his two younger siblings, both girls, had already left the area to marry and make their own way in the world, he kind of inherited it by default. It wasn't as big a farm as Brent's, but he still needed help with it, and he hired John to work with him."

"Ooo! Ooo! Ooo!" Jimmy waved his hand in the air, but he didn't wait for anyone to call on him to begin talking. "About 25 years ago—I was still in high school—Brent Booi changed the Willoopah business logo. They went from a plate of oysters on the half shell to a black, gold, and green Coat of Arms. It made the front page of the North Beach Tribune.

"The Coat of Arms was granted to the family in Holland and depicts a black bird on a gold star, on a green shield. In heraldry, black denotes constancy, and sometimes grief, gold was a symbol of generosity and elevation of mind, and green signifies hope, joy, and sometimes loyalty in love."

"Loyalty in love?" I mused. "That seems a little incongruous for a man who never married."

"Don't tell me you're interested in Brent Booi?" asked

Mercedes, the ever-ready pot stirrer.

I felt the heat in my face begin to intensify, and I dared not look to either side. If the truth be told, I had had a minor crush on Brent back in high school, but that was a very long time ago, and I was quite content to leave the past in the past.

"Cat got your tongue?" teased Mercedes, somehow sensing she'd hit a nerve. She exaggeratedly looked from left to right and back again at the men who flanked me on both sides. "Don't you have your hands full enough right here?"

OYSTER SPAT

CHAPTER 4

Surprisingly, it was Meredith who jumped back into the conversation and effectively let me off the hook.

"Yes, it's funny that Brent never married," said Merri. She spoke as if the unbelievably long and awkward silence had been all in my imagination. "But Tom married Lorraine, his on-again off-again high school sweetheart, within a few weeks of returning to the peninsula."

"On-again off-again?" asked Les.

"Some guys change girlfriends about as often as the stoplight changes at the main intersection of Tinkerstown," said Mercedes, as if she were an expert on the subject. "Then it turns out those new girlfriends, who the guys thought were bright and shiny and exciting, aren't all that much better than the ones they'd had, so they come full circle back to their original gals." She bobbed her head up and down for emphasis. "You might say that the dating scene on the peninsula is kind of like playing Musical Chairs."

"Or maybe Russian Roulette," added Jimmy.

"A lot of guys end up marrying whichever gal gets knocked up when they happen to be sleeping with her," concluded Mercedes.

Having grown up on the peninsula myself, I thought Mercedes' assessment was pretty spot-on accurate, but I could see her blunt way of phrasing it was making Les, Freddy, and Kanji rather uncomfortable. I thought about letting them squirm a little, but I took the high road and had mercy on them.

"It's kind of a small town phenomenon," I offered, trying not to feel the tingling sense of guilt for my own dating behavior as I said it. "The pickins are pretty slim in an isolated place like the North Beach Peninsula, and there aren't that many good relationship candidates to choose from."

"Tell me about it," sighed Jimmy. He bent down and lifted Priscilla into his lap, where she commenced purring almost instantly. Absentmindedly, he scratched her ears, then ran his hand along her back and out to the tip of her tail.

I wasn't sure at what age Jimmy Noble had embraced his true sexuality, but it couldn't have been easy for him, growing up gay on our tiny ocean sandspit. Sure, times had changed some since high school, but the dating scene was pretty hard to navigate no matter what age, or which gender, you ultimately preferred.

"So anyway," continued Meredith, determined once again to bring us back to the topic at hand, "not long after Tom married Lorraine, John, who Tom had hired to help him on the oyster farm, married Julie... I believe her maiden name was Holter... in kind of a rushed ceremony over at the courthouse in South Bend."

"Rushed ceremony?" I asked.

"Sounds like her father must have been pointing a premarital shotgun at poor John," said Merc.

"Oh, no, it was nothing like that," said Meredith. She paused, frowning with thought. "Or maybe it was, only it might have been Tom who was actually holding the shotgun; he probably had the most to gain from their hurried union."

"So the plot thickens!" said Lester. He seemed to enjoy learning about the comings and goings of people who'd grown up in one place and were still there, in stark contrast to his own vagabond beginnings with no real roots.

"Well, it's all part of the north end history," said Meredith with a small shrug. "It's not like I'm telling tales out of school. But there was—and still is—quite a bit of unresolved intrigue surrounding the circumstances of that marriage."

"Oooo, do tell!" said Mercedes.

"Tom's wife Lorraine was… is… well…" Merri struggled for the most tactful words. "I wouldn't exactly call her homely, but she was definitely more 'handsome' than pretty, even as a teenager. Yet Tom was smart enough to recognize a good, strong helpmate and a woman who wasn't afraid of hard work.

"Tom and Lorraine, along with John's help, worked his widowed father's oyster farm until his dad suddenly passed away less than a year after they returned. And since his father had left no will, Tom had to fight his way through probate. His sisters wanted to sell the property back to Brent, collect what they thought would be their fair share, which they considered to be one-third each, and be done with the whole thing."

"Excuse me for just one other moment," said Kanji. "I do not mean to be obtuse, but was this not the same property that Brent's grandfather had given to Tom's grandfather out of the kindness of his heart, many years before?"

"You catch on quick, Kanji!" Freddy reached behind me and gave Kanji a friendly slap on the shoulder.

"It's true what they say," said Lester. "Where there's a will, there's greedy relatives."

"Or in this case," said Mercedes, "where there's no will, you'd better watch your back."

"Greed runs deep in that family," said Meredith. "Not only did Tom want to keep the Diamond Oyster Farm all to himself, but he staked a claim of ownership to some of the area always farmed by Grandpa Diamond, but which he knew good and well still legally belonged to the Booi family. He based his claim on a recently revised tidal map."

"They say possession is nine tenths of the law," piped up Jimmy.

"And this is where John's marriage to Julie comes in," continued Meredith. "John was raised in Ocean Crest, just a few miles south of Willoopah. So was Julie Holter. But Julie was a Native American, with definite ties to the Shallowwater Tribe. Tom thought if his partner John was married to Julie, it would give the Diamond Oyster brand a stronger claim to the tidelands."

Meredith paused, carefully considering her next words. "You know, I never really looked at it this way before, but when Mercedes mentioned that shotgun thing… You know, Tom's pressure for John to marry Julie might have been a condition of John's continued employment."

"You mean he might have fired him if John refused to marry the woman?" asked Freddy. "That's pretty harsh."

"Harsh or not," said Merc, "lots of unholy marriages since time began have been strictly for convenience and/or for profit."

"Geez Louise," said Lester. He scooted his chair up closer to the table and hung onto Merri's every word. "This plot just keeps thickening and thickening."

"From a purely objective standpoint, I'm curious how Tom's manipulation of John's marital status all played out back then," said Freddy.

I turned in slow motion and stared at him. "Frederick Harold Morgan, you are nowhere near objective on this particular issue. You are both Native American and the owner of a casino on Shallowwater tribal land, and you know good and well your inheritance was based primarily on your fortuitous ancestry."

I'm still not sure if Native Americans can blush, but at least Freddy had the decency to stare down into his coffee cup and look a tad bit chagrined.

"And what, may I ask, was the final determination of the courts in this matter?" asked Kanji. "I am most curious as well."

Wouldn't you know it? Kanji to the rescue, even when he and Freddy were in direct competition for my affections, and it wouldn't hurt his chances with me one iota if Freddy appeared a little self-serving in this instance. Another bonus point in Kanji's column. I had to admire a man who set personal issues aside to help someone else save face.

"When it finally went to court," said Meredith, without missing a beat, "a permanent dividing line was drawn between the claims. This was nearly 30 years ago, and neither Tom nor Brent were happy with the outcome. The metaphorical fence has never been mended between them—although Lorraine and Brent have set most of their differences aside and have always been friendly enough. Lorraine would be the first to tell you that in the long run, being neighborly is much more important than being right."

"What happened to the sisters' claim?" asked Lester.

"Tom had to buy them out," said Meredith. "Which nearly bankrupted him, even though he lowballed them on the agreed upon price."

"Lowball," Jimmy piped up. "Another name for swindled, cheated, devalued, ripped off—"

"In other words," Meredith cut in, "they didn't have any idea about the true value of the oyster beds. Both of the girls had left the peninsula the moment they finished high school and never looked back. They viewed the tidelands as nothing more than some muddy, dirty backwater that came in and went out twice a day."

"And in other words," I interjected, echoing Meredith's recent clarification, "they beat feet as quickly as possible to make sure they weren't roped into taking on the responsibility of the family business while Tom was in the service."

Meredith nodded. "Oyster farming is incredibly hard work, subject to so many variables." She started ticking them off on her fingers. "There's weather, natural pests, environmental toxins, market values. Work like that is often feast or famine."

"Mostly famine," said Jimmy, "unless you're eating what you're raising for every meal." He set Priscilla back down on the floor and smacked his lips. "Oyster omelets, oyster stew, oyster shooters, Hangtown Fry, oysters Rockefeller, made a dozen different ways…"

I reached over and put my hand on Jimmy's arm to quiet him, but he just kept going.

"Grilled, steamed, baked, stewed, barbecued—"

"Please explain," said Kanji, finally putting an end to Jimmy's litany of oyster entrees and their various preparations, "how the property dividing line was established in the courts. I am curious, as in my former occupation as an insurance fraud investigator, the end result often comes down to the judge's understanding of not only the law, but of the primary intention of the principals involved."

I am often impressed by Kanji's outsider's insights. He was sincere in his attempt to grasp the variables of the situation, thoughtfully considering each side of the issue. Plain and simple, that man was one smart cookie, and I greatly admire guys with intelligence.

Meredith's brow wrinkled up and she took a long sip of her coffee. "It's complicated."

Jimmy got up and refilled Meredith's cup as if to prompt

her memory. She'd been born right here on the peninsula, and was one of the few who could recite the ancestry of most of the people who'd lived here for generations. Then as a nurse in the community for more than 30 years, she was also privy to all the gossip and the dirty linen most families would rather people forgot.

"The judge ruled that Tom and John did have a reasonable claim to a portion of the tidal lands that Brent also claimed," said Meredith. "This was only in a small way influenced by the weak argument that John's wife Julie belonged to the Shallowwater tribe.

"Brent rotated his harvest fields, so there were many years the lands in question sat without activity on them. Then a couple years before the case landed in front of the judge, Tom and John started infringing on that area, trying to make it look like it had been worked by them all along."

"And is that not called 'adverse possession'?" asked Kanji. "The occupation of land to which another person has title, with the intention of possessing it as one's own?"

Wowza! I started wondering if maybe Kanji had been an attorney in a previous life. He certainly had a wealth of valuable information to contribute on legal issues.

Meredith nodded. "That's it, exactly. The ruling went through numerous appeals, but none of them amounted to much. Then before the ink was even dry on the final piece of paperwork, John disappeared."

"Disappeared?" asked Mercedes. "What do you mean disappeared? People don't just disappear, something bad musta happened."

Meredith looked a little uncomfortable, so Jimmy, having no such reservations about spreading 25-year-old gossip, jumped right in.

"Actually, John went missing immediately after signing over his share of the Diamond Oyster Farm to Tom," Jimmy blurted out. "He didn't even say goodbye to Julie. She claimed he must have come to harm out on the bay, but there wasn't any evidence of that, so most everyone just assumed he abandoned her in shame."

"What? Why would he do such a thing?" asked Mercedes.

"He had an enormous gambling debt he couldn't cover," Jimmy replied.

"Allegedly," said Meredith.

"Allegedly he had a gambling debt, or allegedly he signed over his share of the farm, or allegedly what?" I asked, wondering how much Meredith really knew about all this. "I feel like you're holding out on us, Mom."

"Well, don't look at me," said Freddy. "This happened way, way back before my uncle Harry built the Spartina Point Casino and Resort, so the object of my inheritance was in no way ever even slightly involved."

"That's correct," said Meredith. "The alleged gambling debt was incurred over time out in Tom's gear shed. Rumor had it that when the weather or the tides weren't cooperating, Tom, John, and some of the seasonal, part-time farm workers used to play 'Ship, Captain, and Crew' on a gaming table made out of a sheet of plywood placed upon between two wooden sawhorses."

"Again, I do not mean to be intentionally naive about such things," said Kanji. "But what is 'Ship, Captain, and Crew'? I am not familiar with any such gaming activity at Spartina Point." He looked to Freddy for confirmation.

Freddy actually chuckled. "Of course not, Kanji. 'Ship, Captain, and Crew' is kind of a back alley dice game."

"Then theoretically," mused Kanji, "it is possible that John did, indeed, acquire quite a large debt playing such a game of chance with his rather unscrupulous business partner."

"Theoretically, that's right," echoed Meredith. "Especially since John was a big drinker, and couldn't hold his liquor. But the timing—in fact, all the circumstances surrounding John's disappearance—were very suspicious. There was even a rumor that John and Lorraine were having an affair, and that when Tom threatened to tell Julie all about it, John hightailed it off the peninsula with his tail between his legs."

"So to speak," said Jimmy.

"Well was John or wasn't John having an affair with Lorraine?" asked Mercedes. "Seems to me, you just deny something like that and move on with your life—politicians do it all the time—so there must have been a little something behind Tom's claim."

"I don't know," said Meredith. "Maybe they were involved, but I sincerely doubt it. I'm more inclined to believe that something else prevented John from getting home that night."

"Do you mean something or someone?" I asked.

Meredith shrugged. "Your guess is as good as mine."

"So the case was never solved?" asked Freddy.

Meredith shook her head. "No trace of John was ever located. He didn't even take his truck from the Diamond Farm that night. He just up and vanished, and a few months later, Julie, who was left penniless, decided that it was in her best interest to move out of the area." Merri bit on her lower lip, as if there were more to the story, but remained silent.

Since Meredith had had a long-term nursing practice on the peninsula, and I'd had 30 years in child protective services, I knew we often had more backstory than what you'd read in the newspaper. I also knew there were many times the information we tucked away could get us into big trouble if we publicly shared it. But since we were talking about ancient history, and both of us are retired, I wondered if perhaps the boundaries of propriety couldn't be pushed just a little.

"Mom?" I prodded. "What is it you aren't telling us?"

She sighed. "Since Julie was Native American, and a very bright young woman, she landed a job with GOIA—the Governor's Office of Indian Affairs—over in Olympia. She settled in either Lacey or Tumwater—I get them confused."

But while that answered pretty much everyone else's questions, it only piqued my interest further. There was no reason Meredith would have initially withheld that particular little tidbit of info. I looked over at her, but she purposely didn't meet my eyes, which pretty much waved a red flag in my direction, inviting me to jump in with both feet. "Were you and Julie friends?"

Now Meredith's eyes darted to mine and made contact, but she quickly looked away.

"Mom? Did you ever see Julie again after she moved away?"

This time her sigh was strong enough to cool everyone's coffee. "Yes, honey, I did." She looked around the table, evaluating her audience. "It's a secret I've kept for over 25 years."

Lester reached over and squeezed Meredith's hand. "But why would you have to keep it a secret that you and Julie had further communication after she left?" he asked. "You weren't breaking any laws or anything were you?"

"No, of course not. We just felt it was for the best," Meredith replied. Then she shrugged. "Julie wanted to leave the peninsula, and all its memories, both good and bad, behind her."

"What kind of bad memories?" asked Mercedes and Lester at the same time.

"Julie had been a suspect in John's disappearance," said Meredith. "Everyone knew he had a drinking problem, and

OYSTER SPAT

a wife who finds out her husband has gambled away his share of a business that is their only livelihood might be just a little angry about something like that."

Freddy sat up a little straighter in his chair. "And the spouse is always the first person of interest to be investigated."

"And more often than not, found to be guilty," added Jimmy.

"Yes." Kanji smiled. "In my former insurance fraud investigations, I found it was often the spouse who wanted to claim insurance on a partner they had either killed themselves, or had paid to have killed by a third party."

Oddly enough, Kanji's comment gave us pause for a slight chuckle, as the ladies of The Veiled Rainbow had all come under his professional scrutiny for exactly these types of activities just a few months before. Thankfully, they were all exonerated, none of them had to return any insurance money, and nobody ended up in jail.

But I still didn't feel like we'd gotten to the end of the trail with Meredith. In fact, I felt kind of like a dog worrying a bone. For some reason, I couldn't leave the story be. Chalk it up to the mother/daughter bond, but I could tell she was still holding something back.

"And Julie never set foot on the peninsula again because…?" I drew the last word out like it was a fill-in-the-blank question.

"Because Julie was pregnant when she left," said Meredith. She slumped down a little in her chair as if a large weight were being lifted from her shoulders. "She moved to a new town, with a new job, new friends, and a chance to start fresh, and yet just a few months later she gave birth to a constant reminder of her troubles when she lived here. And on top of everything else, she had a baby girl who would never know her father."

We all fell silent as we contemplated how this might have tragically impacted the young single mother's life.

"Did she keep the baby, or give it up for adoption?" I asked quietly.

Meredith considered once again whether she was violating any confidentiality laws before she slowly resolved the issue in her own mind. Finally, she nodded and answered. "She kept her."

"And you know this because you kept in contact?"

"Sylvia! Someday that overly inquisitive mind of yours is going to get you into a lot of trouble, young lady!"

I laughed. "You were too good a nurse—too compassionate not to follow up and keep tabs on her—at least from a distance."

Meredith sighed. "I visited her many times over the years. Her daughter turned out to be a wonderfully bright, well-centered young woman, and just this past June got her degree from the University of Washington."

"Sounds like you two are pretty good friends."

"We were," said Meredith, "but she died last spring."

Mom's statement set us back into our quiet individual reflections until we were abruptly, and literally, interrupted by Jimmy's growling stomach.

"Time out!" Jimmy said, getting to his feet. "All this talk of forced marriages and intertidal disputes and 'alleged' gambling debts and missing oyster farmers has gotten my appetite worked up. Is anybody else ready for some memorial leftovers?"

OYSTER SPAT

CHAPTER 5

Kanji, arguably the best cook in the group, immediately took over in the kitchen, manning the oven, the stove top burners, and the microwave while instructing Jimmy to pass out paper plates so we "don't find ourselves still here in the morning, finishing up the dishes."

Sheriff Donaldson, as if by some strange type of "dinner's ready radar" came wheeling into the Clamshell Motel parking lot as Kanji was setting the bowls and platters on the table. His 6'4" frame filled the doorway as he entered without knocking, set his Stetson on top of the refrigerator, deftly stepped over Priscilla, bent to give Mercedes a quick kiss on the lips, and pulled the last open chair up next to her at the table.

"I take it I'm just in time," said Carter, smacking his lips as Kanji set a casserole heaping with oysters down on the table right in front of him.

As the group had already established, I'm not an oyster fan, but the smell of saltine crackers, butter, mushroom soup and parmesan cheese mixed together with the oysters in that casserole dish set my mouth to watering. I was considering trying just a tiny little taste of it when I remembered that all I'd eaten earlier were desserts, so at this point, it wouldn't be unusual for the smell of any "real food" to trigger my salivary glands.

"Dig in," said Mercedes, handing the sheriff a large

slotted spoon.

Sheriff D didn't hesitate to do as he was told, offhandedly remarking he sure was glad Nadine had passed in a month that had an 'R' in it, so there'd be plenty of oysters served at her Memorial Service.

"Carter!" Mercedes slapped at his arm. "What a terrible thing to say!"

"And it's actually an old wives' tale," Jimmy piped up.

The two threads of conversation collided like a head-on train wreck. I wasn't sure which comment to direct my attention to, and apparently, I wasn't alone.

"I must beg your pardon for further explanation once again," said Kanji.

Mercedes suddenly switched perspectives and rode to the rescue of Sheriff Donaldson. "I think what Carter meant to say was that Nadine had a long full life and she'd been fighting the cancer many years, and since she wasn't going to get better, he's just glad that... Well, he's not 'glad,' that's not exactly the right word, but..." she looked around the room for someone—anyone—to get her out of the hole she was digging.

Meredith reached over and patted her hand. "It's okay, Merc. We all understand what Sheriff D was trying to say. We all know he's generally a decent human being beneath his uncouth exterior and inability to filter his thoughts."

Man oh man, Mom was dancing uncomfortably close to insulting the sheriff, which is never a good thing to do unless you're absolutely sure you're never going to need him to ride to your rescue ever again. And of course, none of us could ever be too sure of that!

"It was probably just low blood sugar that prevented him from saying it more tactfully," said Lester. He looked like he wanted to put a muzzle on Meredith.

Meredith lowered her voice and whispered, "I got this,"

to Lester and he quickly went back to spooning more cranberry crab salad onto his plate.

Freddy had a bemused look on his face, but was too savvy to offer up anything for the group to scrutinize, and I had also decided to keep mum on the sheriff's lack of refinement at this particular moment.

"Yes, the part about the sheriff's unfortunate choice of words, I understood," said Kanji, bringing us full circle. "What I needed clarification on was Jimmy's statement about an old wives' tale. That is an idiom I cannot manage by myself to apply to Nadine's passing and months with an 'R' and oysters." He smiled sheepishly and shrugged. "Could someone please enlighten me?"

"Sure, I'd be happy to," said Jimmy without a second's hesitation. "An old wives' tale is something that is once believed to be true, but has later been proven to be incorrect."

Kanji nodded thoughtfully, and Jimmy waited while he processed the information. The rest of us weren't waiting to start passing the mountain of food around in a clockwise direction, and I began to wonder if anyone else who attended the service had taken any leftovers home. We seemed to have enough to feed a hungry army all by ourselves.

"Back in the day," Jimmy continued, "people believed oysters were not edible in months that did not have an 'R' in them. That comes from the fact that the summer months— May, June, July, and August—are the oysters prime breeding months—"

"And in the winter," interrupted Sheriff Donaldson, waving a plump oyster around on the end of his fork for emphasis, "we have prime 'oyster *breading* months'."

Mercedes, Meredith, Lester, Freddy, and I all groaned at his attempted humor, Jimmy rolled his eyes, and poor Kanji looked more confused than ever.

But rather than stop to explain the breeding/breading pun the sheriff was going for, Jimmy just took a deep breath and plunged on ahead.

"During the summer months, we have what are called 'red tides.' This is when the large blooms of algae that grow along the coastline have the tendency to spread toxins that can be absorbed by shellfish, including oysters. So oyster season used to be unofficially closed during the R-less months. The oysters also reproduce during this time, and in preparation for spawning, they convert glycogen stores to gamete, which is sperm and eggs."

"And this is a problem?" asked Kanji.

"Well, some people won't eat oysters in the summer because they say they get soft and rank," replied Jimmy, "but Shallowwater Bay is cold enough, and monitored for any red tide influences, so our oysters are safe to eat year 'round."

"Enough of the soft and rank talk, Jiminy Cricket," said Mercedes, waving her hands around in front of her as if to erase his words. "That's way beyond TMI. You'll spoil the sheriff's appetite."

At 6'4" and pushing up there close to 300 pounds, I was pretty sure nothing could ever spoil the sheriff's appetite, but again, I managed not to say a word to the contrary. Somewhere, somehow, I was hoping to save up karma points for all my uncharacteristic restraint.

Relative silence descended around the table as we chowed down on oysters, Chinese food, enchiladas, pasta crab salad, and crab and cranberry salad as if we hadn't just eaten a few hours before. Sheriff Donaldson was the first to speak when we finally came up for air.

"Sorry I couldn't be two places at once today," said the sheriff to nobody in particular, "but somebody had to keep the law and order on the peninsula this afternoon."

Freddy took that as his cue to thank Sheriff D once again

for giving him the time off so he could attend Nadine's service.

"No problem, son," said the sheriff.

I involuntarily wince every time Carter refers to Freddy as "son." While it was certainly true the sheriff was old enough to have a son Freddy's age, it was also true that Carter and I were closer in age than Freddy and I, and that often gave me a considerable self-inflicted heartburn when I considered any possible future with Freddy.

As if reading my mind, Freddy turned and winked at me, causing a flush to start at my shoulders and course up my neck to my face. I shot a look over at Kanji to see if he was taking this in, but fortunately, Kanji was back up and wrapping up what little was left of the leftovers of the leftovers.

"So I heard through the grapevine I missed a little oystermen drama in the church reception room," said Sheriff D. "Is that what you were discussing before I got here?"

"Pretty much," said Lester, shrugging. "The North Beach Peninsula is its own little Peyton Place, no doubt about it."

Mercedes got up and artfully arranged a tray of desserts on a platter before setting it on the table in front of us. She squeezed the sheriff's shoulder as she retook her seat. "Wouldn't want you to miss out on all these lovely sweet treats we brought back."

The sheriff leaned over and gave her a kiss on the cheek. "As if you're not sweet enough..."

"Hey!" said Jimmy. "If you guys want to rent a room, just say the word. I got no renters in four of my six units tonight."

That wasn't surprising, considering the aging cinderblock-construction motel wasn't exactly a 5 star—or even a 1 star—peninsula destination, but Jimmy had made his point.

Freddy quickly spoke up, and steered us back to the conversation we'd been having before our dinner break. "We were just saying that every time you turn around, one of these oyster guys is filing a lawsuit against the other, when what they really ought to be doing is joining forces and working together to save the fishery."

Sheriff Donaldson nodded thoughtfully as he set a large piece of apple cranberry crisp on his empty dinner plate. "Some wounds go pretty deep."

I wasn't sure what he was talking about, but Meredith's head was bobbing up and down in agreement, and I couldn't stand being on the outside of some of their insider information. "What kind of wounds are you talking about?"

The sheriff and Meredith exchanged glances, and by some nonverbal agreement, Mom spoke up first.

"There were rumors—" she pursed her lips for a moment, then shook her head. "No. Best to let some sleeping dogs lie."

"Like hell!" I blurted out. "You can't just lead us all to the brink like that and then not finish the story."

But Meredith was set on keeping her mouth closed, at least for the moment, and instead of answering, helped herself to a slice of carrot cake. An uncomfortable silence fell among us.

Jimmy cracked first. "Once," he began, "Tom even insisted that Brent couldn't sell food to eat on his oyster farm. Brent had set out a couple picnic tables and chairs on his back deck so that people could enjoy a snack as they enjoyed the view out on Shallowwater Bay."

"So what was wrong with that?" asked Mercedes.

"It wasn't zoned to be a restaurant, or even a seafood market back then," said Jimmy. "The Booi family had been selling fresh oysters for literally decades without a problem.

OYSTER SPAT

They argued that they were grandfathered in, despite any zoning changes. But then Tom Diamond decided to press the issue and took Brent to court."

"Did Tom want to sell foodstuffs at his farm, too?" asked Freddy.

"No," said Meredith. "He just didn't want Brent to be able to do it."

"Oh for crying out loud," Mercedes huffed. "Why couldn't they just live and let live?"

I could tell Kanji was busting with questions, but he held back, his hands folded on the table in front of him, perhaps hoping if he listened long enough, some of it might make sense.

"I vaguely remember this." I scrunched up my forehead as I strained to recall the circumstances more clearly. "The day the judge was about to give his decision, wasn't there a bomb threat at the courthouse?"

"Yes, Sylvia, you are correct," said Sheriff D. "That case, with all its dirty laundry and speculation, was front page news for months." He chuckled. "I was in attendance at the court the day the decision was coming down, just in case tempers flared on either side. I was a wet-behind-the-ears deputy back then, and I always suspected I drew the short straw for that duty."

"Do tell!" said Mercedes, as she popped a big chunk of double chocolate brownie into her mouth.

That brownie looked awfully good, and I helped myself to the last one on the platter before anyone else could beat me to it, rationalizing that my brain needed sugar refueling.

"The closing arguments had been made, and the judge was orally reviewing the major points of each position," began the sheriff. "The court clerk quietly came in, went around the back of the bench, and whispered something in the judge's ear."

"Oooo," said Mercedes, "that couldn't have been good."

"The judge got a strange look on his face," continued Sheriff D. "He kind of puckered up and turned red, and if the guy could have spit nails, we all would have been in his way."

I looked around the table. All of us—Mercedes, Meredith, Lester, Freddy, Kanji, Jimmy and I—were anxiously leaning forward in our chairs. The lovely desserts in front of us were forgotten for the moment as we focused our attention on the sheriff's story.

The sheriff, however, seemed to be enjoying stretching the tale out, and took a big forkful of his fruit crisp, chewed it thoroughly, swallowed, and washed it down with coffee before going on. Talk about a Drama King!

"The judge sat up even straighter in his chair. He peered with laser precision at the attorneys, their clients, and those in the gallery. I remember this as if it were yesterday." Sheriff Donaldson smiled, then used his right index finger and thumb to press his mustache down from the middle to the ends. "Finally the judge said, 'Ladies and gentlemen, it appears there's been a bomb threat made on the courthouse, and we've been advised to evacuate'."

"And did you?" asked Mercedes. Her eyes were big and round, and she sounded as if this had all happened yesterday and not a couple decades ago.

The sheriff shook his head. "Nope. The judge told us he doubted the threat was credible, that all this falderal had gone on far too long, and nobody was going anywhere until he said so. I can still hear him spouting 'the bomb's not going to go off until I've ruled on this case, and that's final!'"

Freddy grinned ear to ear. "Now I remember this," he said. He pointed at Jimmy and then himself several times, his index finger flying back and forth. "We were still in high school, but all we talked about in our classes for days afterward were what big kahunas that judge had!"

OYSTER SPAT

"That's right," said Jimmy, nodding enthusiastically. "The front page headline that week read, 'Judge won't be bullied,' and my debate teacher used the incident as a springboard for our lessons that week. The two sides had to support whether his decision not to evacuate right away was gutsy or foolish."

Several of our group spoke at once.

"Gutsy!" said Freddy and Lester.

"Foolish!" said Meredith and Mercedes.

I opened my mouth to weigh in on the fact that the men in our assembly were thinking macho and the women were thinking safety, but I was temporarily struck dumb. I was trying to wrap my mind around the fact that Freddy—the man I called my sometimes boyfriend—had still been in high school when I was out of college, working for Child Protective Services, and often advocated for the local high school students.

Kanji did not weigh in on the choices given either, but I could see he was giving the whole ordeal some serious thought.

Meanwhile, the sheriff was softly chuckling. "Sylvia," he began, "aren't you going to jump in here and make a point that what we have here is a classic case of a gender division decision, with Freddy and Lester saying it was gutsy, and Meredith and Mercedes saying foolish?"

Actually, I did want to say something to that effect, but other issues about dating ageism and being a potential cougar and sleeping with a man who was but a boy in high school when we might have first met were clouding my thought processes.

"May I ask," said Kanji, "how the judge ruled?"

"Yes, of course," said Sheriff D. "It was a complicated issue, but in the end, he ruled in favor of Brent Booi at Willoopah Oysters. Being allowed to have a place to sit on the deck and eating oyster shooters and oyster chowder and washing it all down with beer or wine was a natural business development of what his grandfather visualized decades ago."

Kanji nodded. "I believe that to be the most reasonable judgement."

"But not everyone agreed," said Meredith. "The letters to the editor filled up page after page for months, and the community was pretty adamant, and divided, with their opinions."

"If I am to understand this correctly," Kanji said slowly, "Willoopah was—and still is—an extremely small community."

His statement was greeted by nods of agreement all around the table, so he continued. "And the number of tourists that drove to the north end of the peninsula before the installation of the casino was relatively small."

Again, Kanji saw nothing but support for what he said. "So why was it important for the people of the middle, or south end, of the peninsula to want to try to stop a few people from enjoying a snack or light meal at a working oyster farm in which they, themselves, had no vested interest?"

"And therein lies a great deal of the problem," said Sheriff Donaldson. "We have always had plenty of code-enforcement issues in this county, from illegal garbage dumping, to junked vehicles, to abandoned or abused animals, to inadequate housing, you name it. The whole thing boggles my mind to consider the amount of the county's time and money that was wasted on this ridiculous court case."

"So what was Tom Diamond's actual issue?" asked Lester.

"I honestly don't know," said Sheriff D. "But the ruling sure pissed him off, and the feud was refueled and continues to this day."

"Maybe it had something to do with jealousy," said Mercedes. "Maybe he was sorry he didn't think of opening a little retail operation first."

"Not allowing Willoopah to be turned into a heavily commercialized area on the most pristine bay in the whole country was one of the big issues for the letter writers," said Meredith. "They thought that ruling in Brent's favor opened up a whole can of worms."

"Well," said Mercedes, "I know it's true that once you've squeezed the tube of toothpaste, you can't put the paste back into the tube."

Mercedes had a point, but it was buried somewhere in that analogy, and nobody seemed to have a good comeback for it.

Sheriff Donaldson just shook his head and signaled to Jimmy for more coffee by tapping his empty coffee cup impatiently with his fingernail, and Jimmy immediately got up to retrieve the pot. I was more than a little surprised that Jimmy didn't tell him, in no uncertain terms, that he wasn't the waiter or the manservant here, and the sheriff could get his coffee himself!

"You know," said Sheriff D, contemplating the situation, "that case divided the community pretty deeply. It was even made an issue in the next election."

"How so?" asked Freddy.

"The prosecutor took an awful lot of heat for pursuing that case," said the sheriff. "But he didn't have much of a choice when he took it on. It's his job to represent those who elect him, and all he did was follow the letter of the law. Anyone in that hotseat would have had to do the very same thing. I kinda felt sorry for the guy."

"But he was reelected, wasn't he?" I asked.

Sheriff Donaldson nodded. "By a wide margin, as it

turned out. And so was the judge. But—" the sheriff hesitated. When no one jumped in to interrupt him, he reluctantly finished his thought. "But the judge—he was a great guy—he retired shortly after that. He said it was for health reasons, but I always wondered if he'd been personally threatened, or if it had something to do with the bomb threat."

"It was just a threat, wasn't it?" asked Lester. "There wasn't an actual bomb found, was there?"

"No bomb," said Meredith, "but the issue got statewide attention, and lots of security changes were made in most of Washington's 39 county courthouses."

"An event such as that certainly gives one pause to consider one's mortality," said Kanji. "The judge could not be blamed if he decided to spend more time pursuing a quality retirement."

"True," said Sheriff D. He shot a look at Freddy. "But now that we've taken this trip down memory lane, I'm left wondering if perhaps the bomb threat we received at Willoopah Oysters a couple months ago was a decades old aftermath of the judge's ruling."

"Carter? What in the world are you talking about?" asked Mercedes.

"I don't believe in coincidences," Sheriff D said.

"Do you have any evidence that the two incidences are connected, Sheriff?" asked Freddy.

"Let's just say, I don't have any evidence that they're not."

"Now you're talking in riddles," said Meredith, a little impatiently. "Just spit it out, Carter. How do you think these two bomb threats, many years and miles apart, could possibly be related?"

"Well," said Sheriff D, "I can think of one pretty important fact that might tie them together a whole lot tighter than anyone imagines."

"And what would that be?" prompted Mercedes.

The sheriff got up and put his paper plate into the trash. Then he turned, looked each of us briefly in the eye, and said, "Tom Diamond's specialty in the Navy was demolition."

CHAPTER 6

I went to pay my respects again to Goodie and Patrick a couple days later. I know from experience that the "after the memorial let down" can be the toughest part of any grieving process. Once the family and friends have drifted back to their own realities, it can be the loneliest time of all, and I was grateful Goodie had Patrick to lean on. And vice versa.

I found them in the kitchen, amicably bickering like they were an old married couple. Trays, bowls, and platters were stacked on the table, the counters, even on chair seats, and Goodie was waving a roll of masking tape around in one hand and a black felt marker in the other.

"Sylvia!" Goodie immediately set her tools down to embrace me tightly. "Thank goodness you're here! We need a tie breaker!"

"A tie breaker?" I asked. "For what, exactly?"

Goodie huffed. "Patrick was so stoned at the memorial, he took all the nametags off the serving dishes of food, and now we can't figure out where to return the kitchenware!"

I bit my lip to keep from smiling too broadly. If this was their biggest challenge today, then there was hope for them to emerge from their individual loss still friends.

I picked up a large, two-handled aluminum kettle. "This came with the Cinco Amigos," I said. "It was filled with Mexican oyster soup."

"Sopa de Ostiones!" exclaimed Patrick, smacking his

lips. "Boy, do I remember that soup! I asked Julio if he would share their recipe. He said I'd have to do a lot of math to cut it down to a meal for just one or two people, but he said he'd get it for me."

I laughed. "I'll help you with the math, Patrick. It looked and smelled really good." I hadn't actually sampled any of it, but Patrick didn't need to know that at the moment.

Goodie was standing with her hands on her hips. "Will you two little Suzy Homemakers please focus on one problem at a time? We need to get all this stuff," she waved her hands around, vaguely indicating the various pots and pans, "returned to the rightful owners, along with a little thank you note for each of their kindnesses."

"You want me to write individual thank you notes?" Patrick was suddenly on red alert. "Holy guacamole! Can this day get any worse?"

"Relax, Patrick," said Goodie. "I've got all the notes written already; I just can't get them matched up to all the things that need returned."

"What have you got so far?" I asked. "Maybe if we moved the things ready to go out into the living room, we could narrow down the items that are left."

"A solid plan," said Patrick, nodding. He looked at Goodie and winked. "But I think I've got a better one."

"Do tell," said Goodie. "I'm all ears." And she promptly plopped down on the only empty kitchen chair.

Patrick turned to me. "You headed up north today?" he asked.

"Well, you know I live halfway up the peninsula anyway, but yeah, I'm planning on going on up to Spartina Point this afternoon. Why?"

Patrick grinned. "Then would you mind returning the things that need to get back to the good folks who live way out in Willoopah?"

I could see where this was headed. "You mean you'd like me to stop in and personally deliver your appreciation for their kindnesses at the residences of the Hatfields and McCoys?"

"Well, no," said Patrick, scowling and shaking his head. "I was thinking that you might stop in to see Brent Booi and the Diamonds."

"Same thing," said Goodie, smiling. "You're just not old enough to catch that reference."

Patrick shrugged. "I guess not." Then he turned to me and brightened. "So you'll do that for us, Syl? Huh? Pretty please?"

"Of course," I replied. "No need to bat those baby blues at me, Patrick. I'd be happy to help. And I can take a lot of this other stuff too. Freddy sent quite a few things from the casino restaurant. All we need to do is remember which dish came in each bowl or on what tray."

"Which is what we've been trying to do all morning," said Goodie. Her heavy sigh indicated she was nearing her wit's end.

"I think I might be able to help you with that," I said. "I assisted Kanji when he loaded up a lot of the food for the memorial Saturday morning, and I think I can remember what foodstuffs the casino sent, and therefore what pan or tray it must have come in or on."

"Bless you!" said Goodie and Patrick in unison.

And Goodie followed up with, "You're just the angel I was praying for!"

It didn't take as long as I feared to get most of the kitchenware labeled, and the mustang trunk and back seat brimming with the items to be returned. Patrick offered me "a couple of puffs for the road," but I gracefully declined and was headed north by early afternoon.

The drive up Sandspit Road was as beautiful as always.

OYSTER SPAT

When the leaves are off the trees in winter there are little peeks between the houses at Shallowwater Bay to be enjoyed all along the route. During the summer I sometimes forget that the water is so near, simply because I can't see it through all the leafy foliage.

As I passed my own driveway, which turns off on the west side of the road, I gave a little wave. The west side of Sandspit Road is affectionately called "the cheap seats," because no homes on that side have a view of the water, but I don't mind paying half the property taxes.

I didn't need to pick anything up at home, so I just kept on driving. My first stop would be at Willoopah Oysters, followed by the Diamond Oyster Farm, followed by Spartina Point Casino and Resort. With any luck, I'd be there in time for an early dinner with—

My continual stream of thought while I drove came to an abrupt halt. To have an early dinner with whom, Sylvia? I asked myself. Was I looking forward to seeing Kanji in the kitchen more than Freddy in the main casino? One of these days I was going to have to sort out my feelings for those two men, but that wasn't on the top of my to-do list for today.

Today was a gorgeous December day, and I veered east near the end of Sandspit Road and entered the quiet little burg of Willoopah. There's not much to this little town—never has been. But there's still a quaint little church with bell tower, the building which once housed one of the first schools in Washington territory, and a couple dozen homes with name plates and homestead dates on their gates. This part of the town is a quiet, almost reverent nod to the past. Several hundred newer residences are a few blocks west, and don't have a long history, even though they all boast having the Willoopah address.

I took a hard right at the end of the historical district and came face-to-face with the sparkling water of Shallowwater

Bay and the dark forests of Elk Island beyond the water. Then another quick turn north, right along the shoreline, and I felt like the oyster farms in front of me had been painted into the landscape. Such a pastoral picture postcard! I smiled, and let the peaceful scene wash over me.

The first farm I came to was Willoopah Oysters. There were at least a dozen cars parked across the lane from the cluster of buildings, and I parked among them. Brent must have seen my car coming down the narrow, and in some places, one-way lane. He walked out from the gear shed to the little parking strip wiping his hands on a mechanic's rag, and grinning ear to ear. "Sylvia!! So good to see you!"

"Good to see you, too, Brent." I clicked my key fob and my trunk popped open. "Gee, I bet we haven't seen each other since—well, last Saturday."

Brent chuckled. "Yeah, well, today we meet under much more pleasant circumstances."

"And speaking of the memorial—" I lifted the lid on the mustang's trunk. "I could use some help carrying in your casserole dishes. Goodie and Patrick sent me to return them and thank you again for your generosity." I handed him the handwritten thank you card.

Brent laughed good-naturedly and tucked the card into his back pocket. Then he assumed the lion's share of the work toting in the trays and casserole dishes. We carried everything through the entry to the small farm store adjacent to the gear shed, walked clear through to the back, and set the dishes on a counter behind the cash register. I was embarrassed to admit it, but it had been years since I'd visited Brent's farm, and I was anxious to take a little look around.

As if reading my thoughts, Brent said, "Would you like me to give you the nickel tour?"

"Only if you have time to do that," I replied.

OYSTER SPAT

Brent laughed. "I'm the boss; when I want to take time off, I do."

I smiled in return. "Then by all means, lead the way." I half-bowed, and made a grand, sweeping gesture, hoping it would look like a flourish, with my arm.

"First off," said Brent, taking me out back and onto the deck that wrapped around the small seafood store, "just take a moment to enjoy the view."

I'm pretty sure a small gasp escaped me as I was suddenly confronted by an uninterrupted expanse of winter-gray dune grass, untrodden mud flats where a number of shorebirds scurried for their next meal, the darker calm water of the bay, and in the distance, the outline of Elk Island, a deep, conifer green that rose up out of the water, both foreboding and majestic. It was essentially the same view I'd seen as I'd driven the last mile, but now it was extremely up close and personal, from the smell of the fresh salt air to the numerous bird sounds you just don't hear when you're driving by in your car.

Brent saw my reaction and smiled. "Welcome to my office."

"Wow," I said softly. "Some view."

I walked between a couple picnic tables to the edge of the deck where there was a line of four metal stools placed along a short wooden counter built into the railing. I just stood there, taking it all in. Smaller birds chirping, the sound of the water lapping against the dock that stretched straight out from the gear shed, the screech of an eagle perched on a nearby piling, and out on the water, the rhythmic hum of a scow's engine. At least I think it's called a scow. Overall, the scene was breathtaking, almost surreal, like something you'd see only in a Hallmark movie.

I pointed east, out across the tidelands to the boat. "Is that your crew?"

"Yes, it is," replied Brent. "At least for today. The farm employs 6 or 8 workers at a time. Most days, my guys are out on the bay in the process of spreading seed or harvesting oysters ready for market."

"Your guys??" I gently teased him. "Aren't you an equal opportunity employer?"

"Funny you should say that," Brent replied. "Just a few months ago, I hired a gal—a recent graduate from the University of Washington's Aquatic and Fishing Sciences program. But for the most part, oyster farming is hard, physical labor, and women don't often apply."

That made sense, so I cut him some slack. "So those are all your guys' cars out front?"

Brent nodded thoughtfully. "More or less."

For some reason, his vague answer got my curiosity aroused. "Which is it Brent, more or less?"

"I'll be frank, Sylvia," said Brent. "Most of my employees are Mexican laborers. They're hard workers, every one of them. And if they don't have the necessary documentation to work legally, I will still hire them, as long as they agree to getting, and maintaining, the correct documentation as soon as possible."

"You mean to tell me that ICE comes all the way out here just to round up an oyster picker or two?" It didn't seem cost-effective for the government to send out at least two men, in a publicly owned vehicle, just to harass workers who were trying to make a living for themselves and their families doing work few others wanted to do.

"Since Washington allows the privatization of tidelands, the ICE guys have to catch them before they get onto Willoopah Oyster Farms property." Brent smiled. "That's where all those extra cars come in. It makes it harder for the agents to recognize, and target, anyone they might be seeking to detain."

OYSTER SPAT

"You mean some of those cars are decoys?"

"You might say that." Brent laughed. "Or you might call it a carpool safety net. From time to time, I drive a few of them myself, the guys ride to and from work in one or another throughout the week, and my new hire also parks out there."

"Can't say as I blame you," I replied. "But I had no idea your workers couldn't be picked up if they were physically on your farm property."

"As I said before, Washington is the only state that allows the privatization of the tidelands," said Brent. "The only state. And it turns out to be a good thing all around. If the oyster farmers didn't own the land, it's a sure bet there'd be high rise condos lining the shores of Shallowwater Bay, and commercial businesses and strip malls would spring up not too far from the water's edge as well."

Brent's chest swelled with pride. "I'm happy to say that Shallowwater Bay is the cleanest, most pristine ecosystem in the entire United States. That's one of the reasons our oysters taste so much better than those grown anywhere else."

"Ever the promoter," I said, smiling but shivering slightly in the bright sunshine but cold temperature of December.

Brent saw me shiver and motioned for me to return inside. He drew the sliding wooden door closed behind us. "And in here, we sell quite an assortment of oyster products, plus smoked salmon, salmon dip and crackers, an assortment of beverages—everything you'd need for a midday bayside picnic pick-me-up."

"And this is what got the county all up in a tailspin?" I asked before thinking.

Brent scowled, then shook his head as if to clear the dark thoughts. "I can't blame the county, exactly." He looked out the small window to the north, up towards the Diamond

Oyster Farm. "Some people just can't leave well enough alone; they have to go stirring the pot, trying to create trouble for some of us who are just trying to eke out a living without compromising the holiness of the bay."

"The holiness of the bay," I echoed thoughtfully. "That's exactly how it feels out there—as if you're in nature's church."

"I'm glad you understand," said Brent. "And I understand why there must be regulations and rules concerning the development along the shore. But I fail to understand how someone buying a Willoopah embroidered hoodie sporting an oyster on it endangers the environment."

When I didn't respond, Brent continued.

"The county wanted to make a list of what I could and couldn't sell here," he began. "Back when my grandfather ran the business, it was mostly fresh oysters still in the shell. Then my grandmother got the idea to keep a pot of oyster stew going for the crew, and for those who came out to see a working oyster farm in action. Over time, one thing led to another and…"

Brent stopped talking while he straightened up the cellophane packages on a display rack of quality handmade pasta, which I knew to be locally made. "The county even challenged me on why pasta should be allowed at a seafood market." He sighed. "Hello? Has anyone ever heard of seafood fettuccini?"

I wanted to laugh, but the reality wasn't very funny.

Brent looked out over the bay again. "Too damn bad the burrowing shrimp aren't edible. I could make a fortune harvesting them. Those pests are taking over the tidelands. They're going to be the end of oyster farming on this bay if the government doesn't hurry up and get its act together."

Brent looked me in the eye. "Don't ever play poker, Sylvia."

OYSTER SPAT

Startled at this quick shift in the conversation, I asked, "Why not?"

"It's obvious you don't have a clue what I'm talking about."

"Oh. Um. Well, you're right. Until just this minute, I didn't know there were different types of shrimp—other than salad shrimp and jumbo prawns, that is."

Brent chuckled. "Not many people do." Then he sighed. "And part of the problem is that the oyster fishery hasn't kept the public educated about the challenges we have on the bay. As far as most people know, oysters come in a little pint jar at Thriftway. They don't have any idea how long it takes to raise them, and what intensive labor is involved, or anything at all about the way ghost shrimp are threatening to take over all the usable oyster beds."

It was a rather long speech for Brent, and he expelled a huge breath as he pulled off his ball cap with one hand and ran his other hand up through his graying hair. "Sorry. I get pretty passionate about this particular topic."

I smiled. "Yes you do, but I believe that's justifiably so."

"Thanks for understanding," said Brent.

"Now don't go jumping the gun," I replied. "I still don't really understand much of anything you said. So why don't you start by giving me the CliffsNotes on how the shrimp in the bay are taking away the oyster beds. Did you say they were burrowing shrimp? Or was it ghost shrimp?"

"The terms are used pretty interchangeably," said Brent. "In fact, burrowing blue mud shrimp is probably the best answer, but whatever you call them, they are 100% bad news when it comes to maintaining the ecological balance in the bay."

I knew my naivety was showing, but I had to ask, "What makes them so bad?"

Brent motioned toward the bay. "They destroy the

oyster beds."

"And… um… how do they do that?"

"Like their name implies, the burrowing shrimp dig down on the bay's bottom looking for their next meal. The burrows, or tunnels, turn the bottom of the bay into nothing more than an ooey gooey mess—a lot like quicksand, but usually only about three feet deep.

"Then when we put out the oyster seed, the mushy ground can't sustain the weight of the growing oyster shells, and the oysters sink down into the gunk and suffocate."

I thought back to the way Nadine's husband had died—confused by his Alzheimer's, he mistakenly thought he could walk over to Elk Island at low tide and pick his wife some flowers. The silt on the bay bottom had sucked his feet down into the murk, and he'd drowned.

"So what can you do to control them?" I asked Brent.

He sighed. "And therein lies the sixty-four-thousand-dollar question."

"Don't the shrimp have any natural predators?"

"They used to," Brent began, "but the sturgeon in the bay have been overfished, the birds can't keep up with the multitude of shrimp, and the effect of damming the rivers that emptied their fresh water into the saltwater of the bay plays a part too."

"I kinda hate to bring this up," I said, "but what about spraying chemicals? Isn't there some kind of 'Shrimp-B-Gone' spray you can control them with?"

Brent groaned. "Chemical toxins to control the burrowing shrimp has been an ongoing debate for half a century." He abruptly started for the door that led back onto the deck. "Come with me. I'd like you to meet the gal I hired from the UW. She seems just as interested in keeping Shallowwater Bay the cleanest saltwater ecosystem in the United States as I do. She gives me hope for the future of the oyster fishery."

And although I knew I had one more stop to return bowls and trays before heading for dinner at the casino, I was suddenly anxious to "meet the future" and learn more about the kind of people who are going to college to become better oyster farmers.

CHAPTER 7

Brent slid the door open on the gear shed and went on in ahead of me. It took several moments for my eyes to adjust from the bright December sunshine to the darkened workroom, but when they did, I was more than a little surprised by what I saw.

Along the far wall were eight gigantic gray plastic barrels, maybe 12 feet high and 8 feet across. The barrels were numbered in descending order. Along the wall perpendicular to that were the same size black barrels, some with green or clear hoses sticking out the tops and some with ladders leaning against their sides. A scaffolding of what appeared to be "grow lights" was strung above the gray vats.

In the middle of the room were an assortment of mismatched desks and tables, looking like the leftovers from a "going out of business sale" at a thrift shop. Unfortunately, none of the desks had their table lamps on at the moment, but I could make out piles of papers, file folders, and clipboards stacked high on several of the half-dozen desks.

Helter-skelter around the office cubicle without walls were four filing cabinets, none of which matched another one, two computers attached to separate printers, two microscopes, and quite an array of oversized beakers and test tubes. My first impression was that it would look like a mammoth Mr. Science Chemistry Set to a young child. Or even someone like me.

OYSTER SPAT

The whole place smelled overwhelmingly of bleach, seaweed, and saltwater, but not in a bad way. Each smell was so strong it threatened to overtake the others, but somehow they all seemed to work together, as if they belonged here.

"Nautika!" Brent called out. "Are you in here?"

"I'm over here, Boss!" a young woman replied. "Behind seed vat number two."

"Watch where you step," Brent said over his shoulder to me. "There are electrical cords and hoses strewn everywhere."

He didn't have to tell me twice. I'd already felt the tug of a cord around my ankle several times as I tried to follow him across the darkened room.

Nautika came out from behind the line of gray barrels and flipped on an overhead light switch. "Sorry about that," she said. "I wasn't expecting company." She wiped her hands on a work rag and extended her right hand. "Hi. I'm Nautika."

"And I'm Sylvia," I replied. I noted not only Nautika's firm handshake, but also how strangely feminine and pretty she looked at the same time. Her long dark brown hair was tied back, but even a ball cap couldn't keep the wispy strands from escaping around both ears. Her eyes were also a deep dark brown, and they constantly darted here and there, taking everything in at once, and I got the distinct impression that nothing much ever got by her.

"So what's going on in here?" I asked, looking around at the now-illuminated interior of the gear shed. "It kind of reminds me of our high school biology lab."

"As well it should," said Brent, with just a touch of pride. "And Nautika is our head mad scientist."

I laughed. "Well, I hope you're both using your super powers for good, and not looking for a new way to take over the world."

"Actually, the work we're doing is very, very good, when you consider the impact on the future of the world's natural water systems and the fisheries that depend on them," said Brent. "And right here and now, Nautika is proving herself to be a true pioneer in finding ways to sustain the local oyster industry."

"We're raising our own oyster seed in the gray barrels," said Nautika proudly. "And that means we have to cultivate our own nutrient-rich formula to feed the little buggers." She pointed to where the hoses led from the second line of black barrels back to the first.

"Wow! That's a pretty ambitious plan," I said admiringly.

"You better believe it!" said Brent. "And I'm not sure I'd have taken on such a mammoth project without the help and expertise of my new number one assistant."

I could tell Nautika was pleased by Brent's praise, but she was also humble. "I'm just part of the team here," she said. "If Brent hadn't been willing to think outside the box, we'd never have gotten this off the ground. Someday soon, we'll be able to supply not only our own oyster spat, but we'll have enough to export to other growers."

"Brent was telling me you've hired on here to help bring his farm into the 21st century, but I had no idea how quickly you'd be catapulting him up to speed."

Both Brent and Nautika got a good chuckle out of that.

"So if you haven't been raising your own oyster seed, where has it been coming from?" I asked.

"In the beginning, Japan was our primary resource," said Brent. "But now there are some farmers right here in Washington who are putting us on the cutting edge of self-sustainment." He grinned. "And soon to be leading the pack is our Nautika."

At the mention of her name again, my curiosity got the

best of me. "Forgive me for asking, but Nautika is such an interesting name. Are you Russian?"

Nautika shook her head. "Nope. Not even an eyelash." She smiled. "My father, John Henry, was in the Navy, so Mom chose a name to honor his military service."

I was nearly struck dumb by her answer. So this was the young woman Meredith had referred to as a bright, educated young lady, the daughter of John and Julie Henry! Talk about small worlds! But not wanting Nautika to think I'd just recently been gossiping about her with a group of overly curious locals, I carefully asked, "Would your parents have been in the oyster industry before you were born? And would your mother's name be Julie?"

"Right on both counts." Her eyebrows knitted together. "But how did you know?"

Brent laughed. "I told you it was a small community."

I ignored his interruption and continued. "My mother knew your mother when they both lived here back before you were born. Your mom and dad lived in Ocean Crest, didn't they?"

"Yes, they did," said Nautika. She seemed a little ill at ease with my insider knowledge, so I rushed to explain just enough to make her feel more comfortable.

"I went to school with your parents," I explained. "And with Brent and Tom too, although Brent and Tom were a year ahead of me and John and Julie were a year behind. We didn't socialize much, but we knew each other."

"That's right," said Brent. "We're all grads of Unity High." He smiled. "And after our military stint, Nautika's dad was partners with Tom Diamond over at Diamond Oysters, but... well... that's a very long story for another time."

"Yes, a very long story," agreed Nautika. "Then after my dad left us, Mom moved to Olympia to take a job there a few months later."

I was considering letting things lie and asking Meredith about it later, but since Nautika had brought her father's disappearance into the forefront, I decided to seize the opportunity. "Did you say your dad left you?"

Nautika and Brent exchanged glances, but neither one of them spoke, so I plowed on ahead. "Do you know where he is? Is he still alive?"

"I wanted to believe that for the longest time," said Nautika. "But Mom said there's never been any kind of paper trail since the day he disappeared 25 years ago, and it's extremely unlikely he wouldn't have surfaced in some form or another, long before now."

I made a mental note that "surfaced" was an interesting choice of words, given that the peninsula is surrounded by water, and that no sign of him had ever been found.

"Well, I, for one, am very grateful Nautika's come back to her family's roots here on the bay," said Brent. He leaned toward her and gave her shoulder a friendly squeeze.

My former position with Child Protective Services directed my focus compass to high alert. The shoulder squeeze had appeared innocuous enough, but there was something that just didn't set right with me. I tried to ignore it, but my intuition was too often spot-on under such circumstances. Brent was a confirmed bachelor, and 30 years Nautika's senior.

"So where are you staying?" I asked. The question sounded natural enough, but I was searching for any additional information that might have kicked my sixth sense into suspicious activity gear.

Nautika's face lit up. "I've got the shortest commute ever! Brent is renting me a room in his house right next door. Isn't that great?"

Whoa! My hinky meter went sky high on that answer,

OYSTER SPAT

but Nautika was legal age, so it would serve me well not to pursue my line of thinking any further. At least not at the moment. It was clear she wasn't being held against her will, so I backed off and listened carefully to her answers to my questions rather than supply my own, based on nothing concrete.

"May I ask why you chose to come work for Willoopah Oysters and not follow in your father's footsteps at the Diamond Farm?" I hoped I didn't sound like I was digging for dirt, even if that's exactly what I was doing.

"My mother died last year from Non-Hodgkins Lymphoma," said Nautika.

I started to express my condolences, but she waved me off. "It's okay. We knew for a long time the disease was going to catch up with her, and we had plenty of time to prepare ourselves."

She shot a look over at Brent and smiled. "Fortunately, just before she passed, she wrote me a letter of introduction to Brent. She said he'd always been kind to her when she lived on the peninsula, and she knew he'd do right by me." Nautika sighed. "I just wished she'd lived long enough to know what a perfect job I've landed here, and how happy I am."

"How could I not hire her on the spot?" said Brent, who for all the world looked to be beaming with pride. "Her credentials are impeccable. Nautika was the top of her Marine Biology classes and plans to spend her life protecting the native flora and fauna in and along our state's waterways."

I looked at Nautika from my own 30-year idealistic distance and hoped life wouldn't throw her too many curveballs. She looked like a wonderful kid, standing there in her snug-fitting jeans with bedazzled back pockets and Xtratuf boots, which, I noted with surprise, were also bejeweled.

I made a comment about her boots not being oyster farmer regulation and she laughed.

"Oh, these boots are definitely work boots," she said, with her charming smile. "They're unisex, insulated, and with special nonslip soles. But you can't blame a gal for wanting to jazz them up a little, can you?"

I laughed too. "Well, when you put it that way, I guess not."

"And besides," Nautika continued, "my mother's name was Julie, but her friends called her Jewels, so this is a special nod to her, too."

"It's perfect," I said, and truly meant it. "It's been lovely meeting you, Nautika, and I hope I see you both again real soon, but right now I've got to get a move on."

"More pots, pans, and trays to return?" asked Brent.

"You know it!"

I gave them both a quick wave as I hurried to my car. It gets dark pretty early in December, and I wanted to be finished at the Diamond Farm and on my way over to the casino with the trays and utensils Freddy had supplied for the memorial long before the sun set.

Tonight would be a great chance to visit with both Freddy and Kanji, and I selfishly hoped it was Kanji's night to take over the kitchen for one of his spectacular Indian Feasts. My mouth started watering as I already imagined his signature dish: Chicken Tikki Marsala. And as a reward to myself for helping out Goodie and Patrick by returning a trunk and backseat full of pots and pans, I might just decide to indulge in the casino's signature drink, too: a classic Spartina Point Spartini.

The Diamond Farm was only three quarters of a mile farther down the road that branched north from Willoopah, so it was only a couple minutes before I pulled up in front of their modest bayfront home. Their farm had significantly fewer outbuildings than the Booi's, but the traditional house, gear shed, and oyster processing structures were lined up right along the water's edge, pretty much the same as their neighbor's buildings down the road.

The Diamond's dock extended from the oyster shed straight out into the water, and at the moment, there was only one boat tied up there. I didn't know how many dredges, barges, skiffs or scows the Diamonds owned, so I didn't know if they might be out on the water or not. Then I suddenly realized I couldn't positively identify one type of boat from any other out there. Really! What self-absorbed rock had I been hiding under that I wasn't familiar with the different types of boats used out on the bay? Good grief and gravy! I did a mental head slap, and vowed to fix that oversight "one of these days soon."

Unlike the fleet of vehicles parked across the road from Willoopah Oyster Farm, there was only one elderly blue pick-up truck in the driveway at the Diamond's, and I pulled up next to it and turned off the ignition.

"Hello?! Lorraine! Tom!" I called out as I stepped from my car and started pulling kitchenware from my trunk. "Hello?! Anybody at home?" I'd overhead some talk at the memorial about Lorraine and Tom riding down to the church in the only vehicle they owned, so I assumed the beat-up pick-up was it. Therefore, I quickly deduced that either they were both in one or another of the buildings on the property, or that Lorraine was around here somewhere while Tom was out working on the bay. I'd also heard that Lorraine rarely worked out on the water anymore. Something about having occasional vertigo and being unsteady on her feet.

I really didn't care which of them was nearest to the house, only that someone was here to take all this cookware from me. I filled my arms with everything marked

"Diamond" and quickly headed for the front door before I started losing my grip.

But when no one answered my knock, I backed off the porch and took a closer look out on the water. I could see several dredges—at least I thought they were dredges—and some hand pickers, but there was no way I could tell if any of them was Tom Diamond.

I stepped back up on the stoop and tried knocking again. "Lorraine? Hello? It's Sylvia. I have some things here to return to you from Goodie and Patrick."

No one came to the door, but I was sure I heard movement coming from inside the house. Forgetting for a moment that lots of people on the peninsula had excessively large dogs, I impulsively tried the doorknob, and the door swung open.

Holy Criminitly! The door opened directly into their living room, which showed clear evidence that either a violent struggle had recently taken place on the premises, or someone living here was in contention for the world's worst housekeeper.

There was no sign of a Christmas tree, or any seasonal decorations, and I stood there uncertain if I should leave the pots and pans in the kitchen, or out on the front porch with Goodie's thank you note and pretend I'd never tried the doorknob.

Tentatively, I tried calling out again. "Lorraine? Hello? It's Sylvia."

This time I distinctly heard Lorraine call out from behind a closed door that might have been a bedroom right off the main living quarters. "Sorry, Sylvia, I'm right in the middle of some delicate work on my newest quilt, and I can't take the time to come out and visit with you."

"It's ok, Lorraine," I said to the closed door. "I'll just leave your cranberry salad bowl and the blackberry pie plates and the rest of these items in your kitchen."

"Thanks, sweetie," said Lorraine. "This room was never meant to be a quilter's sewing room. It's so small the frame takes up the whole space and then the door is completely blocked until I put everything away, and I just don't have the time to do that today. The quilt show is this weekend, you know."

"I totally understand," I replied, although I really didn't understand. For my money, the expansive windows in the large living room would have been a great place for needlework—lots of natural light and a great view. But what did I know?

I cleared a space on one end of a kitchen counter and stacked the clean cookware and utensils there. The kitchen sink was full, and every surface had the remnants of a meal that was either coming or going. Although I didn't know her that well, this scene seemed totally out of Lorraine's character.

"Thanks again for making Nadine's memorial reception so special," I called out, to which Lorraine hollered through the door that I was very welcome and to give her love to Goodie and Patrick the next time I saw them.

"Will do," I said, but when I got to the front door, something made me hesitate. Dang my gut for being so super sensitive today! "Uh... Excuse me again... Lorraine?"

"Goodness, Sylvia! Are you still here?"

My retired CPS gut clenched hard for the second or third time today. "Lorraine? Uh... Do you need any... uh... any help or anything?"

"Help?" echoed Lorraine. Her voice came out a little like the whimpering bark of a tiny Chihuahua, but she recovered quickly. "No, Sylvia, I've been doing needlework most of my life, and I'm sure I can handle the trim on this quilt just fine, thank you."

I was pretty sure she knew that I wasn't asking to help her quilt, as it's well-known throughout the entire peninsula community that I don't know how to sew a button on straight, but I let it go for the time being.

"Okay, then. You take care!" I called out.

"You too, Sylvia. Drive safely!"

I went down the two porch steps, but instead of going directly to my car, I decided to take a look around Tom's gear shed. The sliding panel door on the side closest to the house was padlocked shut, but at the east end there was a solid door with a tiny, useless peep window in it. The door was opened just far enough for me to stick my head inside. But like Brent's gear shed had been earlier, it was pretty darn dark in there. Much too dark to see anything.

I pushed the door back a little further, letting a little more late afternoon light in. Now I could see a lot of large blue plastic totes, some wooden pallets, a forklift that would definitely be needed to move the pallets and totes around or put them on trucks, and a lot of dark-colored barrels—maybe 15 or 20 of them. These barrels were made of metal and not nearly as big as the ones over at the Boois'—these were more like your standard 55-gallon drums.

As my eyes adjusted a little, I could see two outfits, hanging side by side hooks on the nearest wall that looked like suits for a spacewalk. A clear plastic helmet of sorts, a backpack apparatus, and some hoses connected to a large sprayer nozzle. Were these suits used to disseminate some type of weed killer out on the bay? And if so, were the chemicals approved by the Environmental Protection Agency, or something Tom had cooked up just for himself?

And no sooner did the thought enter my mind that I needed to get the heck out of here than a smelly gloved hand suddenly clamped down hard over my mouth and I was roughly pushed farther inside the building.

OYSTER SPAT

"You little snoop! You just had to go sticking your nose into things that are none of your business, didn't you?"

Tom Diamond slammed the door closed behind him, pitching us both into nearly totally darkness, but as it was his gear shed, he had the distinct advantage of knowing where the light switches were. He flipped on a glaring overhead fluorescent panel of tubes and glowered at me.

The look on his face instantly told me, as Meredith had predicted, that my perpetual nosiness was about to get me into more trouble than I'd bargained for. I felt the bile rise in my throat as he tightened his grip on my upper arm and deepened his scowl.

With his head, Tom nodded toward a metal sign hanging on the wall near an old work desk. "You look like a smart enough gal to be able to read what that sign says," he sneered at me.

I nodded, but held my tongue. The large white sign with red letters boldly proclaimed: "Trespassers will be shot on sight."

CHAPTER 8

Freddy and Kanji stood side by side looking out over the tidelands from the big bay windows of the casino's restaurant and lounge. The December dusk cast long shadows, even in the almost treeless marshland, and what color was left in the scenery would soon be drained with the setting of the sun.

"Does this mean we will have to change the name of our signature drink?" asked Kanji.

"No. Not necessarily," Freddy replied. "Spartina Point Casino and Resort is the go-to place of the entire southwest Washington and northwest Oregon coast. The name is already a brand, and the Spartini has become a real big hit with the locals and tourists alike."

"But you are telling me that the Spartina has been all but eradicated in the bay. Is that not true?" asked Kanji.

"Yes, it's quite true," said Freddy. He stuck his hands in his jeans pockets and rocked back and forth on his heels, still gazing out the window. "It took some doing, and there were many camps of opinion about how it should and shouldn't be accomplished, but in the end, the Spartina simply had to go."

Kanji turned from the window and thoughtfully ran a clean, dry towel across the gleaming wooden bar. "And what was so wrong with the Spartina that it had to be removed? Isn't it just a type of marsh grass?"

OYSTER SPAT

"Yes, it's a grass, but it's not a grass native to this area," said Freddy. "It's also known as cordgrass, and it is an aggressive, noxious weed. It displaces native species, destroys wildlife habitat, and interferes with recreational activities. Spartina posed a huge threat to Shallowwater Bay because it was choking out the native grasses that are beneficial to the ecosystem."

"This is most interesting," said Kanji. "Would you mind sharing with me some of those methods that were employed, and ultimately rejected?"

Freddy hesitated, and Kanji added, "I am sincere in my wish to school myself in the history of the ecology of this area. I'd like to know what didn't work, and then what did." He smiled. "I am what they call a life-long learner; I am perpetually curious."

Freddy nodded. "Sure. No problem. First off, Spartina is difficult and expensive to control. They tried mowing it, but just like when you mow your lawn, in a few weeks it needs done again, so that's not very cost effective.

"Then they tried pulling it out by its roots. They even offered to pay high school students to assist with this, but apparently no amount of money, or even extra class credit, could keep the kids interested enough to show up consistently for very long."

"And so they resorted to spraying herbicides?" Kanji prompted.

"Yes," said Freddy. "When confronted with the facts making it necessary to eradicate the Spartina, only one private owner balked at allowing the spraying on their land. So for years there were about 85 acres that kept re-infesting the entire bay. Finally, legal action was taken, and now, at least for the moment, Spartina is kind of a non-issue in Shallowwater Bay."

"Your uncle must have known of the controversy," said

Kanji. It was a statement, not a question, but Freddy didn't mind telling Kanji about his uncle, and what had transpired in recent years because of his uncle's unfounded pride and enormous ego.

"Yes, I'm quite sure Uncle Harry purposely named the casino after a noxious weed just to stick it to the county commissioners who wanted to prohibit his building the resort here on the upper north end of the peninsula." Freddy sighed. "I'm afraid he really wasn't a very nice man."

"But I am sure your uncle must have had at least some redeeming qualities," replied Kanji.

Freddy snorted. "I'm not so sure. In fact, it was Uncle Harry's refusal to adhere to the county height restrictions on new construction that ultimately led to his own demise."

"Oh dear," said Kanji. "I am so very sorry that I brought up such a painful memory."

"No worries, Kanji," said Freddy. "It's ancient history." He shrugged, and blew out a deep breath. "Uncle Harry's passing is also how I came to inherit the resort." He looked around the room, admiring all the changes he'd made since becoming the owner of this place. He hoped some of the shadiness of its past reputation would eventually be forgotten.

"You know," said Freddy, pointing to the tasteful seashore murals now obscuring the glass panels above the bar, "my uncle had a window there where the lounge patrons could watch the underwater escapades of the people in the pool—without their knowledge."

"Oh... my!" said Kanji. "Perhaps you are correct in your assessment of him."

"The county wouldn't allow him to build a traditional pool due to the potentially unstable ground here at the point," said Freddy. "So he put a small pool and hot tub in the center of the building. The pool room, as you know, spans two floors, and it was no accident the architect's plans provided entertainment for the voyeurs in the bar."

Kanji looked horrified. "Were there not some type of privacy laws in place to protect those who took advantage of the swimming pool during their stay?"

"Well, there are now!" Freddy laughed. "Like I said, Uncle Harry's illegal and immoral actions here at the resort became a moot point once I took over."

Kanji nodded thoughtfully, and turned the conversation back to the original topic. "Was there no other resistance to the spraying of chemicals on the Spartina?"

"Oh, there was plenty," said Freddy. "But it could be easily proven that the herbicide they used was too diluted to build up in the water and is rapidly broken down by sunlight. Even the EPA says it's a miniscule amount of risk to the environment, compared to the risk posed by Spartina continually infesting, and eventually killing, the entire bay."

"But what about the honeybees?" asked Kanji. "I have heard much debate and concern over the loss of honeybees due to the chemicals being sprayed on weeds which are also toxic to many beneficial insects."

Freddy smiled. "Honeybees do not go into the saltwater marshes, Kanji. There's nothing there for them; there are no flowers they normally gather pollen from."

"I see." Kanji again looked thoughtful. "So returning once again to my initial question, are we, or are we not, going to be changing the name of our most popular drink?" he asked. "It would be a pity, since the name Spartini, like the name Spartina Point Casino and Resort, sounds so classy and elegant." He chuckled. "But I am also certain that you do not wish for there to be any political backlash from the local community or the tourists who visit here."

"Fortunately for us," said Freddy, "few people know what a truly noxious weed Spartina actually was, and even fewer can tell the difference between native eel grass and Spartina, which, as I already mentioned, is a cordgrass." He grinned conspiratorially. "Especially those people not raised around here."

Kanji thought for another long moment before asking, "Am I to assume we've been using this native eel grass as the garnish for our Spartini drinks all along?"

"I cannot either confirm or deny that," said Freddy, grinning from ear to ear. "But like I said when we were over at Jimmy's place, you catch on quick." Then he glanced up at the clock on the wall behind the bar. "Did Sylvia happen to tell you when she'd get here today?"

Kanji shook his head. "No, she did not. She texted late this morning and said she was going to check on Goodie and Patrick and be up here later on. I'm afraid her text did not specify how much 'later on' she would be, or when she would arrive."

"I guess we got basically the same text then," said Freddy. He sighed heavily. "But I really thought she'd be here long before now. I've got a funny feeling in my gut that Syl not being here by now means that something's not quite right."

"Hhmm," said Kanji, "I have tried both calling and texting during the past hour, but have not managed to connect with her. Perhaps you have a number for Goodie or Patrick?"

"That I do," said Freddy, and he pulled his phone from his pocket. In mere moments he'd discovered that Syl was running a few errands for the two roommates returning kitchenware used at Nadine's memorial, but, according to Goodie, she'd left "hours ago" and probably should have been there already.

"But I wouldn't be too worried," Goodie rushed to continue, realizing that she might have upset Freddy. "You know how Sylvia loves to talk. I'm sure she just lost track of time and that she'll be along any minute."

Freddy thanked Goodie for the information, hung up, and continued to stare out the window at the quickly descending December darkness.

Meanwhile, back at the Diamond Oyster Farm, I was trying in vain to talk myself out of any conflict or controversy with Tom Diamond.

"Look, Tom, I don't know what you think I saw, or what you think I know, about anything. And I certainly didn't mean to trespass. I just came to see Lorraine and thank her for the yummy cranberry salad and blackberry pies she brought to the service last weekend. Everybody said how good the pies were. She must have saved several quarts from her berry picking last summer, because you can't get those little wild Pacificas this time of year and I—"

Tom gave a hard jerk on my arm. "Just shut up, will you? Rambling on like that isn't going to get you out of this; it's only going to make things a lot worse."

I knew what he said to be true, but I couldn't help myself. I often babble when I get nervous, and right now I was so nervous I thought I'd wet my pants. "And that crust. Just like Mother used to make—I mean if my mother ever actually baked. But hey, I promised Goodie I'd return the pans and now I've done that, so I guess it's time for me to be heading out of here."

If it were possible, Tom's grip tightened twice as hard, and I realized he was going to leave one heckuva bruise, if not actual fingerprints, on my upper arm. He roughly turned me so that his body was between me and the door. "So you saw Lorraine?"

The way he said it made the hair on my arms stand up and my stomach ball into a tight knot. Just the way he spit out his words made me glad I had not actually "seen" Lorraine, and that I could truthfully deny setting my eyes on her this afternoon.

"No, I didn't get the opportunity to speak to Lorraine face-to-face. She was holed up in her sewing room. She said she was working on a quilt she's going to finish for the show next weekend and she didn't want to take the quilting frame apart just to be able to get the bedroom door open, so we just talked through the closed door."

"Hhmm." Tom stared down at his feet, deep in thought. Then he began mumbling to himself. "You and that self-appointed do-gooder Nadine." He shook his head. "Both of you, nothing but trouble."

He looked up. "Maybe I'll just go collaborate your story with Lorraine before I decide whether or not to let you go."

He had me sit on a metal folding chair near a wooden desk that must have dated back at least a century. Then he took a roll of duct tape off a nail on the wall and bound my hands behind my back, then around and around my torso. He tore off another piece, started to put it over my mouth, then thought better of it. "Out here," his throaty chuckle gave me goosebumps all over my body, "no one can hear you scream, so you needn't bother."

Tom turned off the overhead light on his way out, and I heard another padlock click into place on the outside of the door. There was only one small window on the west side of the building giving me any light at all, and the tiny window in the door on the east side was useless for any light except first thing in the morning when the sun was coming up. The evening's full darkness wasn't that far away, even though it was only late afternoon. My goosebumps turned into full length body shivers as I contemplated my few options.

I took solace in the fact that he'd forgotten that my cell phone was most likely in my jacket pocket. It was oddly

OYSTER SPAT

comforting to know he wasn't all that astute at detaining people. Apparently, Tom didn't watch nearly the amount of crime show TV that I did. But it was probably a pipedream that there'd be good cell service way out here on the bay anyway.

As my eyes became a little more accustomed to the dim interior of the shed, I racked my brain trying to remember what all was here inside the building with me. I remembered a forklift, totes, pallets, barrels, and something that resembled a spacesuit. But there was also a desk, chair, table strewn with papers, a filing cabinet, a large, funny-looking radio system with a lot of dials on the front, and an old-time headset.

Nowhere in my recent memory did I recall seeing any type of landline telephone or even a desktop computer. The window was high up on the wall, and was built with many small panes, not one with a big piece of glass I could break out and crawl through, even if I could manage to stack enough pieces of furniture and totes together to climb up there. If I could get the forklift started, maybe I could crash it through the wall... Maybe.

All the while I was trying to figure out an escape plan, I'd been wiggling my wrists and twisting my arms around, pulling at the duct tape that bound me. As it was an ancient metal folding chair, I hoped that perhaps the stoppers on the ends of the frame might have been lost over the decades. And, as luck would have it, I was right about that. I successfully maneuvered around and was able to start using a raw metal edge to saw at my bindings.

It didn't take nearly as long as it does on TV to cut oneself through duct tape handcuffs, and I was able to get my hands free in nothing flat. Chalk another lucky point up to the fact that Tom hadn't known what he was doing when he'd restrained me.

My cell phone was right where it should be, and the battery had a pretty full charge. But there were no service bars showing and no way to call for help. Most likely, being inside in a steel construction building didn't make it any easier for my phone to find a nearby tower from which to pull a signal.

I didn't waste any time trying to unwrap my legs or torso, but cow-hopped in the chair to the desk. Using the flashlight option on my cell phone, I discovered a walkie-talkie handset. But just seconds before I pressed the receiver button down, I realized that this was only a two-way radio, and probably set up for Tom to contact Lorraine inside the house, or for her to call him out on the bay, and I hastily dropped the walkie-talkie as if it had burned me.

The other electronic equipment on the desk turned out to be a HAM radio set up. These are common worldwide for amateur radio operators to contact each other. A HAM was an amateur radio operator. HAM equaled Amateur. That much I was sure of. And I knew they used call signs to contact one another. But unlike a person's name, every call sign is unique to each HAM; no two are ever the same.

I briefly considered that Tom might have a second system set up inside the house, but quickly dismissed it. His gear shed was clearly his man cave, and it was here he probably spent most of his leisure hours—if oyster farmers had any such thing.

I turned the radio on, and was rewarded with a crackling and hissing that told me I might actually have a shot at getting out of this gear shed alive. I was pretty sure logging on to the system wasn't all that different from logging onto the Internet, but I didn't have a password—or rather a call sign—to get my distress signal out onto the airwaves.

Racking my brain, I remembered the uncle of a friend of mine who was a HAM back when I was a kid in elementary school. It's funny how memory works when one is under a great deal of stress. I clearly remembered his call sign because it was an easy one to remember, and also because he had spent time with our class at school teaching us how to spell our names in Morse Code.

I looked at the little electronic button, or key, or whatever it was officially called. Tentatively, I tapped it, and was rewarded with a short "dit" noise. I pressed it again, a little longer this time, and got a definite "dah" sound. Dits and dahs. Morse code is a binary system, so every letter of the alphabet had to be some combination of short and long sounds. There were only two choices. Short and long sounds, otherwise known as dits and dahs.

For the life of me, I couldn't remember the correct combination to signal an SOS. I couldn't even remember my own name in Morse Code. All I could remember was my elementary friend's five-letter first name: Dit-dah-dah-dah, dit-dah, dah-dit, dit, dah. Janet.

But I was pretty sure signaling Janet! Janet! Janet! wasn't going to bring the necessary help. And there was no way I could figure out how to rearrange the letters in Janet to make any other words that might make sense or signal distress. Janet, Jane, Jan, jet, net, ant, ante, ten, tan, an, eat, ate, at, a. Nope. With only those five letters of code, I'd likely be stuck here all night—or at least until Tom returned, whenever that would be.

The headset was my next option. I plugged it into the radio, settled it over my head, and listened to the static. No one was there, already speaking, so I depressed the microphone button. "This is W7HUG. Hello? W7HUG here, trying to patch a message through to Nova Johanssen on the Estrella Nueva in Unity, Washington. Ms. Johanssen, come in please! Come in, Nova Johanssen. Can you read me? This is W7HUG over and out!"

I'm not sure how many state, federal, or international laws I was breaking, but I figured since it was life or death, and that this was an amateur radio club, I'd probably get off with a warning, a fine, or community service. Right now, I just needed for Nova to be out on her boat crab fishing and have her radio turned on.

I waited, listening to the crackling and buzzing, and distant sounds of life out there somewhere in the universe. If this was what social media was like before the advent of Facebook, I'm glad I wasn't born any sooner. But now I wasn't sure what to do next. Should I resend the message? Should I just press the down the microphone button and start yelling SOS, SOS, SOS at the top of my lungs?

"This is Nova Johanssen on the Estrella Nueva," said a voice I could not recognize through all the static. "W7HUG, how can I help you?"

Relief flooded through me, and I wasn't sure if I were going to burst into tears, or pee my pants, or both. Nova was only a radio transmission away! But I didn't dare use my own name over the radio, still fearing that Tom might have a simple monitor set up inside the house. Too late I realized I had only partially thought this through.

"This is Stella Larsen," I said, after pressing the microphone button. "I need you to relay a message to Frederick Harold Morgan. Please tell him that Señor Oscar Sierra would like to meet him *RIGHT AWAY* at the place just north of where the pink sandverbena were discovered growing last summer. Do you copy? Frederick Harold Morgan must meet Señor Oscar Sierra near the pink sandverbenas immediately. *DO YOU COPY?*"

My plea for help was met with crackling, popping, buzzing, and plenty of static, but no response or any kind of confirmation that Nova had received my message. I felt a wave of nausea starting up into my throat, but if Nova had heard even half of my call, she'd still be my best chance to be rescued. "W7HUG, over and out."

I took off the headset and clawed at the rest of the duct tape binding me to the chair. Whether my coded message got through or not, I needed to be prepared for Tom's eventual return. Prepared, and more than ready to fight for my life.

CHAPTER 9

Tom and Lorraine Diamond were not expecting anyone to come calling after dark. Living at the end of the road, it was unusual for them to get even a casual visitor, and certainly not one who had not called first.

As it turned out, they were just finishing up dinner when the knock sounded on their front door. They looked dumbly at one another, and Lorraine shrugged. "I'm not expecting company," she said.

"Yeah, and you weren't expecting company when that snoopy little trespasser came to return your pie plates and bowls this afternoon either," said Tom.

"No harm done," said Lorraine. She gently placed a hand to her face and lightly touched the swelling around her eye. "She didn't see me."

"Nonetheless," said Tom. "We don't need no snoops hanging around." He got up from the table and started for the front door.

Freddy, in his usual jeans, button-down shirt, quilted vest and cowboy boots, stood on the doorstep, shifting from foot to foot. Damn! It was cold out here, and he knew with 100% certainty that not only were the Diamonds at home, but that Syl was somewhere nearby, too. He looked back over his shoulder at her mustang parked between his red Mazda and Tom Diamond's ratty old blue pick-up truck.

As soon as Freddy received Nova's odd message, he had

OYSTER SPAT

hightailed it out of the casino for nearby Willoopah. At the Booi farm, Brent had told him that Syl had been by earlier in the afternoon, and that she'd left there headed for the Diamond's to continue returning various kitchenware.

Now standing on the Diamond's porch, Freddy wondered if he'd need the revolver he had tucked into the back of his jean's waistband, or if Nova had misunderstood an apparent distress call for help.

Tom turned on the porchlight, flung the door open, stepped outside onto the stoop, and closed the door tightly behind him. "You lost?" he asked Freddy.

Tom showed no recognition on his face, although it had been Deputy Morgan who had separated Brent and him at Nadine's memorial less than a week ago. Perhaps, thought Freddy, he's one of those guys who only sees the uniform, and not the guy inside it.

"No, I'm not lost," said Freddy, "but I'm thinking maybe my girlfriend is." He gestured with his thumb back over his shoulder. "That's her car parked over there."

"You mean that snoopy little trespasser who was lurking around here is your girlfriend?" asked Tom, feigning surprise. "Man, some guys got absolutely no taste in women."

Freddy balled his hands into fists, but kept his cool. "Do you happen to know where she is?"

"Well, I ain't seen her, but maybe she got locked in my gear shed when I closed up for the night," said Tom. "Let me pull on a jacket, and we can go take a look around."

The men's voices carried quite a distance in the chill December air, and before they got too close to the gear shed, I stashed the pipe I'd been ready to swing like a baseball bat at the first head through the doorway behind one of the 55-gallon drums. I recognized Freddy's voice, and was about to weep with joy, but instead I had the presence of mind to start rapidly flashing the overhead light switch on and off and on and off and on and off.

When Tom removed the padlock and swung the door open, he pretended a second time to be surprised. "Well, well, well, little missy. I don't know how you got yourself trapped in here today, but I'm sure glad someone knew to come looking for you."

Freddy stepped up and hugged me, whispering in my ear, "You okay?"

I nodded my head against his shoulder, and once again fought the urge to cry.

"Woulda been mighty cold out here tonight," said Tom to no one in particular, but glaring at me with his eyes narrowed. "I guess this is your lucky day."

"I guess so," I muttered contritely. There'd be time enough to go over things with Freddy later. Right now, I just wanted to put some distance between Tom Diamond and me. For the moment, I was more than grateful that Freddy was following my lead and not going all "cop mode" on me.

Freddy and I walked over to the cars while Tom stood with his fists on his hips and watched us leave. "I'll follow you to the casino," Freddy said softly. And again, I just nodded.

Once we took a table in the bar, and I had a hot cup of chamomile tea to wrap my hands around, Freddy wanted to hear the whole story. "And don't leave anything out," he warned.

"Is Kanji making Chicken Tikki Marsala tonight?" I asked, before I agreed to anything. "Thinking about having Indian food here tonight is about all that kept me going the past few hours."

Freddy motioned to the bartender, who called an order in to the kitchen, then turned to me with his dark, piercing eyes. "Now," he said, "no more excuses."

OYSTER SPAT

"I was returning pots and pans for Goodie and Patrick. I stopped at the Booi farm first. I met Nautika Henry, his new assistant who just graduated from the U Dub. It turns out she's the child Meredith told us about, born to Julie Henry 25 years ago.

"Then I went to the Diamond farm, and something wasn't quite right with Lorraine. I think she was hiding in the bedroom, pretending that her quilting frame was blocking the door, so that I wouldn't see her. I stopped by Tom's gear shed to see if Tom were around, and... And then I guess I got accidentally locked inside when he went into the house for dinner."

"Not buying it," said Freddy, sipping a cup of black coffee.

One of his eyebrows had an arc to it that told me he wasn't going to go along with my story until I told him the entire truth, and even then, he would decide for himself on the next course of action. That eyebrow always spoke volumes.

But before I could add anything more to what I'd told him, Kanji appeared at the table with a tray loaded with Indian food—plenty enough for all three of us. He started by setting plates and silverware on the table, then without waiting for an invitation, pulled up a chair and sat down. He handed me a fork. "I believe the proper expression for a moment like this is 'dig in.'"

Kanji's smile was genuine, and I was grateful he was there to buffer the tension between Freddy and me, but I was also grateful that when I did tell the whole story, I'd only have to tell it once for both of them to be satisfied that I was alright, and I knew what I was doing.

The food was beyond delicious, and not just because I hadn't had a single bite of anything since breakfast. Kanji was an excellent chef, among other things, and Freddy had been smart enough to capitalize on his expertise in both hospitality and cooking when he hired him. Although as I recall it, Freddy had hired Kanji more to keep an eye on him—a new guy in the community, and his possible competition for my affection.

When there wasn't another piece of naan to be had, or sauce to dip it in left on any of our plates, Freddy returned to what I considered my interrogation.

I quickly brought Kanji up to speed, watching as his eyebrows knit together in concern for my welfare as I tried again to pass off my detainment in the Diamond gear shed as just an unfortunate accident.

"Yeah, still not buying it," said Freddy.

"Perhaps Miss Sylvia would like to review the facts of her containment in the gear shed and consider that we are both on her side and are here only to help her?" asked Kanji.

Well, when he put it that way... I took a deep breath. "Fine."

And then, so help me, there was nothing I could do to stop my shoulders from shaking and the tears from streaking down my face. So much for my competent woman who can take care of herself posturing! My bravado flew out the window like jet-propelled pumice stones leaving Mt. St. Helens during the volcanic eruption.

Freddy handed me his cloth napkin, and Kanji reached over to gently squeeze my shoulder. "I was here when the call came in from Nova," said Kanji. "We already know you were in considerable danger and that time was of the essence."

I nodded and blew my nose. "Yes. I was afraid Tom was going to— Well, I'm not exactly sure what Tom was going to do, but I'm sure it wasn't going to be very pleasant."

"I wonder what he was going to do with your car parked right out there in front of his house," said Freddy. "And the fact that there were two witnesses that could place you in the car, and headed his way, earlier this afternoon."

"Yes," said Kanji. "Miss Sylvia drives a very distinctive car. I have never seen another one like it, and it would not be an easy thing for anyone to hide."

"Unless Tom used his backhoe to bury the car—and Sylvia—deep in the marshlands out there somewhere," Freddy replied.

"I'm right here!" I said indignantly. "And I'm safe and sound, and nobody's burying me or my car out anyplace on the peninsula any time soon!" I nearly spat out the final words.

"Good," said Kanji. "The color has now returned to her face."

"That's my girl," said Freddy, reaching over to pat my hand. "Now are you ready to tell us exactly what happened at the Diamond farm this afternoon?"

"And please," said Kanji, "think carefully so that you do not accidently leave anything out."

I looked from one lovingly concerned face to the other and shook my head. "I don't know what I did right to have you two care so much about me, but I'm really glad you do." I wiped the back of my hand across my cheek where a stray tear or two was trying to escape.

"Do you need to call Sheriff Donaldson?" I asked Freddy, "Or can you take my statement without involving him?"

Freddy smiled. "I already spoke with him. As long as you don't mind me recording our conversation, that's all I need to do at this point."

"Good." I nodded slowly and thoughtfully. "So let's start when I pulled up at the Diamond farm."

Freddy put his phone on record, and neither of the men said a word for the next few minutes, although I could see by their expressions there was plenty they wanted to say, and I was probably going to get an earful when I finished my report.

"I tapped on the door a couple times, and called out for both Lorraine and Tom. Then I tried the door, because I thought maybe I could set the dishes down inside and just leave, and not have to make a second trip to return them."

Freddy and Kanji both silently nodded.

"Then I heard someone in a back bedroom. It was Lorraine. But she said she was working on a quilt and couldn't take down the whole frame to come out at that moment, and she thanked me for coming, but I had a feeling…"

"A feeling?" prompted Freddy.

"A bad feeling. Something just wasn't quite right. I could feel it in my gut. The house was a mess—like it had been ransacked or something. No Christmas tree, no decorations. Just not the kind of homey atmosphere I'd expect from Lorraine."

"Because of her work with the quilting guild?" asked Freddy.

"No. Yes. Well—" I huffed. "I'm just not sure."

"It may be hard to imagine a woman of high standing in her church and community groups to be less than a stellar housekeeper," Kanji offered.

"I just felt—in my gut—that something was very wrong in the Diamond home."

"Okay," said Freddy, nodding. "I think I understand. It was Tom, not Lorraine, who answered my knock tonight, and he stepped out on the porch and pulled the door closed behind him. It was as if he didn't want me to see inside the house, or to see Lorraine, or for her to see me, I'm not sure which. In fact, I'm not even sure he knew exactly who I was, since I wasn't wearing my uniform." Freddy paused. "And I'm pretty sure he'd been drinking."

OYSTER SPAT

It was my turn to simply nod my understanding. "So instead of getting in my car and leaving right away," I said, "I went to see if Tom was out in his gear shed. I don't know why. I just wanted to know where he was at that moment."

"And did you find him?"

"No." I looked down at my hands, folded tightly on the table. "I went into the shed—"

"Uninvited?" asked Freddy.

"Yes, uninvited." I glared at him. "But the door wasn't locked, just like the door to their house wasn't locked. In fact, it was slightly ajar."

"So you were trespassing," said Freddy. "Just like Tom said you were when I got there and asked him about you."

"Do you want to hear the rest of what happened or not?"

"Please continue, Miss Sylvia," said Kanji. "Our deep concern for your welfare has made us both a little on the edgy side."

I nodded. "The gear shed held things that were vastly different from the things in the gear shed at the Booi farm."

"How so?" asked Freddy.

"The Booi gear shed is set up for research and innovation. The Diamond shed was filled with a lot of totes, and pallets, and a forklift to move them, but there were no research vats for growing algae or oyster seed." I paused, trying to put my feelings into words. "It just felt... different... dirty... ugly... sinister..." I closed my eyes and tried to remember why I felt that way. "There were 10 or 15 big, dark 55-gallon drums of something. And two outfits that looked like spacesuits hanging on hooks on the walls."

"Can you describe these 'spacesuits'?" asked Freddy.

"A plastic or rubber kind of helmet— or hat— or head covering, with a full face shield, and a one-piece waterproof bodysuit with attached boots..."

"You mean like a commercial fisherman's survival suit?"

"Yes, but they didn't look like they were buoyant. Just protective. And there were backpacks, kind of, that had hoses coming out of them, with the end of the hose connected to a sprayer-like attachment."

"Okay, so Tom sprays his property for weeds," said Freddy. "No crime there."

"Maybe not." I sighed. "And right about then, Tom came in and grabbed my upper arm and called me a do-gooder like Nadine, and that I was nothing but trouble."

I rolled up my sleeve, and as I'd suspected, there was a sizeable bruise on my upper arm. I started to shiver, reliving the experience, but pressed on. "He bound me with duct tape to a folding chair and left me there, padlocking the door from the outside."

I could tell both Freddy and Kanji were getting red-faced and agitated over my treatment, but they kept quiet.

"I got loose, but there's no cell service out there. No phone in the shed, either. But there was a HAM radio set up…"

"A HAM radio?" asked Kanji.

"Uhhh…" I looked at Freddy for help explaining, but he looked as clueless as I felt. "It's a bunch of amateur radio enthusiasts who connect on frequencies that are set aside for them to send messages to their friends without the internet or cell phones, or…stuff like that." I shrugged. The one time I needed Jimmy's encyclopedic resource mind, and he wasn't there!

"So a HAM is an amateur broadcaster, and anyone can do this?" asked Kanji.

"They have to have a license, and there are rules, but yes, I guess it's open to anyone who passes their test," I said.

Freddy smiled. "You're not licensed to operate one, are you?"

I rolled my eyes and my temper flared. "After all I've

OYSTER SPAT

been through today, are you telling me you want to arrest me for operating a HAM radio without a license?"

"No, no, of course he does not," soothed Kanji. "We are both just so thankful you knew how to operate such a survival mechanism as to affect your own rescue."

"Yes," said Freddy. "Now about that convoluted message you sent to Nova."

"Nova's the only one I know who monitors the HAM frequencies," I replied.

"But you identified yourself as Stella Larsen," said Freddy.

"Who, may I ask, is this Stella Larsen?" asked Kanji.

"Stella is... or was... Nadine's special needs papillon dog," said Freddy.

"Oh my," said Kanji. Then he smiled. "That was most clever of you, Miss Sylvia. If someone were listening to the transmission who did not know about Nadine's most pampered pet, they might not know you were actually signaling your distress and calling for help."

"Well, I couldn't very well use my real name—"

"So you used the name Stella Larsen because...?"

"Because I figured that Nova would know something was really wrong. And I used your middle name because I knew if she called you, you'd know the message was from me, because not too many people know your middle name is Harold."

Kanji smiled again at that. "So you were named after your Uncle Harry?"

"Yeah," Freddy answered Kanji, "but don't hold it against me." Then he turned to me. "What Nova had the most trouble with was figuring out the part about Señor Oscar Sierra."

"S-O-S!" I said. "Señor Oscar Sierra! That should have been the easy part!"

"Uh... Okay..." Freddy wasn't sure if he should laugh or not. "But if you were using the NATO alphabet, it would have been 'Sierra Oscar Sierra.' So why did you use Señor?"

"Because Nova speaks Spanish!" I couldn't believe how Freddy could be so obtuse.

"Uh, right..." Freddy shot a look at Kanji that clearly said he wasn't following my reasoning at all, then asked me about the pink sandverbena.

"You know, those little pink native flowers that have begun to reestablish themselves along the bay shore between the casino and Willoopah? We saw some along the bay last summer," I looked from Freddy to Kanji and back again. "Everybody thought the plants were extinct, but once the Spartina was cleared out, they started making a comeback. I figured you'd remember where we saw them when we were out riding our motorcycles together."

"Oh. Right. Yes, of course."

Freddy seemed to be patronizing me, but at this point I didn't even care. He'd found me, saved me from god-only-knows-what at the hands of Tom Diamond, and I was safe and warm and back among friends.

"So are you going to press charges against Tom for unlawfully detaining you?" asked Freddy. "Because if you do, it's quite likely that Tom will file a criminal trespass complaint, mistaking you for a rabid environmentalist out to sabotage his equipment, and that he was just holding you in the gear shed until he could notify the police."

My mouth opened and closed several times like a guppy out of water. "Whatever would have given him that crazy idea?"

"There was a bomb threat at the Booi farm just a few months ago, remember? And Tom figured those... what did he call them?... those pinko commie radicals...were probably coming after him, too." Freddy paused briefly. "And don't forget the fact that you WERE trespassing, Syl."

I glowered. "No, I'm not pressing charges, but not because I'm afraid of him—at least not for myself. I'm afraid that Lorraine would suffer the consequences later. Really there was no harm done— Well, no physical harm besides this one big bruise." I had already rolled my sleeve back down. "So I guess I'll just let it go."

Freddy nodded. "You can let it go, for now, but by filing this report, we'll have a paper trail in case anything else comes to light later."

"What do you mean by 'anything else'?" I asked.

"Like if Lorraine wanted to get a restraining order on him or something like that."

Geez, I should have realized that. With 30 years in the business of protecting those who couldn't protect themselves, I should have realized Lorraine might need me as a character witness or a personal advocate somewhere down the line.

"Can we just list this as a big misunderstanding, and go on with our lives?" I asked.

"Sounds good to me," said Freddy.

"For now," added Kanji. "But if I am to understand what you are saying here, there may be a time when you can no longer keep quiet, Miss Sylvia. Is that correct?"

"Yes, Kanji, that is correct. And it's the one time I hope I'm wrong in my assessment of a situation. But I'm pretty sure Tom uses Lorraine as his personal punching bag with regularity. I think that's why she didn't come out to visit with me when I stopped over there. She didn't want me to ask about any marks or bruises."

"And the county sheriff can't do much about it if Lorraine doesn't report the abuse," added Freddy.

I was about to launch into a tirade about women who just take the abuse and then blame themselves for causing the problems instead of standing up to someone who mistreats them, but I stopped myself just in time. Of all the men I knew, these two were the least likely to ever touch a woman in anger. And of that, I was absolutely certain.

OYSTER SPAT

CHAPTER 10

Brent had already cleared the table and was busy putting the leftovers into smaller containers for the refrigerator. Nautika stood at the sink, doing their dinner dishes and staring out the window at the dark expanse looming out there that she knew to be Shallowwater Bay.

"When there's no moon, it's kind of ominous out there at night, isn't it?" Nautika asked him.

Brent walked up behind her and looked out the window over her shoulder. He nodded. "Uh-huh. Sometimes it feels like a reflection of a big black hole in outer space. Then daylight comes, and it returns to the welcoming landscape we call home."

"Home," said Nautika. "Yes, there's certainly something about this place that just feels like home, alright."

Brent opened the bottom drawer beneath the counter and brought out a clean dish towel. He picked up a handful of silverware to dry, but suddenly he flinched, abruptly pulling his hand back as if he'd cut himself, dropping the forks and spoons and one other utensil onto the floor.

"Hey!" admonished Nautika, "I just washed those!"

"Sorry," said Brent. He put the forks and spoons back into the soapy sink water and held up the item that had startled him. "Where did this oyster shucking knife come from?"

Nautika smiled. "It was my mother's. Why?"

Brent turned the beautiful knife over in his hands, admiring the fit of the handle in his grip and the craftsmanship that had gone into making this tool. "Do you know the story behind it?" he asked.

Nautika rinsed the silverware off a second time and put them into the dish drainer. She wiped her hands on a dishtowel and nodded. "Yes, I've heard the story many times." She laughed. "To hear Mom tell it, the birds were singing, the bells were ringing, and it was the most beautiful late summer day the world had ever seen."

"It was," said Brent, leaning back on the kitchen counter. "Blue sky, warm but not too warm, and with just enough breeze along the bay to call it balmy. We don't get a lot of days like that, but when they show up, we enjoy every moment. That day, the community was celebrating the 150th anniversary of the commercial oyster fishery on Shallowwater Bay. And to that effect, 150 commemorative oyster shucking knives were given out during the festivities."

Nautika chuckled. "At first, Mom thought she'd gotten the very last one, because it has the number 150 engraved on the handle..."

"...but it turned out that all the knives had the number 150 on them." Brent also chuckled at the memory as he finished the sentence for her.

"You know, Nautika, you look just like Jewels did at your age."

"I'll take that as a compliment."

"You should. She was a beautiful woman."

Nautika blushed slightly. "How well did you know her?"

"Well, she and... John... were part of the Diamond Oyster Farms lawsuit against me and my ancestral claim to some of the oyster tidelands back then." Brent took a deep breath. "But I never held it against her personally." He sighed. "In fact, I'm sure now that Julie was secretly on my side during the whole ordeal, but of course, she'd never publicly say so."

"That's sounds about right," said Nautika. "Mom was very worried about what others thought of her, and speaking out against her husband or his employer would have gone against her code of ethics."

"Very true," Brent replied. "Jewels was a woman of the highest moral standards." He paused for just a fraction of a second before softly concluding, "For the most part."

"For the most part?" Nautika frowned. "What is that supposed to mean?"

Brent smiled. "I was quite fond of your mother back then."

Nautika's brow furrowed. She pulled out a chair at the kitchen table and sat down. "Just what are you saying, Brent?"

"Don't go there," said Brent, holding a hand up to stop her. "It's not what you might be thinking."

"Then why don't you tell me what I *should* be thinking?"

"Alright, I will." Brent nodded, and he put his hand on the back of the chair that faced her, as if to steady himself. "I think it's high time you knew the truth." He pulled out the chair and sat down. "I was in love with your mother long before John came upon the scene, Nautika, but I was shy, painfully shy, and I could never bring myself to ask her out back in high school.

"Then when the three of us returned from the Navy, Tom pushed John into marrying Julie as quickly as he could, over at the courthouse. He thought it would give Diamond Farms a stronger claim to the tidelands if one of the partners was married to a Native American woman."

Nautika scowled and crossed her arms over her chest. "So they weren't madly in love. I already knew that. But Mom didn't see a whole lot of other men knocking her door down."

Brent shook his head. "I could never get up the courage. I was so busy working. Time… and life… just flew by while I was working my butt off out on the bay."

"So you had an unrequited love?"

"Not exactly…"

"What do you mean by 'not exactly'?" asked Nautika. She grabbed the edge of the table so hard her knuckles turned white. "Are you saying my mother cheated on my father?"

"No, nothing like that. Your mother, as I've said, was an honorable woman."

Nautika loosened her grip just a little, but the tight foreboding in her chest did not lessen.

"Please, Nautika, just hear me out."

Wordlessly, Nautika nodded.

"I was the one who found a single rubber boot in the mud along the bay one afternoon about two weeks after John disappeared," said Brent. "It had his initials, 'JH,' in marking pen on the inside rim of the boot. I called the sheriff's office right away so I could turn it over to them, and was told the sheriff was busy at the other end of the county. They said he would be out to collect it later that night. The dispatcher told me to meet the sheriff at the Henry's place in Ocean Crest.

"So I went down to Ocean Crest to console Julie, but she took the news really well. She had accepted the fact that John was just gone, and that was that."

"She wasn't grieving? Or worried? Or upset or anything?"

"No." Brent shook his head. "She just went about the business of fixing us some dinner as if we ate together every evening. We talked about high school, and how we'd had mutual crushes on each other, and that we were sorry that neither one of us ever acted upon it.

"We talked about our views on the right way to go about

oyster farming without jeopardizing the fishery. We talked about all sorts of things. She even apologized for how John and Tom had treated me, before, during, and after the lawsuit.

"We shared our deepest feelings, our biggest regrets, and then one thing started leading to another, but..." Brent paused, searching for just the right words.

"But what?" Nautika was halfway up and out of her chair. "Don't tell me that you and my mother..."

"No, no, nothing like that. Before things went too far, the sheriff arrived, and I went out to my truck and got him the boot I'd found. Then the sheriff asked Julie if she could positively identify the boot. Jewels sadly smiled and nodded and went out to the carport and brought a boot back in that matched the one in the sheriff's hand.

"It turned out it was her who had lost a boot, not John. JH. John Henry, Julie Henry. Same initials. Unisex boots. I should have thought of that before I notified the sheriff." Brent shook his head. "For such a big man, John Henry had pretty small feet." He grinned. "And your mother's feet, well..." He looked down at Nautika's feet sticking out from under the table and his grin widened. "I see your feet take after your mother's. Good and sturdy."

Nautika was still scowling. "Never mind about my feet. What I want to know is if you're saying what I think you're saying. Are you implying you think my mom might have killed my dad or something?"

"No, no, certainly not. Nothing of the kind. What I was trying to say is the sheriff arrived before your mother and I got too close that night.

"As for her missing boot, it was August. If ever there were days you just wanted to kick off your boots and squish around barefoot along the bay, it would be then." Brent smiled. "Julie asked the sheriff if she could have her boot back, but he said he needed it for evidence."

"Evidence of what?" asked Nautika.

"That's exactly what your mother said." Brent laughed. "She jutted out her chin, put her hands on her hips, looked him square in the eye, and said, 'Why do you need any evidence of the fact I like to go barefoot in the summer? It's no big secret; I've always loved going barefoot, ever since I can remember.'"

Nautika returned Brent's smile. "So you two bonded over making the sheriff look foolish?"

"Well, yes, that too. But Nautika—" Brent couldn't make himself look her in the eye. "That wasn't the only time your mother and I spent together after John disappeared."

Brent looked down at the oyster knife in his hand, turning it over and over, as if weighing the consequences of his thoughts, his words, his actions. "Well, sweetheart," he mumbled quietly, "I guess the time has come."

"The time has come for what?" asked Nautika. "Please, just spit it out."

Brent lifted his eyes to hers. His sigh came from deep within his chest, maybe all the way from his toes. "You remember that letter of introduction you brought me?"

"Yes," said Nautika. "Of course. Mother made me promise not to open it, but to give it directly to you when I came to interview for work here."

"How long was that before she died?" asked Brent.

"Not very long—a week or so at best." Nautika's eyes teared up. "We'd talked a lot about what I was going to do after graduating from the U. We discussed a lot of options. But when I told her I really wanted to return to her roots here, and work to preserve the oyster fishery as well as the clean water of the bay, I think it kind of pleased her. She said that would bring everything 'full circle'," said Nautika. "I'm not exactly sure what she meant by that, but she wrote the letter then, and I tucked it in with my resumés and transcripts to have when I needed it.

"Unfortunately, Mom died a few weeks before I graduated." Nautika sighed heavily. "After packing up the house, I called to set up the interview with you." She shrugged. "And here I am."

Brent nodded. "Full circle. Yes, indeed." He absentmindedly tapped the oyster knife against the palm of his hand.

Nautika studied his face. "You know what she meant by that, don't you?"

"Yes, Nautika, I do. Your mother left it up to me when to tell you about her time here on the peninsula, the circumstances of John's disappearance, and the real reason she left the area."

"But I've been here almost five months," said Nautika. "Why haven't you said anything before now?"

"Because I've been selfish," said Brent. "I've liked the way things were going. I've enjoyed getting to know you. I didn't want to rock the boat too soon, and risk you deciding to look elsewhere for employment." Brent gnawed on his lower lip. "I didn't want to lose you."

"Mom told me my dad abandoned her after gambling away his share of the Diamond farm," said Nautika. "And that she never heard from him again. She said it was better for her, and me, if she moved away to start fresh somewhere else."

"And that's pretty much all true," said Brent.

"Pretty much?"

"John disappeared in late July, 26 years ago," said Brent. "Your mother moved to Olympia in November, saying she didn't want to spend the holidays here on the bay. But in fact, she didn't want her neighbors in Ocean Crest to find out she was pregnant, so she left before she started to show. The county nurse, Meredith Avery, and I helped her move, and we both went up to visit her a few times the following year."

"Meredith Avery?" asked Nautika. "Is she related to the Sylvia Avery I met here earlier today?"

Brent shrugged. "It's a very small county, Nautika; Meredith is Sylvia's mother."

"No kidding," said Nautika. Now it was her turn to chew on her lower lip, and Brent briefly wondered if that trait was transmitted genetically—her mother often did that too, when she was deep in thought. He did it too. Maybe everyone did.

"It was very nice of you," said Nautika, "helping her move, considering you'd been on different sides of the property dispute. I'm sure my mom really appreciated your kindness."

Nautika unfolded her arms and rested her hands in her lap. "But do you know why in the world she wouldn't stay here where she had some kind of support system? Why didn't she want her friends around her through her pregnancy, and to help her learn to be a single mom?"

"Both very good questions," said Brent. "And they deserve honest answers." He set the knife down, propped his elbows on the table and rubbed his forehead with both hands for a minute or two before he spoke again. "Your mother didn't want the neighbors all talking, speculating, gossiping. And after she got that great job in Olympia, there really was no reason to return. She knew she could do better by you if she made a good living for the two of you and lived a lot closer to good schools and colleges and what she called 'civilization'."

"I... I guess that makes some sense. But Mom was all alone in a new city. She had no one to share her joy with."

"That's not entirely true," said Brent. "She had me, and in a different way, she had Meredith. We were both there when you were born, honey. Your mother and I picked out your name together." Brent's eyes misted over. "It was a beautiful June day; the day of the solstice. The longest, most beautiful day of that year."

Nautika scowled. "I still don't see what any of this has to do with—"

Brent's voice came out in a soft, husky whisper. "Nautika… You're a smart girl; you can do the math."

"What are you saying?" Nautika's scowl deepened. "What are you— NO! Oh my god, are you telling me that John is not my real father?" She jumped up from her chair, indignant. "But his name is on my birth certificate!"

"Julie thought it would be easier that way," said Brent. "No questions, no whispers behind anyone's backs. I couldn't leave the oyster farm, and she couldn't leave the future she was determined to build for you."

Nautika silently plopped back down in the kitchen chair, visibly shaken and adamantly shaking her head. "No. No! It just can't be."

"Your mother was afraid people would think that either she killed John, or I did. Can you understand what kind of scandal that would have been?"

Nautika took a paper napkin from the holder on the table and blew her nose. "It's not true. It can't be true. All my life—"

"I know, honey, it's a lot to take in." Brent picked up the oyster knife again, carefully considering his next words. "You know that June's birthstone is a pearl," said Brent.

Nautika nodded. "Yes, she told me that's why she chose Pearl for my middle name."

"But you also know that pearls are found in oysters."

"Yes, but Pacific Northwest Oysters aren't the kind that produce the pearls that are used in fine jewelry," said Nautika.

"It's no secret that your mother had a wonderful sense of humor," continued Brent. "And if things had been a little different back then, your full name on your birth certificate would have been Nautika Pearl Booi.

Brent hoped Nautika would see her mother's playfulness in that, but instead of comforting her, his words had somehow produced an adverse reaction.

"NO!" Nautika violently shook her head as if the pure force of her will could change history. "No! That just can't be! Why would my mother lie to me about this my whole life? It doesn't make sense." She glared at Brent. "What kind of a scam are you trying to pull?" Her eyes narrowed, and she nearly spit her next words at him, "Before I trust that anything you're saying is true, buster, I'm going to need a DNA sample from you."

Brent barely contained a big old belly laugh. He just got up and went to his desk at the back of the kitchen, opened a lower drawer and pulled out a manila envelope. 'That's exactly what your mother thought you would say." He handed Nautika the envelope. "The results are right here, and we won't be needing Maury Povich to tell you that I AM your father."

Nautika took the envelope and set it on the table in front of her, the wind totally taken out of her sails. "Then I guess I don't really need to open the envelope, do I?"

"When Julie first told me she had cancer, I promised her I would see to it you would always have a place to live, and a job to do, if you wanted it," said Brent. "We agreed I would reveal your true paternity when the time was right, and tonight, when you were standing at the sink looking out at the bay, I felt your loneliness, and I was thinking then about telling you. Then, after seeing that oyster shucking knife, well, it felt like Jewels was sending me a sign."

They sat in companionable silence, each contemplating

their next move. After a while, Brent went again to his desk and brought back his business ball cap. "You see the Willoopah Oyster business logo on this hat?" he asked.

Nautika nodded.

"I created it right after you were born. The Booi's come from Holland. This is the Booi Coat of Arms: A black bird on a gold star on a green shield. Black is for constancy, or sometimes grief; gold is a symbol of generosity and elevation of mind; and the green signifies hope, joy, and loyalty in love."

"I remember seeing this logo on some of the mail Mom got," said Nautika. "I never thought to ask her who the letters were from."

"The logo was a symbol of my love—of your mother's and my love—and of my love for you, too. You've always been a part of me, Nautika. But I realize this is quite a shock, and we can keep it just between us for as long as you wish."

Again, Nautika nodded. "Thank you. I appreciate that. And if you don't mind, I'd think I'd like to keep our familial relationship quiet until I can fully embrace it."

"Of course," Brent readily agreed.

"I really have no reason to doubt you, Brent, but I need some time to take it all in. It's quite an adjustment to suddenly set aside who I thought I was and figure out who I really am. Don't worry. I'll be okay after I get used to it. I know you have nothing to gain from telling me all this."

Brent's eyes misted over. "Nothing to gain but a daughter."

Nautika stood up and moved toward him. Brent was still holding the oyster shucking knife, so he quickly stuck it into his pants pocket. He wanted both hands free so he could fully enjoy embracing his amazing adult daughter for the very first time.

CHAPTER 11

The Veiled Rainbow belly dancing troupe was originally scheduled to perform at the North Beach Peninsula's Holiday Quilt Show at the casino the following weekend, but the ladies' hearts were understandably just not into it. Nevertheless, Meredith, Orpha, Goodie and Nova showed up to give their support to Lorraine and the quilting guild.

The show was well-attended, the quilts were nothing short of amazing, and we rendezvoused in the lounge for cocktails and appetizers when the show closed mid-afternoon.

I'd already explained privately to Nova that my SOS from the Diamond Oyster Farm was just a big misunderstanding, and got her to pinky-promise me she wouldn't bring it up in front of anyone, ever. No sense worrying Mom or anyone else. It was just water under the bridge. No big deal. End of story.

Nova, at a young 68, was a little more astute than the rest of the geriatric troupe, but she good naturedly went along with my request for silence, after teasing me no end for my lack of skills in both the HAM radio operation and the NATO phonetic alphabet.

Kanji delivered the first round of beverages to our table, quietly setting everyone's favorite drink in front of them without a word. I nodded my thanks to him, and the quick wink and smile he gave me in return would have curled my

OYSTER SPAT

toes, had I been looking to have my toes curled that particular afternoon.

"Here's to our dear, sweet, precious little Deenie," said Meredith, lifting her glass.

"Here! Here!" we all chorused, each taking a sip afterwards.

Lorraine Diamond fluttered into the room right as we were setting our glasses back down. She was wearing a tropical print caftan that moved every which way as she walked, giving the impression she was more ethereal than mortal. She slid into an empty chair next to Orpha, and motioned to Kanji to bring her "one of those tasty Spartinis you're so famous for."

Anyone with decent vision could see that Lorraine was trying to hide something, and most likely, it was her entire face. It was covered from her chin line on up with heavy foundation, and the shoulder-length auburn wig she wore had the bangs combed down to the tops of her extra large half-tinted tortoise shell framed glasses.

Orpha looked at Lorraine as if she were seeing a ghost. "What the hell are you all dressed up like that for?" she asked. "Are you applying to fill Nadine's spot in the dancing troupe?"

"I beg your pardon?" asked Lorraine.

"Well, Nadine loved mixing up her hair colors, and her vision was bad, so she always wore those half-shade sunglasses like the ones you've got on. Your muu-muu is all leafy green and tropical looking," said Orpha, nearly running out of breath as she rushed on, "so if that ain't a pitch to take over Nadine's recently vacated green spot in our ensemble, I don't know what is."

"Heavens to mercy, no!" admonished Lorraine. "As the president of the quilting guild, I have a duty to add a flourish of class to the event by dressing professionally." She looked at the rest of us for backup. "Surely you ladies understand the value of power dressing."

"Power dressing?" Orpha quipped. "What kind of a salad do you put that on?"

Kanji arrived with Lorraine's Spartini, and told her it was on the house for all the work she'd done to organize such a fabulous quilt show.

"Why thank you," gushed Lorraine. "Thank you very much. It IS a lot of work, and it's good to know that it's appreciated."

"And am I to understand that you are the singular crafter of several of those intricately designed patterns?" Kanji asked.

"It's true," Lorraine gushed, obviously pleased, but feigning a modest blush. "No rest for the wicked!" She giggled like a schoolgirl. "In the summertime I'm often out helping Tom with the oyster farm, but during the shorter days and longer nights of winter, I keep myself busy with my sewing crafts."

"They are indeed most lovely," said Kanji, bowing slightly to her. "In fact, there were several exquisite quilts in the display that I would not mind owning for myself," he said as he left us.

Lorraine fanned herself with her cocktail napkin. "My goodness gracious, that man's charm can certainly warm up a cold winter day."

"No argument there!" Orpha piped up. "But Sylvia would probably know a little more about that than the rest of us."

My face flamed beet red, but I held my ground. "Kanji and I are good friends," I explained to Lorraine, but my eyes were taking in the rest of the women at the table. "And I don't know why everyone always wants to make such a big deal out of our friendship."

OYSTER SPAT

Meredith smiled, batted her eyelids, and elbowed Goodie. "The lady doth protest too much, methinks."

"Methinks so too," Goodie said back to her, with an equally ridiculous amount of eyelash batting.

And then the two of them erupted into fits of giggles. Had I not come in with them, I would have sworn they'd gotten a head start on our happy hour.

"Ladies! Shhhhush! Our handsome Indian bartender is headed back in this direction," said Nova.

Without an ounce of shame, Meredith, Goodie, Orpha and Lorraine turned in unison to greet Kanji with ogling eyes and big, welcoming smiles. If he felt like a fresh piece of meat thrown before the wolves—or in this case, cougars—he sure didn't show it.

"What's on the appetizer menu tonight, Kanji?" asked Meredith.

"I was just coming to tell you about our early bird specials." Kanji bowed to the table, somehow making each of us feel special and specifically singled out in his all-encompassing gaze.

"As I am sure Lorraine is the most aware, here at the Spartina Point Casino and Resort, our menu runs by the tide, bringing the freshest seafood selections to our tables every night.

"This afternoon we have fresh Shallowwater Bay oysters, served any way your heart desires. There's also an opportunity to share, or enjoy all for yourself, a pound bucket of today's steamer clam harvest drenched in white wine and butter. Or perhaps you're more in the mood for our Pacific razor clam fritters served with a garlic lime aioli dipping sauce.

"And of course," Kanji concluded in his lyrical, velvet voice, "everything on our usual menu is also available if you'd prefer to have a full meal service."

I could feel my salivary glands shifting into overdrive just listening to Kanji as he described the menu. That was not a voice one would consider kicking out of bed for eating crackers. Not even oyster crackers.

"My oh my," said Meredith, exaggeratedly running her tongue over her lips, "who doesn't just love those tabasco-sauced little oyster shooters? I could eat them all day and all night." Then her eyes caught the expression on my face. "I mean," she quickly amended herself, "who doesn't like oyster shooters, besides Sylvia?"

"Mom!" I rolled my eyes, a bad habit I'm sure I inherited from her. "You five can have the shooters all to yourselves. I'm just going to order a cup of chowder and a couple clam fritters."

"And I'll pass on the shooters, as well," said Lorraine, "since I can have oysters at home any time I want, you know." She smiled up at Kanji as she handed him her empty glass. "Now I'm afraid I can't stay any longer, ladies. Tom likes his dinner on the table promptly at 6 o'clock every night. I'm sure you all understand."

Although everyone in our company nodded, I'm pretty sure none of us professing to be independent women of the 21st century actually understood. But just for today, we weren't going to call her out on it.

After Lorraine took her leave, Mom, Nova, and Goodie settled on four oyster shooters each, and Orpha and I opted to stick with the tried and true clam chowder, and splitting an order of Pacific razor clam fritters. Kanji took our order, and before he returned with it, we'd already danced around the elephant on the table several times.

"Ok, fine," said Goodie at last. She took a deep breath. "I know I'm probably going to have to go to confession for even bringing this up, but did anyone else notice Lorraine was trying to cover up a black eye with all her eye shadow?"

OYSTER SPAT

The silence was deafening. I knew for sure I had to keep my mouth tightly zipped shut so I didn't end up having to explain what I'd seen and done out at the Diamond farm when I'd been sent to return the kitchenware. Nova shot a quick look at me, and I held my breath, hoping she wasn't going to betray my confidence and open up that whole can of worms.

Thankfully, Orpha piped right up with, "Everybody knows that Tom's always had quite the temper. He's used Lorraine to take out his aggressions on for as long as I can remember, which, even on a bad day, is pretty far back."

Goodie frowned. "Has she reported him to the police?"

"Most women are afraid they've created the situation," said Meredith. "They think it's all their own fault. Some don't think they can do any better, and they don't think they can survive on their own. Consequently, they live their lives walking on eggshells."

"Or in Lorraine's case, oyster shells," said Orpha.

I couldn't take it anymore, and decided it might be time to open my mouth and add my two cents to the conversation. Fortunately, I was saved from doing so by Kanji's return to the table with our happy hour snacks.

All talk abruptly ceased as we enjoyed our food, along with the twinkling white lights of the holiday-decorated lounge, as darkness started falling outside the huge bay windows overlooking the wetlands. None of us really liked to drive after dark anymore, but staying long enough to see the magic of Christmas come to elegant life in the casino lounge was worth it.

"Now don't forget!" said Nova, as we gathered up our belongings and headed for the door. "Tomorrow night's the Crab Pot Tree Lighting down at the port in Unity! Please promise me you'll all come and join in the singing of the Crabby carols. I know you'll have a great time!"

We all dutifully pledged to be there, hugged all around, and it felt like we'd regained a little of our Christmas spirit after a pretty sad week.

"Miss Sylvia!" Kanji called out just as I approached the casino lounge exit. "A moment of your time, please."

"Sure thing, Kanji. Just give me a minute." I held the door for the others to pass through, waved good-bye, and stepped back inside the lounge.

"If I may ask," Kanji began, "what is this Crab Pot Tree Lighting to which Nova referred?"

I laughed. "The Crab Pot Tree is a stack of actual crab pots, piled more than 20 feet high into a pyramid shape, then decorated with Christmas lights and garland. At 5:00 tomorrow night, the frivolity begins with the lighting of the tree, and then the world's shortest fireworks display." I laughed. "It's the traditional start of the holiday mini-bazaar along the Unity waterfront where locals sell their crafts. Santa will be there for the kids, and the adults will be singing something we call 'Crabby Christmas Carols.' Our joyful noise always contributes to the fun."

"I see," said Kanji.

But by the look on his face, I could see he clearly didn't see anything at all. "The words of the carols are changed to reflect our local communities," I said. "It becomes a silly kind of parody when you sing about Santa arriving on a crab boat, or Billy wanting a fishing pole for Christmas." I paused, finding it rather difficult to explain. "Well, maybe it's something you just have to see to believe," I said.

Kanji immediately brightened. "Then, my dear Miss Sylvia, would you be so kind as to agree to be my date to tomorrow's festivities in Unity?"

Whoa! Kanji had used the word "date" in a way that there was no doubt he was asking me out. I opened my mouth to refuse his offer, but just as suddenly realized that

OYSTER SPAT

Freddy was going to be busy working his deputy shift the next night, so what was really stopping me from attending the tree lighting with an attractive male escort? Without giving it any more thought, I heard myself saying, "Sure, Kanji, I'd love to!" and was glad I did.

The next evening, Nova, dressed as Mrs. Claus, led the caroling with gusto: "Snow on the arches, and crab pots for trees... Oysters on half shells, all fresh from the sea.... Cranberry chutney, and salmon in spring... These are a few of my favorite things!"

I felt deliciously happy and hopelessly content just being there, enjoying the myriad of twinkling colored lights, as well as their reflections on the water in the port. I was surrounded by people I love in a community I love. The songs were funny and festive. And after the singing we toured the market stalls, and ate perhaps more than our fair share of Christmas cookies.

And when the night was drawing to a close, and Kanji reached over and took my mitten-covered hand in his, I saw no reason to pull away, despite who might be watching.

A short while later, when we drove into my driveway, I decided, for once, to "play the part of the girl" and stayed seated inside the car until Kanji gallantly came around his vehicle to open the door for me. He then took me by the hand and walked me up the walk and onto the stoop at my front door. And then came the inevitable awkward moment.

Kanji cleared his throat. "Miss Sylvia, I would very much like to ask your permission for a good night kiss, but I am fearful that you will not grant me permission, so if my actions now are too impertinent, you will have to let me know later."

And then he leaned in for a most lovely kiss, a swoon-worthy kiss, a kiss that left me breathless and weak-kneed, and all kinds of hot and bothered in a crazy, hormonally-driven and kaleidoscope-invoking way.

When I finally stepped back, it was my turn to clear my throat. "I'd invite you in, Kanji, but you know I'm kind of dating your boss, don't you?"

"I am well-aware of your relationship with Freddy," said Kanji. "And still I find myself wanting an answer to just one more impertinent question."

"Which is?"

"Which is," said Kanji, leaning in again and brushing my ear with his lips, "have you and my boss agreed upon a mutual understanding and acceptance of exclusivity?"

Lord, have mercy. I froze, unsure how to answer such a forthright question, until a little voice inside my head prompted me to tell him the absolute truth. "Well, now that you mention it, no, I am quite sure your boss and I have come to no such agreement."

"Ahh," Kanji whispered, "I thought not." He kissed from my ear down my neck and toward my shoulder. "Then what happens next, dear Sylvia, will be totally up to you."

The horrific howling of the wind in the trees and the pelting of hard-driving rain against the bedroom window abruptly awakened me the next morning. The "major winter storm" that had been promised during the Portland weather forecasts for several days had finally arrived. I suppose we should have counted our blessings it had waited just long enough for the Crab Pot Tree Lighting to take place before slamming face-first into the coastal communities of the North Beach Peninsula. But by now, I suspected most of the ornaments had been blown so far out to sea that little Japanese children would be finding them on their beaches in the days ahead.

I rolled over to check the time on the bedside clock and

realized the power was out. I probably should have realized that already by how cold it was in my bedroom. I involuntarily shivered, then reached up into my headboard for my industrial flashlight.

I jerked my hand back with a little squeak of a squeal when my hand came in contact with someone's bare arm, curled protectively around the back of my pillow.

"Good morning, my dear Sylvia," said Kanji. His voice was soft and warm, like melting caramel. "I trust you slept well?"

"Kanji..." But before I could formulate my scattered thoughts into some type of comprehendible words, Kanji's cell phone rang.

The light from his phone display was the only reason Kanji managed to locate it on the bedside table in the dark room. "It's Freddy."

I flushed from head to toe, afraid Kanji might be tempted to share exactly where he was at this precise moment, but that would have been grossly underestimating the good manners of Mr. Kanjirappally Kumera. He was all business, and fully professional, clear down to his naked little toes, which just happened to be still tucked under my bedcovers next to me.

"Uh-huh," said Kanji. I could only hear his end of the conversation, which wasn't more than a word or two at a time, followed by more listening, then another few words. "I understand. Yes. Of course. That is not a problem. I will be there to help just as soon as I am able to find a clear roadway to the casino. You are most welcome."

While he'd been talking, I'd located the LED emergency lantern I keep in my bedroom and the light now cast a neon-eerie glow over the two of us. But the soft lighting didn't warm the room up any, and I dove back under the covers and wiggled in close to Kanji for warmth.

"Apparently, we slept through the beginnings of a major hurricane heading our way." Kanji smiled, reached over, and tucked some of my hair back behind my ear. "The power has been out for most of the night all over the peninsula. The hospital and high school in Unity have been marked as warming and homeless shelters, as are the rest of the school district classrooms and churches. Midway up the peninsula, the Senior Center will open its doors for the hungry, and the Spartina Point Casino and Resort is now the major designated north end shelter."

"A homeless shelter with slot machines?" I almost laughed. Almost, but not quite.

"The storm is still gaining momentum," said Kanji. "I am sure the generators at the casino will not be employed for gaming purposes at this time."

"No, of course not." I felt bad for preying on Kanji's literal interpretation of my words.

"Freddy wants me to come in and help," continued Kanji. "He said that—"

Kanji's words were interrupted by my own cell phone ringing, but the ringtone told me who it was well before I could grab it to pick it up: "Bad boys, bad boys, whatcha gonna do? Whatcha gonna do when they come for you?"

I pressed the green button. "Hello Freddy." Now it was Kanji's turn to try to make sense out of only one side of a conversation. "Yes, of course. Oh, that long? Uh-huh. Yes, I have several of those. Yes. And I'll bring my 5-gallon gas can too. Uh-huh. It's full. Ok. I'm going to stop and check on Meredith and Les, and I'll be there as soon as possible."

I hung up, looked at Kanji, and gave him an apologetic little shrug. "So much for us sleeping in this morning."

Kanji chuckled. "Sleeping in is one of the farthest things from my mind right now." He traced my ear lobe with his finger and sighed. "However, facing my first major winter storm on the beach isn't what I had in mind for today, either.

I kissed his cheek and slid from the warmth of the bed back into the chill of a room which had been without a heater for many hours. I quickly wrapped myself in a bathrobe and sat on the edge of the bed to pull on my socks. "Freddy wants me to bring anything in my freezer that needs to be cooked and eaten. He said the peninsula could be without power for several days, and we need to be able to feed anyone who walks in the door and needs a hot meal.

"He also wants any extra blankets or sleeping bags I have, and my spare gasoline can. We'll need to keep the generators running up there 24/7 until the power's back on."

Kanji sat up and put his arms around me from behind, lying his head on my shoulder. "Sylvia..." His voice was uncharacteristically husky. "About last night—"

"We'll need to talk about last night some other time, Kanji. Right now, it's all hands on deck on the North Beach Peninsula." I looked at the battery level on my cell phone. "It's a good thing I can charge my phone in my car."

"Of course," said Kanji, answering my request to talk about our night together at a later date.

We pulled the rest of our clothes on in silence. I didn't dare look at Kanji. I was too busy wondering how I was going to keep from looking Freddy in the eye a little later on.

CHAPTER 12

Kanji helped me empty most of the contents of my freezer into two plastic camp coolers and then we loaded them into my car trunk. In the back seat, we piled sleeping bags, blankets, pillows, and my personal overnight bag. At the last minute, I added a heavy-duty plastic garbage bag filled with thick, fluffy socks, a few extra sweatshirts, and nearly a dozen knitted or crocheted stocking caps in a wide variety of colors.

"Tune your radio to 91.9," I told Kanji. "That's our community radio station. They're generator powered, and they will have the ability to keep the North Beach Peninsula fully informed with weather reports, road closures, and other emergency information. Otherwise, we'd be pretty cut off from the rest of the world."

I was glad Kanji was there to help me hoist up the garage door, since it too ran on electricity, and he made sure it stayed open until I'd backed my car outside. Although my home is fully surrounded by trees, the wind was really blowing out there, and I couldn't even get my car door open against its push. So I rolled down my window just far enough to tell him, or rather, yell at him so he had a chance of hearing me, to drive safely and I'd see him later.

"There are going to be a lot of trees down across many of the roads," I hollered at the top of my lungs. "Just stay in your car and wait for the next pickup truck to come along.

Most of them have a chain saw with them. They will cut a path for cars."

Kanji reached inside the window and pulled my left hand tight against his chest. "You be careful, too," he said into my hair. The howling wind was so strong, I could barely hear him.

"See you soon." Then I pulled out of the driveway and turned north on Sandspit Road, while Kanji turned south so he could gather a few things up at his home in Tinkerstown before heading to the casino.

It took me almost two hours to get from my house to Ocean Crest. Usually the drive takes me only 7 or 8 minutes, but usually there aren't over two dozen trees down across the road during the 5-mile drive. Fortunately, the community woodcutters were out in force, and they braved the winds and flying debris to keep the major roads clear.

I parked behind Les's Prius in Mom's driveway. Her red Saturn was parked inside her carport. Had it not been for the fact that a tree had fallen directly on the carport, slamming it down on top of her car inside, I might not have noticed anything out of the ordinary. But seeing that flattened carport on top of her squished car, well, that really scared me spitless. And when I saw the offending tree wasn't all that big around, my heart started racing to beat the band. John Phillips Sousa in three-quarters time, overtime, or just holy hell, is Mom okay? time.

I jumped out, and the wind jerked the car door away from me, nearly catching both my legs in it as the door springs bounced it back in my direction. "Mom!" I started hollering as I ran toward her front door. "Mom! Les! Hello? Are you guys all right?!"

Meredith opened the door, grabbed me by my jacket front, and quickly pulled me inside. "Honey! What in the world are you doing out in weather like this?"

"What am I doing out in—" Apparently, Mom and Les had everything under control at their place. A nice bright fire burned in the fireplace, and the Scrabble board was set up on the coffee table in front of the couch. Les was sitting cross-legged on one end of the couch, looking happy and relaxed in a comfortable sweat suit. In the recliner, Chuck, Harlan, and Bob, Mom's three cats all named after her three deceased husbands, were amicably curled up together, totally unaffected by the screaming sounds of the storm outside.

Mom saw my wild-eyed look and pulled me into a tight hug before I could deny I'd seen the flattened car and been frightened for her.

"It's okay, honey." She used both her hands to smooth my hair. "I should have called to tell you about the tree hitting the carport. Then it wouldn't have been such a shock for you. We're fine, Sylleegirl." She pulled back and looked me in the eye. "I promise. We're both fine."

I took a couple deep, gulping breaths, and wordlessly nodded. "I know. I just—"

"Would you like a glass of wine, or maybe something a bit stronger?" asked Les.

I shook my head. "No, thank you. I'm on my way to Spartina Point. The resort has been called into service as a storm shelter. Freddy called Kanji and me to come help."

"So you've spoken to Kanji this morning?" asked Meredith.

Her question was innocent enough, but enough to start a blush at the bottom of my neck racing upwards, and I didn't know exactly how to answer her.

"We saw you two at the tree lighting," said Les. "How did Kanji like the Crab Pot Tree?"

Oh. Gee. Of course. There was no way for Meredith to know how our night had ended—or where our morning had begun.

OYSTER SPAT

"He enjoyed it just fine." I started for the door. "Now I need to get going."

"Of course." Les sagely nodded. "But would you do your mother and me a favor?" he asked. "Would you please call her when you get there safely? You're not the only one who worries."

I promised to do so, then fought my way against the wind and air filled with flying leaves and twigs and who-knows-what-else back to my car. Wind patterns along our little peninsula are not always predictable. Where one neighbor might lose the entire roof off her house, the neighbor on the other side might not lose even a single shingle.

I drove extra carefully the last few miles, picking my way around various sizes of tree branches and kids' toys and rolling garbage cans and so on and so forth on up to the casino.

My first stop on casino property was to check in on Mercedes, who lives in a large, self-contained motorhome in the far parking lot. Sometimes she calls it her apartment on wheels, and at other times she insists she was way ahead of the tiny house craze. She only drives the motorhome a few times a year, and that's only when she deems it an emergency. Like when she hoped to be hired as an extra in a movie being filmed near the boardwalk in Tinkerstown.

I climbed the two short metal steps and pounded with my fist on her door. Since she has no other vehicle, I can't always tell if she's home, but this time, as soon as I knocked, I was certain she was not there. Brutus, her long-haired dachshund, set up a wailing and a whimpering I could hear above the sounds of the storm. Poor baby. I hoped Mercedes would return before too long to comfort him. For a dog, he really was a scaredy cat.

The main casino parking lot was completely full, except

for two of the four designated VIP spaces right up front next to the bridge to cross the moat at the main entrance. The spaces had originally been reserved for Uncle Harry, and his fleet of four Lincoln Town Cars, but now those spots were home to Freddy's red Mazda RX-8, his official county cruiser, my chameleon mustang, and Kanji's Scion xB. Today when I pulled into the third spot, the fourth spot was still empty, and I said a silent prayer that Kanji would arrive without incident.

Except for my four years away to attend college, I have always resided on the North Beach Peninsula. Some might call that living a little myopic, but the way I look at it, why look for anyplace else, when what you have is far superior? But in all that time, I had never—and I mean never—seen and heard sustained winds at over 100 miles per hour. Until today.

The road north had been treacherous. Even though it was daylight, it was difficult to see, with the rain, leaves, limbs, larger branches and whole trees stalling my progress on the road. The world in front of my car was a thick carpet of green and brown vegetation, and in some places, I hadn't been able to tell where the pavement ended, and a deep ditch lurked below.

As neighbors will do, many of them were out in force, using their chain saws to keep the major roadways clear enough for emergency vehicles, cutting at least a one-way path through a virtual horizontal forest across the streets.

My phone was fully charged by the time I arrived, and as promised, I called Mom first thing, letting her know I'd made it safely to my destination.

Rain slammed at me sideways as I hurried for the front door, my arms loaded with bedding. I was glad the bridge across the moat was so sturdy, and that the handrails were also thick and strong. Freddy had made many improvements to his uncle's castle/fortress motif, and I was doubly grateful today for the rough nonslip strips that covered the otherwise slick wooden walkway. Safety first!

Once inside, I found volunteers eager to help everywhere, and in one more trip, six of us had emptied the linens and clothing out into the main hall of the resort, while the foodstuffs went with four more helpers directly into the kitchen.

I briefly wondered if I'd ever see any of my blankets or sweatshirts again, but shrugged the thought off. It was a small price to pay to assist those in unfathomable need.

Juanita, one of the casino's full-time housekeepers, told me she thought "Mr. Freddy" could be found in the kitchen. She took my overnight bag from my hand and told me with a wink that she'd personally see it was secured up in the penthouse, room 552.

I thanked her, but couldn't help but feel a wave of deep guilt flush my face. Not eight hours ago, I was sleeping in another man's arms, and tonight, unless the weather cleared and the power came back on, it was quite likely I'd be shacking up with Freddy for the night. Good grief and gravy! What kind of a person was I turning into?

I was still pondering the question of my morality when I entered the kitchen. Coleman stoves lined the counters. Large pans of soups were being prepared at every station. The volunteer "cooks" were wearing their coats and hats, directing an army of "sous chefs" to chop and slice all sorts of fresh peninsula-grown vegetables to add to their individual cauldrons. Despite the helter-skelter look about it, the kitchen seemed to be humming with teamwork.

Freddy, however, was nowhere to be seen, and I moved into the dining room, where every table looked a little like a kid's blanket fort, and families were quietly huddled together playing cards or board games by the light of their portable camping lanterns and flashlights.

I suddenly heard music, and followed the sound into the main ballroom. It shouldn't have been a surprise to see Mercedes pounding away at an ancient baby grand piano, but without her amplifying sound gear, her songs were all but lost on the company in attendance.

Old habits are hard to break, and when Merc saw me come in, she immediately started playing a rousing rendition of "If I Knew You Were Coming, I'd Have Baked a Cake." The song was kind of an inside joke, just between the two of us, but enough people there knew the words, that it suddenly became a full-scale sing-a-long.

The song concluded with the words, "How-ja do, How-ja do, How-ja do!" And everyone started cheering and clapping. Mercedes blew me a kiss before launching into another tried and true crowd-pleaser, "She'll be Coming 'Round the Mountain."

Freddy, however, was still nowhere to be found, and I was rapidly running out of places to look for him. I exited the main hall, passed the gift shop, which was naturally closed, and ruled out heading toward the indoor pool. The pool would have been the first thing Freddy pulled the plug on when the storm struck, conserving as much energy as possible.

On a whim, I decided to pop my head into the room containing the gaming tables and slots. Naturally, the power from the generators was not being diverted to this room, but the emergency exit signs and the glow from the battery-powered LED lights along the carpeted walkways made it light enough to navigate around the room and avoid stumbling into the dark slot machines.

It did not, however, keep me from tripping over a man's feet sticking out from behind the craps table. I sent up a small shriek as I went sprawling, ass over teakettle, and made a hard two-hands and one knee face-first landing on the floor next to the inert body of none other than Frederick Harold Morgan.

"Freddy!" I rolled to the side, sat up, and grabbed for his wrist to check his pulse. Yes, there was one, and thankfully, it was good and strong. "Freddy!" I took my phone out of my pocket and used the flashlight function, planning to see if his eyes were dilated, or if he might be unconscious. But the light illuminated the fact that the entire side of his face was a glistening bright red. "FREDDY!"

"Hey," said Freddy, in not much more than a whisper. "I'm right here, Sylleegirl. You don't have to yell."

"Oh my god, Freddy." And despite my tough gal exterior, I started to cry. "You had me so scared." I pulled off my jacket, and then my sweater, as well as my well-worn Mariners t-shirt underneath, leaving my top half covered by only a black lacy bra.

"Uh, Syl? You sure you want to do this right here? You know I've got a whole room upstairs. In fact, you witchy woman, I've got an entire resort full of rooms, so you can take your pick."

I wanted to take a swing at him, but it wasn't his fault he had misinterpreted my intentions. Or maybe he just wanted to interject a little lightheartedness into the situation. Whatever. What I really needed to do right this moment was tear my t-shirt into strips to use as a compression bandage against his head wound, which could, if not checked, cause him to pass out from lack of blood if I didn't act fast.

I hated to lose my lucky Mariner shirt like this, but maybe it was just lucky I was wearing it. Without another word, I folded a strip of it into a palm-sized bandage and pressed it tightly against Freddy's head. He winced at the pressure. "Hold this right here, tough guy." I said to him, putting his own hand on the bandage. "And stay put. I need to go get some help."

As luck would have it, the first person I ran into between the gaming room and the main event center was Kanji, who was just entering the building through the front door out by the gift shop. He took one look at me, and I swear I saw his Indian complexion pale. His mouth dropped open, and he stuttered, "S-S- Syl- Wh-where are you h-hurt?"

I looked down at my hands and what little clothing I still had on and realized I was half naked, and half covered in blood. "I'm okay, Kanji. It's not my blood, it's Freddy's."

"You've killed Freddy?" said Kanji, his eyes nearly popping from his head.

"I didn't touch him. I swear. I'm not sure what happened, but I found him on the floor of the gaming room, and he needs medical help, ASAP."

That snapped Kanji right out of the horror movie obviously playing out inside his head. "Of course, Miss Sylvia." His head bowed slightly. "Please lead the way."

Once we got Freddy up to his room and cleaned his wound, we could see that it was mostly superficial, but as head wounds are prone to do, it was a true bleeder.

When I was satisfied he was not in immediate mortal danger, I washed my hands, pulled my sweater back on, and ran my fingers through my hair, hoping my efforts would erase the images both Freddy and Kanji had been privy to a short while before.

Unfortunately, Freddy couldn't tell us exactly what had happened. He remembered taking the short cut through the gaming room to access the back hallway to the lounge. And he remembered hearing someone—or make that two someones—trying to break into the slot machines with something metal. Maybe a crowbar or a hammer or something.

When he called out, "Who's there?" all noise stopped,

and he'd suddenly realized he had no back up, as he never wore his service revolver into the casino. He'd turned around and started for the door when someone had clobbered him from behind. And that's all he remembered until, as he put it, "Sylvia fell pretty hard for me."

The joke would have been a lot funnier if I hadn't been so overcome by guilt from the previous evening's activities with Kanji. Undeniably enjoyable activities, but nevertheless shameful. I guess. Or maybe that's just what a remorseful woman was supposed to feel. I really wasn't too sure how I felt, only that I really didn't regret for a single minute having had an amorous roommate share my bed the previous night.

"Do you know how long you were lying there?" asked Kanji.

"No," said Freddy. "I'm sure I passed out, but I don't even know what time it is now." He shook his head, but made a painful face when he did so.

"Usually when there's a storm," said Freddy, "the vandals break into the abandoned or evacuated homes on the peninsula. I can't believe they'd think they could get away with robbing the slot machines when hundreds of people are gathered a few rooms away."

"I dunno," I volunteered. "It might be tempting to try. Sometimes there's quite a bit of cash in those machines."

"True," said Freddy, "but they're emptied regularly, and—" he started to chuckle, but winced again in pain— "and each of those machines is built like a miniature Fort Knox. There's no way you can beat the money out of them. It's just not possible."

"So are we talking kids, or just really stupid grown-ups?" I asked.

"Perhaps," said Kanji, "the perpetrators, of whatever age, realized your security cameras would not be functioning during the power outage and sought to take advantage of the situation."

"Of course," said Freddy. "I hadn't thought of that." He sighed. "But it was pretty darn ballsy of them attempting to rob a casino owned by a County Deputy."

My indignation flared. "A County Deputy that has opened his doors to the homeless and hungry during a damn hurricane. What the hell's wrong with these people?!"

"Easy Sylleegirl," said Freddy. "It's alright. I'm okay."

"It's *NOT* alright, and whether you're okay or not remains to be seen, dammit!" The quiver in my voice was almost visible in the air between us. Finding Freddy with his head bashed in, lying helpless on the casino floor, triggered every one of my wounded mother bear hormones. I wanted nothing more than to find out who had done this, rip his arms off with my bare hands, and beat him senseless with them. And I'm pretty sure encompassing protectiveness showed up on my face, for both Freddy and for Kanji to observe.

And the moment it occurred to me how Kanji must feel as I flew to Freddy's defense, I stopped talking. Little did he know I would be just as outraged, and just as scared, if it had been him that had been assaulted.

"If I may inquire," Kanji calmly said to Freddy, "are you choosing to call this a crime merely of opportunity, and without premeditation or a planned escape route?"

Freddy narrowed his eyes and stared at him, mentally filling in the blanks of what was not being said. "Kanji? Are you thinking the perps might still be in the casino?"

Kanji rallied the regular security guys, and a search was done for the "weapon of assault," as Kanji called it, or anyone who might have been looking to score from taking advantage of the situation in the gaming room.

After hours of investigation, nothing and no one turned

OYSTER SPAT

up on the radar, and Kanji gave up the hunt, at least temporarily, calling it a random act of north end vandalism, and concluded the weapon, perhaps a crowbar, was most likely at the bottom of the moat by now. Then he began apologizing profusely to Freddy for not getting there sooner, saying his presence might have made a difference just by his proximity.

"I would have been here somewhat sooner had I not taken Elvis to stay at the Clamshell," said Kanji. "The poor animal is most terrified by this storm, and you said we might be here for several days. Although I knew you would welcome him here, I thought I would be of more useful service if I were not distracted by also having my pet to attend to."

Good grief and gravy! Selfish me had never given a single thought to Kanji's adolescent black Lab in the past 24 hours. "You were absolutely right to take him to the Clamshell," I said to Kanji, lightly touching his forearm as I spoke. "Elvis will feel right at home there; it was his first home, and Jimmy and Priscilla both love him."

Only I knew the real reason why Kanji felt so guilty for not "being there" when Freddy needed him. Kanji was undoubtedly feeling a bit of remorse for our time spent together.

Nevertheless, I was absolutely certain that at least one of us would probably do it all over again, given half the chance.

CHAPTER 13

The storm, which by all accounts qualified as a full-on category five hurricane, lasted another two days and nights, and by then, those of us taking refuge at the casino all had a pretty good idea of who played a mean game of charades, and who couldn't draw a tandem bicycle to save their soul. But other than Freddy's robbery-gone-bad encounter on the first night, there was no other bloodshed, and we all managed to get along quite nicely, sharing the "chores" and responsibilities, and being on our best behavior.

Lorraine Diamond, whose husband Tom refused to leave the homestead in Willoopah, turned out to be a real hoot when it came to playing Pinochle, and confided she hadn't had this much fun out socializing in decades. I was hoping she'd confide a bit more to me before our exile ended, but she was pretty tight-lipped about her home situation.

Most of us stayed hunkered down until the fourth morning. By then the local PUD had at least 75% of the peninsula's power back on. And in all that time, we found no clues as to who had assaulted Freddy, what their motive might have been for trying to break into the slot machines, if they had left the premises that first night, or if they were lurking around waiting to complete their mission, whatever in God's green acre that might have been.

Their unknown whereabouts was enough to give me the freakin' heebie jeebies, leaving me as jumpy as a long-tailed

OYSTER SPAT

cat in a room full of rocking chairs. Freddy and Kanji, however, seemed to take it all in stride.

As for sleeping arrangements, Mercedes and I battled the wind, the rain, and the flying branches to walk across the parking lot together each night. There I shared her couch with the perpetually quivering and shivering Brutus, the dog she'd originally gotten "for protection."

Believe me, when we finally heard the "all clear" siren after almost four days of isolation with several hundred of the northern half of the peninsula's population, I couldn't wait to get home, take a hot shower, and get about 15 hours of nonstop sleep!

Freddy, bless his heart, hired a professional cleaning company to restore the resort to some semblance of its high-end luxury status, explaining it offered a win-win situation.

"The cleaning company can use the work, and everyone I know who was here can use the time to go home and recharge. It's only three days until Christmas Eve, and on Christmas Day we've still got a full community dinner to host!"

I'm sure my eyebrows arched right up through my hairline. "As if you haven't just hosted an all-expense paid Air BnB for the past four days?" I admit, I sounded a bit snarky, but exhaustion will do that to a person.

"I made a commitment," said Freddy, "and I'm sticking to it." He lowered his voice and leaned closer. "And I've got a room full of toys for the kids in the small exhibit hall that need to find new homes via Santa's sleigh in the very near future!"

Well, when he put it that way…

I was tempted to cross my fingers and my toes as I turned into my driveway. My home is surrounded by large trees, and if I'd known the words, I'd have said a few Hail Marys that they'd all stayed standing in my absence. The last thing I needed was to find that several of them had given up the ghost during the hurricane and landed on my roof. But praise be! Everything was still standing, and my house had gotten through the worst of it unscathed. Whew!

Fortunately, power had been returned to every single peninsula home by Christmas Eve, and the children were all resting easier knowing that Santa could still make his rounds, with or without Rudolph's red nose to guide him.

I returned to the casino kitchen and spent Christmas Eve afternoon peeling potatoes, while Freddy, Kanji, Sheriff D and Mercedes baked enough hams and turkeys to feed half the county, which, when I thought about it, was exactly what they were planning to do.

Late in the afternoon, when I was about to call it quits for the day, Jimmy and Julio arrived in the Five Amigos Chinese Cuisine take-out truck.

"Guess what we brought?" Jimmy asked Freddy, as he bounded through the casino's back kitchen door.

"I'm guessing it's not Chinese food?" asked Freddy, playing along.

I smiled. I knew Freddy had already received a call from Juan, down at their restaurant in Tinkerstown, making sure that what the Mexican families had chosen to bring for the Christmas dinner table tomorrow was going to be welcomed.

Jimmy and Julio came in and took two of the big catering carts out to their truck. They returned bringing five huge double-handled pans of "estofado de ostras del equipo de ostras," which, roughly translated, is "oyster stew from the oyster crew."

Many of the Five Amigos' relatives worked for Willoopah Oysters. Today they had commandeered the Chinese restaurant kitchen to slice and dice carrots, potatoes and open bushels of fresh oysters so they could bring this special offering to the community meal. Five enormous

OYSTER SPAT

cauldrons of oyster stew, one for each of the guys who had left the oyster industry to become successful restaurateurs, were their way of giving back.

The Spartina Point Casino and Resort also employed a large number of Hispanics, and I knew from my work with CPS that speaking Spanish was becoming a necessity among the major county employers. Hard working and ready to take on the less than glamorous jobs of oyster pickers and motel maids, I was glad they were feeling at home in our community. Their work ethic and willingness to get the job done right was a breath of fresh air.

Christmas Day, I was happy to have Nautika working beside me on the serving line. She was wearing a new pair of bedazzled jeans, of course, and I was glad I'd chosen one of my traditional "ugly Christmas sweaters" so that I didn't feel old enough to be her mother—which was ridiculous, because I was, quite literally, just exactly that old.

"Did Santa bring you those jeans?" I teased her.

To my surprise, Nautika actually blushed. "No, uh, well, not exactly." She chuckled nervously. "They were a gift from Brent."

Again, my warning lights and bells and buzzers went off, and I made a mental note to check a little deeper into the goings on behind closed doors on the Willoopah Oyster Farm. Not that it was any of my business, of course, since they were consenting adults, but something just didn't set right in my gut about those two working and living so closely together.

So between delivering scoops of mashed potatoes and gravy, I tried to nudge Nautika in the direction of meeting more young people her age here on the peninsula. I told her, as I would have told a daughter of my own, that it wasn't good for her to work and live with all those much older oystermen out on the bay, and she must be lonely for kids her own age.

"Oh, well, since you brought it up, I did meet a nice guy at the grocery store the other day," said Nautika. She gave me a conspiratorial wink. "He's in the band that will be playing here at the casino on New Year's Eve."

I wasn't sure where musicians fit in among the oystermen on my hierarchy of eligible bachelors, but I was willing to give this new guy on the horizon the benefit of the doubt. "What's his name? Where does he work? How old is he? Is he cute?"

"Oh geez." At first Nautika laughed, then just as suddenly her face crumpled up and she had to wipe her tears away with the back of her gloved hand. "I'm sorry."

"No, I'm sorry." I shook my head. "Did I just say something that might have somehow upset you?"

"No, it's just that…" Nautika groped for the words. "Well, for a minute there," she shot me a sideways look, "you sounded just like my mom."

A lump formed in my throat about the size of Nebraska. "This is your first Christmas without her, isn't it?"

Nautika nodded. "She'd been sick for a long time, and I'm glad she's not in pain anymore, but I didn't know how much I'd miss her when the holidays came around. That's why when Brent suggested we come volunteer here for the community dinner, I agreed right away. It just felt like that's what she'd want us—I mean me—to do."

I nodded thoughtfully. "I saw Brent was moving tables earlier, and I'm glad he's the one refilling our serving tubs. I can't even lift one of those pans of mashed potatoes."

Nautika laughed. "We both stay in pretty good shape lifting and toting all those oysters around out there. It's hard work, the pay isn't very good, but the mussels are terrific."

"The muscles?" I flipped my hip over to connect with hers. "Okay, smarty pants, I get it. That's an oysterperson's joke."

Nautika giggled like the young woman she was. "Do you know how oysters communicate?"

I started laughing simply because she was laughing. "I have absolutely no idea."

"With shell-phones."

"Nautika! I almost missed that guy's plate with my potatoes."

"Okay, just one more. What do you call an oyster that flies?"

"I'm not even going to attempt a guess."

"A shell-icopter."

Jimmy and Julio suddenly appeared next to me. "Freddy says you two are having way too much fun out here; he can hear you laughing all the way into the kitchen. He says Julio and I are to take your place dishing the spuds up, and you gals have been ordered to grab a plate and fix yourself something to eat before the next wave gets here."

I looked at Nautika. "Apparently, we've been replaced—at least for the moment."

"Good deal," said Nautika. "I'm starved!"

I filled my plate with turkey, stuffing, cranberry sauce and yams, while Nautika selected ham, pineapple carrot salad, and a yeasty dinner roll. We found a small table with two chairs and gratefully plopped down to eat. But before I could take my first bite, I caught her warily eying my plate of food. "Is there something wrong, Nautika?"

"Nope," she said shaking her head. "Not a thing. I had exactly what you're having on Thanksgiving, so now I'm choosing to have something different."

I laughed. "I had exactly what I'm having today on Thanksgiving, too. I enjoyed it so much, I wanted to eat it again before next November!"

We ate in amicable silence for a few minutes until I

ventured to ask her again, "So what's his name, where does he work, how old is he, and is he cute?"

Nautika grinned from ear to ear. "You're just not going to let that go, are you?" And she took another big bite of ham, pointing to her mouth as she chewed, her eyes wide and shaking her head, indicating she couldn't talk with her mouth full.

I could tell she wasn't mad or upset this time, so I patiently waited her out.

"Okay. Fine." She set her fork down, took a drink of water, and gave me her full attention. "His name is Cliff Evert, I met him when I was shopping at the Thriftway in Ocean Crest. That's his day job. He's a year older than I am, and yes, he's cute—if you happen to go for guys who have dimples to die for."

"Glad to hear it," I said. I almost blushed myself, as I couldn't help but think about Freddy's dimples. "And I hope you don't think I'm being too personal."

Nautika shook her head. "Compared to everything Lorraine wanted to know about him, you've hardly scratched the surface."

I nearly choked on my soda. "So Lorraine's been mother henning you too?"

"I really like her," said Nautika, thoughtfully. "She's got a big heart, kind, compassionate, and it's nice to know someone who was a friend of my mother's when she lived here." She smiled. "Do you know that 'back in the day,' my mom Julie went by Jewels, and Lorraine's nickname was Gem?" She looked at me to see if it was sinking in. "Lorraine Diamond was called Gem. Get it? Diamond, Gem?"

"Yes, I get it," I said, smiling back at this delightful young woman. "And I'm sorry I can't add anything to what 'Gem' is telling you about 'Jewels.' I barely knew your mother in high school. She was a year behind me, and we didn't have any of the same classes. But I do remember she was more bookworm than sports enthusiast because she often had her nose in a book even at pep assemblies!"

"Yep, that sounds like Mom alright." She nodded. "And don't worry about not knowing her. Where I grew up, we didn't even know half the kids in our own grade, much less anyone else. From what Lorraine's told me, there were more students in my graduating class than in the combined grades of 9 through 12 at Unity High."

"That's very true." I smiled at her, and when she smiled back, I remembered that same soft but determined smile on her mother's face. "But I must say I'm really glad you've got yourself another woman friend out there to talk to."

Nautika nodded again, then went on. "I don't care so much for Tom, though." Her eyes narrowed. "There's something about him that's ugly and mean."

Wow. I wasn't sure it was the right time or place to bring this up, but she's the one who'd opened the can of worms, not me, so I jumped in with both feet. "Do you suspect Tom has been hitting Lorraine?"

Nautika, bless her heart, didn't flinch. "Yes, I do. And I've asked Gem about it. Of course, she denies any such thing, but if I ever hear or see any real proof, I won't hesitate to turn him in. My generation doesn't stand for men beating on women—" She caught herself and rephrased. "Or anyone beating on anyone for that matter."

"I'm very glad to hear that."

Nautika was suddenly chewing on her lower lip, and I wondered if she'd regretted confiding in me. "Sylvia..."

"Don't worry," I replied. "I won't say anything to anybody unless I absolutely have to."

She expelled a huge sigh of relief. "Gracias."

"De nada."

"Oh my gosh, do you speak Spanish, Sylvia?" she asked.

I laughed. "You've just heard at least ten percent of all the words I know."

"I've been learning the language out on the bay," said Nautika. "Working alongside some of the Mexican laborers from both farms, I've picked up a lot of useful words."

"You can never be too educated. You never know when something you've learned, like algebra or speaking Spanish, might come in handy."

Nautika grinned, and this time the smile went clear to her eyes. "You're sounding like my mom again," she said. "But really, I don't mind."

"Okay, then let's talk about your work with the oyster fishery out on the bay."

"I'm loving every minute of it!" Nautika sat up a little straighter in her chair. "It doesn't matter to me that the property lines are a little fuzzy out there. A good marine biologist doesn't let an imaginary line in the sand—or in the water—get in the way of thorough research. And I'm pretty sure, with a united effort against the burrowing shrimp, we'll have a thriving oyster industry in Shallowwater Bay for generations to come."

I admired her youthful enthusiasm. But before I could ask any specific questions about Nautika's work, Orpha, Goodie, and Patrick arrived, and I looked around for a larger table.

"Better find us a table for eight or more," advised Orpha. "Meredith and Les will be joining us shortly, and you'll probably want to make room for at least one of your honeys, too."

I deftly dodged Orpha's unfiltered comment by simply ignoring it and directing Patrick to help me pull another table over beside the one where we already sat. Of all the Rainbow Gals, Orpha was the one most insistent that I hurry up and decide which beau I wanted to court me, if that expression wasn't even older than she is.

I'd known Mom and Les wanted to have a quiet Christmas dinner at home, just the two of them, since this was their first holiday season together, but she'd told me they'd be sure to stop by for dessert before the day was over.

"Nova and Rich won't be coming, though," said Goodie. "They're out on the Estrella Nueva trying to recover some of the crabbing gear lost in the storm."

Patrick shook his head. "Good luck with that," he said. He shucked out of his down jacket and hung it on the back of his chair. "Most of that gear is gone for good. I don't know how anybody makes a decent living out on the ocean anymore. Too many variables."

Nautika cleared her throat.

"Oh! Where are my manners?" I introduced Nautika to the gathering group, then pointed them toward the buffet line, telling them we needed to get back to our mashed potatoes and gravy station before Jimmy and Julio thought we'd abandoned them.

The rest of the afternoon whizzed right by, totally uneventful, except for two major show-stopping events. First off, when Meredith and Les showed up, Merri was all bubbly and flushed and talking exaggeratedly with her hands, very animated. I should have realized something was up right away, but it took a few minutes to zero in on the whopper of a diamond ring she sported on her left hand.

I can't say anyone was surprised by their engagement, and Orpha had apparently been waiting for this so she could start cracking jokes about my birth parents finally making me legitimate by officially tying the knot.

"So when's the big day?" I asked Meredith. I wrapped her in a big hug as soon as I could get my plastic apron off so I didn't get any mashed potatoes on her.

"We haven't set a date yet," Les answered me. "We're

thinking maybe sometime around Valentine's Day."

"If not sooner!" added Meredith, her eyes bright with anticipation. "We've already waited half a century for this to take place.'

"What's the rush?" asked Orpha. "It's not as if you're pregnant or anything."

There was a momentary shocked hush, and then Patrick couldn't hold back any longer. He busted up laughing, which set the rest of us to laughing too.

Kanji and Lorraine were officially in charge of the dessert table, although it was pretty much a serve yourself affair, and it looked to me like Gem was having another fun time being out and about without her husband Tom.

Brent left without joining us for dessert, telling Nautika to stay as long as she liked, but that it was his first chance to get out in some sunshine to check for any storm damage done last week during a low afternoon tide. At first, she'd thought she'd go with him, but then her new friend Cliff arrived and offered to bring her home any time she was ready to leave.

Poor Cliff. He was suddenly the center of everyone's attention, and I have to give him credit for holding his own among such a rabid group of interrogators.

We were down to just the core group of clean up volunteers when the second major event of the day landed at our feet with a resounding thud.

Sheriff Donaldson, who'd been enjoying an intimate holiday off over in Mercedes' motorhome, arrived in full uniform. He pushed his way through the swinging delivery doors, and there was no doubt by the look on his face,—his visit was all business.

"Deputy Morgan," he said, his voice resounding through the kitchen. "I need you in your uniform and come with me."

OYSTER SPAT

"To where?" asked Freddy, his arms elbow deep in soapy dishwater.

"To the Willoopah Oyster Farm," said Sheriff D. "Brent Booi just called it in. Seems while out walking his property this afternoon he discovered—uh—" He cleared his throat and lowered his voice, but every one of us was leaning forward in anticipation. "He discovered some, uh, human remains among the tideland grasses. He's waiting out there now to preserve the scene until we arrive."

CHAPTER 14

In less time than it takes to say "Merry Freakin' Christmas!" Freddy had run upstairs, changed into his uniform, and hopped into his patrol car to follow the Sheriff's Interceptor out to the little bayside burg of Willoopah. Both vehicles left with their lights flashing, but sped east across the peninsula on Willoopah Road without sirens.

And right behind them were Jimmy and I in hot pursuit in my Mustang, followed by Nautika and Cliff in Cliff's little white Ford Ranger pickup bringing up the rear.

"I've always wanted to be in a Christmas parade," said Jimmy. He was practically bouncing in his seat, and I made a quick check to make sure he had his seatbelt securely fastened.

"Then I guess today's your lucky day, Jimbo." I gripped the steering wheel with both hands, my mind racing between the two patrol cars ahead of us, and the pickup behind us. By my calculations, today might very well turn out to be a day in which I'd need every ounce of my background in counseling. I hoped I was wrong, but my gut was telling me these were no ordinary "human remains" found out on the tidelands.

I glanced again in my rearview mirror, and gratefully noted that Cliff was maintaining a safe stopping distance between us. I was also grateful Julio had already gone back to

OYSTER SPAT

Tinkerstown in the Five Amigos' delivery van, or I'm sure we'd have had that vehicle also joining is in Jimmy's fantasy Christmas parade.

My mind flitted back to the casino. Poor Meredith! Her Christmas engagement had been all but upstaged by the announcement of a gruesome discovery along the bay. I guess timing really is everything. Then I wondered for a moment how each of us would best remember this Christmas. Unbridled joy? Unfathomable heartache? Life certainly has its twists and turns.

"Slow down, Syl!" shouted Jimmy, breaking into my reverie. "The sign says there's a sharp left turn ahead!"

"No worries," I replied, deftly shifting the gear down and taking the corner on nothing more than a wing and a prayer.

"Holy crap," said Jimmy. He shot a quick glance over at me and pushed his glasses up with his middle finger. "I thought you had brakes on this car!"

"Don't be silly," I countered, pretending I hadn't seen him giving me the finger. "Mustangs don't come with brakes because Mustang drivers never use them."

Seconds later we arrived at the Willoopah Oyster Farm. We parked in a row across from Brent's gear shed, 1-2-3-4. Then the sheriff, Freddy, Jimmy and I, Cliff and Nautika, flung open the doors and piled out of our respective vehicles at the same time.

The sheriff was none too pleased by so many "civilians" tagging along, but he knew there was nothing he could say that would make any of us leave without a fight. I zipped up my jacket and stuck my hands in the pockets, waiting none too patiently for the men who were actually paid to be here to lead the way along the bay.

Sheriff D put on his non-regulation Stetson and Freddy stuck an also non-regulation Mariners' ball cap on his head.

Together they gathered two rolls of crime scene tape, a half dozen evidence bags, gloves, felt markers, a high-quality digital camera, several pencils and the sheriff's official notepad, and the group started trudging along the trail through thigh-high eel grass. Brent wasn't far from the house, and we could see him standing in his green rain slicker, despite the sunny weather, and florescent orange stocking cap, just a few hundred yards south of his seafood store.

We got within 10 or 15 yards of Brent when the sheriff abruptly stopped, turned an about face, and confronted our entourage. I thought he'd be pissed off we were trailing along like he was some militia mother duck or something, but instead he just started barking orders.

"Sylvia, take Jimmy and—" he blinked several times, apparently at a loss for names, then just pointed at Nautika and Cliff, and said, "and take those two with you—and set the perimeter with this crime tape." He held out one of the bright yellow rolls of "DO NOT CROSS" plastic tape rolls to me. "Give us a radius of 25 feet around Mr. Booi. Can you do that?"

"Yes, sir." I wasn't about to argue that if I followed his directions to the letter, several of us were going to have to wade out at least knee deep into Shallowwater Bay to complete the circle, and we'd have to learn to tread water if the tide came in before we finished. I knew he was just giving us something to do that wouldn't infringe on his ability to collect any actual evidence there might be inside his arbitrary boundary.

Freddy manned the camera, and started moving forward one careful step at a time, digitally establishing the location, then recording the path, clearly marked with a solitary line of Brent's boot prints, all the way to Brent. Meanwhile, the sheriff was undoubtedly following protocol, noting the date, time, approximate coordinates, who was present, who was taking the official photos, etc., in his notepad.

He'd handed the tape to me, so I took the loose end, unrolled a substantial length of it, maybe 25 or 30 feet, and passed the tape on to Nautika, who did the same as I'd done, passing the roll to Cliff, who also did the same, and passed it on to Jimmy, who had no one left to pass it to, so dutifully hung onto the rest of the roll. Since there aren't any trees on the tidelands, we anchored the tape with rocks, driftwood, and whatever else we could find in order to create an approximation of an enclosure in which to concentrate the investigation.

As we finished what I considered our unnecessary assignment, I called out to the sheriff, "Is John Stark on his way?" John Stark is our county ME, a.k.a. coroner. He's also the go-to guy for collection of potential evidence. It's usually up to him to collect and process whatever he can handle in-house, then send the rest of the evidence to the CSI lab in Olympia.

Sheriff D shook his head. "Stark's got his grandkids here for Christmas. I told him this was likely an older cold case, and he needn't bother to meet us here. So it's just us."

"Then what would you like us to do next?"

The sheriff smiled, and just by the way he smiled, I could guess before he said anything exactly what was coming next. "I'd like the four of you to maintain equal distance positions behind the tape and keep any looky-loos from coming closer."

I rolled my eyes. "Come on, Carter, you know we can't see much of anything from way back here, and there's no one else around for us to keep from getting any closer."

Sheriff Donaldson ignored me, and kept right on interviewing Brent. "What time did you discover the skull?

From which direction were you coming? Did you have to move any vegetation to be able to determine that it was a human skull?"

So only a skull, and nothing else? A little of the tension in my gut dissolved. I wasn't sure how Nautika, or Cliff, or even Jimmy and I would have handled it if there'd been a full human skeleton or even just a torso emerging from the sand.

Freddy got down on his hands and knees and took photos from several more angles before setting the camera down and pulling a 3-inch paintbrush from his evidence kit. He slowly brushed away the sand from the portion of the skull that was showing among the grass, then took several more pictures. He repeated the process again and again until the skull was completely visible, even from behind our sheriff-imposed yellow line of demarcation.

I wondered if the skull had originally been buried there, or if it had washed up after months or years of rolling around on the floor of Shallowwater Bay. I wondered if our recent hurricane activity was responsible for a portion of the skull suddenly coming into view. I wondered what Nautika was feeling, considering the fact she could very well be looking at her father's skull. My mind was filled with unanswered, and most likely forever unanswerable questions, and I felt a deep, overwhelming, indescribable sense of loss.

Meanwhile, Jimmy stood on the south side of our circle, directly across from me. For awhile, he was craning his neck to see what he could, but then he got the brilliant idea of using his smart phone to enlarge the scene to maximum magnification before snapping some shots. I was kind of jealous I hadn't thought of that first, but since I'd left my cell phone in the car, it was a moot point anyway.

Nautika and Cliff were huddled together on the west side of our boundary tape, talking quietly. I couldn't hear what they said, but from the expression on Cliff's face, I was pretty certain Nautika was telling him her mother and father had lived on the peninsula before she was born, and the sad story of the disappearance of her father, John Henry, some 25 years ago.

"Sheriff!" Jimmy suddenly called out. "There are some other boot prints over here you may want to take a look at." He pointed to where the trail continued south, beyond where we'd marked off the area, on the other side of the alleged crime scene.

The sheriff scowled, but he and Brent dutifully walked over to take a look. And since it was outside the "do not enter" zone, Jimmy, Nautika, Cliff and I hurried over to have a look too.

There were indeed another set of prints, unlike those we'd followed from Brent's house. They came from the south, heading north, but they suddenly disappeared, just about 30 feet from the skull, which made them five feet outside our Do Not Cross tape.

At least five of the seven of us were not trained to be able to discern just when those tracks had been made, and those who were—namely Sheriff D and Freddy—weren't saying anything loud enough for our ears to hear. The sheriff just barked, "Nobody move," and directed Freddy to take a few more photos of this second set of tracks.

Jimmy, however, thought he had something to contribute to the investigation, and started rattling off the different brands and styles of rubber boots common among the Mexican, Filipino, and Japanese laborers.

"Most of the fishermen on the west coast wear hip boots," he said. "The Filipinos usually wear black knee boots we sometimes call 'farmers boots,' or 'barn boots' with a thick red stripe around the top. The short white ones are favored by the Japanese, and they call them 'shrimpers' boots'. But those are mostly worn by the salmon egg techs in the canneries of Alaska."

Where Jimmy gets all his information is beyond me, but once in a while it actually turns out to be useful. Today I wasn't sure as to the usefulness of his unsolicited information, but I listened attentively and filed it away anyway, just in case.

"My crew all wear Xtratufs," Brent volunteered, pointing to his own feet. "Like mine."

Nautika nodded. "They don't slip as much on the boat decks," she added.

"And did any of you know," said Jimmy excitedly, "that in two states—Florida and Hawaii—they have not only fingerprints, but also barefoot prints on file?"

Sheriff Donaldson blew out a big breath of air. "That's all very fascinating, I'm sure, but it's unlikely that any of that information will do us any good." He put his hands on his hips and turned his face to the sky. "Freddy, just photograph whatever you see, whether you think we need it or not. It's going to be dark here in another hour, and once the tide comes in and out again, nothing will be left of any prints, Hawaiian, Floridian, or otherwise."

Freddy started doing as he'd been instructed, but after a few minutes he stopped and turned back around. "Excuse me, Sheriff? I have a feeling these tracks don't have anything to do with the discovery of the skull. It looks to me, from the obvious starts and stops of the trail, like someone was just out walking, maybe a bird watcher or photographer, enjoying a leisurely after dinner walk on Christmas Day. In my opinion, he or she missed the skull completely, just the same as many people probably have done for some time along here."

Sheriff D critically surveyed the scene again and nodded. 'You're right. Sometimes the simplest solution is the best one." He sighed. "No need to take any more photos of

OYSTER SPAT

the tracks. What you've already gotten will be more than enough."

We'd been too busy to notice an unmarked white van park among our other cars to the north of us until we heard someone trying to hail us. "HELLO!! Yoo-whoo! Sheriff! I'm here!"

John Stark came huffing and puffing up the trail carrying an armload of assorted plastic bags, which he dumped at his feet just outside our yellow tape circle in the sand.

"I thought I told you I could handle it," said Sheriff D.

"You did," said John, "and I appreciate that. Really, I do. But I also appreciated having an indisputable excuse to get away from a houseful of grandkids charged up on holiday sugar for the next couple hours."

Sheriff D made brief introductions, and then Stark asked to see the deceased. Freddy stepped aside, and for the first time, everyone had an equal opportunity to see the entire skull, lying on the sand among the eel grass, bare and white, exposed to the elements.

It was a sobering moment, and we all seemed to be paying our respects by remaining uncharacteristically silent.

"Alas, poor Yorick, I knew him well," said Jimmy, breaking the silence.

Well, at least some of us were quietly paying our respects—at least those of us who were not busy reciting a well-known scene from Shakespeare's Hamlet.

"So how long do you suppose he's been dead?" asked Sheriff D.

"He or she," I reminded the sheriff.

Sheriff D rolled his eyes. "We don't currently have any missing females in this county, Sylvia, so I'm playing the odds this cranium belonged to a man."

"What makes you think he or she was from this

county?" I asked.

A flicker of a sad smile crossed Stark's face. "You know I can't tell you that without a thorough examination when he or she died, Sheriff. We don't know how much the skull has been affected by the elements. It could be it's been in the water or the sand for decades. On the other hand, the crabs and other scavengers pick the bones clean pretty quickly, so it could be someone from just last summer."

I shot a look at Nautika. Her face was ashen, and her knees looked a little wobbly. Would this be how she'd finally find out what had happened to her father? I started to move to her side, but Cliff beat me to it, and put a reassuring arm around her waist. My positive estimation of him was growing by the moment.

Stark bent down to examine the skull a little closer. He looked up at Freddy. "Do you have all the photos you're going to need?"

Freddy nodded. "I believe I do."

"Good." Stark slipped his gloved hand into what would have been the gaping mouth, if the skull still had a mandible attached, and reverently lifted it up, turning it from side to side. "It's apparent he or she had some upper dental work done at some time in his or her life. Not nearly enough, but let's hope we can track down his or her identity through his or her dental records." He turned the skull to examine the back side. "And back here…" He pointed with his free hand. "There's a serious indentation in the back of the cranium, along with a deep crack he or she would not have survived without immediate medical treatment. Maybe not even then." The county Medical Examiner got to his feet and handed the skull to Freddy. "Bag it and tag it, if you would, Deputy."

"Yes, sir." Freddy was already waiting with the open evidence bag, the date, time, and place of discovery printed

OYSTER SPAT

on the tag. This wasn't Freddy's first crime scene, but I couldn't say the same for poor Nautika and Cliff.

"You two okay?" I asked quietly.

They both nodded, but neither one of them said a word. Nautika's eyes were fixed on the skull, now in a clear plastic bag and in Freddy's custody. My heart ached for her as I imagined the thoughts most likely running through her head.

Stark dusted the sand off his hands by brushing them on his jeans. He looked at Sheriff D and raised an eyebrow. "We've never found that kayaker who disappeared last August." It was a statement, not a question.

Sheriff D nodded. "There are those who think that might have been a gay hate crime. The kid was seen drinking at a local watering hole the night he disappeared, and it's speculated he might have propositioned the wrong guy and got his head bashed in for his friendliness. But then some kids found his kayak about a week or so after he was reported missing, and the idea of foul play was set aside for accidental drowning."

"That's right," said Stark. "I was at a state coroner's conference in Olympia, and my temporary replacement ruled that there'd most likely been an unfortunate mishap out on the water, so the investigation was closed."

"Was the kayak paddle ever located?" asked Jimmy.

Sheriff Donaldson rocked back and forth on his heels. "No, it was not."

The sheriff looked at the ME. "So now you're thinking this might be that kid, Stark, and that maybe his own paddle was the murder weapon?"

"Whoa now," said John Stark. "I'm not hypothesizing anything as definitive as that. I was just thinking through the number of missing persons we've had on the books for years."

"You mean like Nadine's husband? Claude Larsen?" I was glad to have something to finally contribute to the conversation.

Stark nodded. "We assumed, from where his car and shoes were found, that Claude died trying to walk across the mud to Elk Island when the tide was out."

When I saw the horrified looks on Nautika's and Cliff's faces, I hurried to fill in an important detail. "Claude Larsen had Alzheimer's. He got confused easily. He probably wasn't cognizant of the idea that the tide would be coming back in before he could return."

"But this skull had some damage done to it on purpose," said Freddy.

"And I don't think this skull is that of a man in his 80s," said Stark. "So we're back to the kayaker, who was in his 30s, or…" He stopped and looked at Nautika, then back to Sheriff D. "Did you say her last name is Henry?"

"That's right," said the sheriff. "And yes, the John Henry case has never been solved, and yes, he would have been around 30 when he also disappeared."

"Well, Sheriff," said Stark, "this is just preliminary, but I'm going to rule this fellow's death a homicide for the time being." He sighed, shook his head, and blew out a very long, deep breath. "You ever wonder how many bodies have been dumped into the ocean?"

"When you swim in the ocean," Jimmy piped up, "and in this case, I suppose Shallowwater Bay counts as a saltwater estuary of the Pacific Ocean, you are actually swimming in the remains of the dead. Those who are missing, and those who choose to be buried at sea, along with the fact that it's the most popular place for murderers to dispose of bodies. It's a fact the ocean contains more human remains then all the graveyards on earth, added up together."

Silently, we all turned and looked out over the bay, each

processing our own thoughts of mortality and even immorality. At the moment, the water was quite tranquil, dark and still, and certainly did not look that threatening. Out on the water, the sound of the Willoopah company dredge made a soft humming background noise.

"Let's get this tape gathered up," said Sheriff D, bending down and pulling at the tape we'd partially anchored with sand. "Don't want to have to arrest any of you for littering."

Most of us knew the sheriff was kidding, and that he probably had used that joke many times before, but Nautika and Cliff didn't know him well enough to think his statement was funny. Together they hurried to wad up the used yellow tape and shove it into an unused evidence bag.

Then as a group, we turned and started walking back up the trail to the parking lot. And as we walked silently along the shoreline, I was relatively certain each of us was thinking pretty much the same thing.

If the skull turned out to be that of John Henry, he'd been right here all along, sleeping with the oysters for two and a half decades. But only time would tell if this skull turned out to be the missing kayaker, John Henry, or someone we didn't even know was missing.

CHAPTER 15

In the early afternoon the day after Christmas, I was scheduled for my biannual dental exam at my dentist's office in Tinkerstown. I know it's a strange time for most people to book an appointment, but I've been going to the same hygienist for decades, and although we've developed a friendly relationship, we never seem to make time for coffee.

I solved that problem by going in every six months so we can catch up with each other. During the kids' Christmas holiday and in the middle of summer vacation had worked best for us for years because I knew I wouldn't need to cancel due to my own work issues.

Nevertheless, I had considered postponing this appointment, what with all the community drama unfolding concerning the North Beach Tribune's headline this morning: "Storm Brings Unwelcome Gift for Christmas." But then I realized the dentist's chair was exactly where I needed to be that day.

"So how's your love life?" asked the woman I fondly refer to as "Nurse Ratchet" as she fastened the apron around my neck.

"Nice to see you, too," I replied.

"Made up your mind yet about which of those handsome hunks you want to call your boyfriend?"

Geez. Was no place sacred? "Cood whee tok abot thumpthin elz?"

OYSTER SPAT

Nurse Ratchet laughed. "Sure. No problem. We don't have to talk about the men in your life if it makes you uncomfortable, but I only get two times a year to catch up with you."

Did dentists and their hygienists take special classes so they could understand what their clients were saying while in a chair reclining so far back all their blood was rushing to their heads and two unfamiliar hands using an assortment of metal probes were groping around in their mouths? Man oh man, she never failed to amaze me.

"I saw in the paper this morning you were present when that skull was found on the tide flats out in Willoopah."

"Uh-huh."

"John Stark brought the skull in at the crack of dawn this morning and we took X-rays of the teeth. Then four of us spent the rest of the morning looking to see if they matched any we had on file."

"Add did day?"

"Considering we're the only dentist on the peninsula right now, and we have literally every dental record of every kid who's ever lived here because we keep all records unless or until someone wants them transferred to another dentist in another city, it's a fair bet we can help identify most anyone who's sat in one of our chairs and had dental work done."

I was glad Nurse Ratchet was in a talkative mood, but she hadn't exactly answered my question. "Did oo get ah mash?"

"We sure did! Had to go back almost 30 years, but there's at least a 95% chance we were able to put the right name on the skull."

I waited while she scraped a little harder behind my lower front teeth. "Add oo waz it?"

"Well, I'm not exactly sure I should be giving that

information out, you know, with the HIPAA privacy rules and all..." Her voice trailed off as she considered her options.

"Pweeze?"

Nurse Ratchet set her instruments down on the tray in front of her and swung the metal arm away from my chin. "I guess it won't do any harm. The guy went to high school here about 40 years ago, dropped out, and joined the Navy, and never returned to our office for any additional dental work." She shrugged. "That's all I know."

I sat up and used the napkin still clipped around my neck to wipe my mouth, hoping not to sound too eager when I asked, "Do you happen to know his name?"

"I don't think he has any relatives here."

"But do you know his name?" I said it a little sharper than I'd intended.

"John Heikkinen," she said, handing me a little bag with toothbrush, paste, and floss inside. "Does that name ring any bells for you?"

Boy did it, but I didn't want it to get back to Sheriff Donaldson that I was leaking insider information about the deceased, so I just shook my head. "Guess we'll both have to wait for the sheriff to finish his investigation." I felt like a cad holding out on her, but it couldn't be helped. It wasn't going to take much time for word to get out that the disappearance of John Henry, a.k.a. John Heikkinen, had been at least partially solved, but I didn't want the information leak tracing directly back to me. Not this time.

So instead of heading home, I decided to stop by the police station to see if they would voluntarily share what they knew. Once they told me, officially, about matching the teeth, I wouldn't have to pretend to be clueless.

Freddy was outside at his cruiser as I pulled into the parking lot behind the cop shop, and we both smiled and waved.

OYSTER SPAT

"So I guess you heard the skull Brent found yesterday belonged to John Henry," said Freddy as I stepped from my car.

"How in the world would I know that?" I asked, feigning innocence.

Freddy shrugged. "I saw your car at the dentist's office."

Small towns! Good grief and gravy, I just couldn't catch a break!

"So is it now an active murder investigation?"

Freddy nodded. "Sheriff Donaldson is up in Willoopah even as we speak. He's interviewing a list of people who may or may not have information on the 25-year-old case, starting with Brent Booi, then Tom and Lorraine Diamond."

"Brent Booi?" My eyebrows shot up a notch. "Wouldn't it be kind of silly for him to report finding a skull of someone he'd murdered 25 years ago?"

"That's exactly what Brent said when the sheriff contacted him to set up an appointment," said Freddy. "But at this point, Sheriff D is only looking to speak with anyone who may have known John back in the day. He's not accusing anyone of anything." Freddy paused. "But you've got to admit Brent had plenty of motive, since John and Tom had used every trick in the book to steal some of his grandfather's oyster beds from him."

"What about Tom Diamond?" I asked. "John allegedly signs over his half of the business to Tom to cover his gambling losses, and then he suddenly up and disappears? I don't buy it."

Freddy nodded. "You're right. There was no way to prove or disprove John Henry's signature on that supposed forfeiture note for his half the ownership in Diamond Oysters."

"Hhmm…" I mused. "Curiouser and curiouser." But before we could continue our conversation, Freddy's collar radio started crackling.

I've never been able to figure out how anyone can understand what anybody's trying to say over those radios, but Freddy seemed to have no trouble at all. He walked a discreet distance and carried on a rather lengthy conversation before saying, "Roger that, Sheriff, I'm on my way," and headed once again for his cruiser.

"Hey! Wait! What's going on?" I called after him.

Freddy stopped with his hand on the car door and turned around. "Remember when Meredith told us that there had been rumors about John and Lorraine having an affair?"

"Yeah…"

"Well, when the sheriff brought the infidelity rumor up during their interview, Tom and Lorraine got into a knock-down, drag-out fight right in front of him. Tom said that nobody'd be dumb enough to believe John would mess around with his butt-ugly wife when he had a cute little gal waiting for him at home, and Lorraine screamed at him that she had put up with too many years of his bullying and badmouthing her character and she was going to get his shot gun and shoot him dead if he didn't take it all back."

"Oh dear," I said, shaking my head. "I take it there might have been some alcohol involved?"

"Good guess," said Freddy.

"So then what happened?"

"Well… I, uh…" Freddy hesitated.

"Freddy, what did you do?"

"Remember that night you got locked in the Diamond's gear shed?"

"Yes, of course. It's not something I'll soon forget."

"Well, I happened to share with the sheriff that you suspected Lorraine might be being physically abused by her husband. So when they went off on each other like that, the sheriff decided it might be a good thing to run Tom into South Bend for a night or two to cool down—and sober up."

"So he arrested Tom Diamond?"

"When confronted with domestic violence, the protocol is that one of the offending spouses is usually removed from the premises. The sheriff chose Tom."

"So where are you headed?"

"I'm the one who gets to transport him to South Bend," said Freddy. He gave me a quick kiss on the lips, and said, "Don't wait up." Then he got into his car and started it up for the trip to the county jail.

After a night in the county lock-up, Tom was released right after lunch without being charged. He called Lorraine, and she said she wasn't pressing charges, but she wasn't going to come get him, either.

Tom asked around the courthouse if there was anyone who could give him a ride, but no one was headed toward the peninsula. Since he hadn't had his cell phone on him when he was arrested, he didn't have any numbers he could call for someone to come get him.

It was almost two o'clock before he decided the heck with it, and just started walking, sticking this thumb out to hitchhike and hoping he didn't have to walk too far before someone took pity on him and picked him up.

An hour or two later, Tom's prayers were answered when a vehicle pulled off the road a few car lengths in front of him and the driver reached over and opened the passenger side door. Tom hustled up and opened it wide, then stopped in his tracks. "Can't say I'm glad to see you, but I sure as hell don't want to have to walk all the way back."

"You going to get in or not?" asked the driver.

Tom got in, pulled the door shut, and fastened his seatbelt.

The driver fiddled with the radio for a moment before pulling back out on the road, hoping Tom would take the hint and not try to carry on any pointless conversation.

Lorraine called the sheriff's office to file a missing person's report the morning after Tom failed to return home. "He's probably just holed up in some bar somewhere," she told Sheriff Donaldson, "trying to make me feel bad for not coming to get him."

"We take all missing person's reports very seriously," said Sheriff D, "but it hasn't been 48 hours yet since he was in custody in South Bend."

Lorraine sighed. "Then what do I do?"

"If Tom hasn't shown up by this time tomorrow, you're welcome to call me back and we'll get the paperwork started," said the sheriff. "Until then, we'll just assume it's like you said—that he's out trying to drown his sorrows, hoping to make you feel guilty."

But the next morning, well before Lorraine planned to put in another call to Sheriff Donaldson, he was standing at her front door, his Stetson clasped in his hand.

"Sheriff?" said Lorraine, as if she weren't quite sure who she was seeing standing there. "You didn't have to come all the way out here just so I could fill out that missing person report. I was planning to come into Tinkerstown to do that this afternoon."

"I'm afraid that won't be necessary, Mrs. Diamond."

Lorraine's gut clenched, and her knees went weak. She grabbed the door frame to steady herself. "Then I guess you better come in."

"I'm sorry to have to bring you this news," said Sheriff D, sitting stiffly at the kitchen table. Lorraine had been insistent upon him coming in and sitting down, and pouring him a cup of coffee before she'd let him say another word.

OYSTER SPAT

Lorraine's lips were pressed together so tightly there was only a fine line to indicate her mouth. Mutely, she nodded, and waited for him to continue.

"Tom's body was found on a logging road not far off Highway 101, about 20 miles this side of South Bend."

Again Lorraine nodded and said nothing.

"He still had his wallet on him, intact with cash and credit cards, so we do not believe robbery was the motive."

Lorraine's brow furrowed, but otherwise her expression did not change.

"Naturally," continued Sheriff D, "John Stark will do an autopsy, so it will be a few days before the body will be released."

Again with the silent nod, Lorraine indicated she'd heard him.

"Is there anyone who can come be with you today?" asked the sheriff. "Any friends or family you wish for us to contact for you? Someone to help you make arrangements?"

Lorraine shook her head. "We didn't have any children, and I doubt his sisters would bother to make the trip." She sighed. "I don't see any point in having a service. Tom didn't have many friends."

Sheriff Donaldson scrutinized her face. Was she in shock? Denial? Relief? He wasn't quite sure what to make of her dispassionate countenance, but it was certainly something for him to consider later when he started his suspect list.

To be polite, he took a big swig of coffee, set the cup down, and stood up. "I'm sorry for your loss, Mrs. Diamond. Please let me know if I can be of any further assistance."

Lorraine walked him to the door. "Thank you for coming," she said, as if this had been a social call. "I appreciate you taking the time to notify me in person."

Sheriff D went down the steps, put his hat on, turned

and touched the brim of it out of respect. "I'll be in touch."

He turned his Interceptor around and headed back out the one-way road. At the Booi farm, he thought briefly about stopping to inform Lorraine's nearest neighbors of Tom's death, but decided his time would be better spent getting the official investigation underway as soon as possible.

Stark's CSI crew should be through processing the area out along the logging road by now, and there might be a preliminary report from the coroner. Anxious to find out what they'd learned, he kept driving, on into Ocean Crest where the cell signal was better.

Although he hated to do it, it was time to call together what he begrudgingly called his "brain trust." Many heads were always better than one, and with the county's meager budget, he wasn't above tapping a couple amateur investigators for help.

But first, he needed to stop at the Ocean Crest Thriftway for donuts. His amateur sleuths gladly worked for free, but he couldn't risk showing up empty-handed.

By the time Sheriff Donaldson rolled into the parking lot of the Clamshell Motel, everyone else was already there. Jimmy had the coffee ready, and Freddy and I sat expectantly at the kitchen table, notepads, pens, and an empty plate and napkins in front of each of us.

"Has Freddy brought you up to speed?" asked Sheriff D as he came through the inner motel office door.

"I've told them everything I know," said Freddy.

I grinned. I knew it was a cheap shot, but I took it anyway. "It really didn't take all that long, Sheriff."

Amid a few guffaws, and Freddy's chagrin, we helped ourselves to donuts, placing our selections on the plates Jimmy had set out. If there's one thing you can count on, it's cops and donuts, I thought to myself, but as bakery goods are one of my great weaknesses, I certainly wasn't complaining.

"So let's review," said the sheriff, after quickly finishing off a bear claw, washing it down with half a cup of coffee, and wiping his mouth on a napkin.

"I transported Tom Diamond to the county jail on December 26th," began Freddy.

I nodded confirmation. That was the same day as my dental exam, and I'd been talking with Freddy when the sheriff had called him into service.

"He was released from jail the next afternoon," began Freddy. "Unable to secure a ride, he began hitchhiking home."

"That was the 27th," said Jimmy, starting a timeline on his notepad.

"On the 28th, Lorraine Diamond called the sheriff's office to report Tom missing, since he hadn't made it home that day," added Sheriff Donaldson.

"And today's the 29th," said Freddy. He shot a quick look at me. "Just two days till New Year's Eve."

I wasn't sure what New Year's Eve had to do with anything, but I nodded anyway.

"I informed Lorraine of her husband's passing this morning," said Sheriff D. "She took the news well—maybe too well, I'm afraid."

"The spouse is always the number one suspect," Jimmy interjected.

"You watch too much crime TV," said Freddy and I in unison.

"But that doesn't necessarily mean he's wrong," added the sheriff. He pulled out his pocket notebook and stubby pencil to check his notes.

"I've already spoken with John Stark. Cause of death was several downward stabs to the right side of the neck, one of them severing his external jugular. He bled out very quickly."

"Ooo! Ooo! Ooo!" said Jimmy. "If the murderer was facing him, since the wounds were on his right side, it most likely indicates a left-handed man."

"Hold on there, cowboy," I said. "Since the stab wounds were downward, you can't rule out the murderer being a woman. Men most often thrust upward, while women are overhand stabbers."

"Now who's watching too much crime TV?" Freddy said softly.

Far from disappointed at my challenge, Jimmy was nodding enthusiastically. "Or, it could have been a man who also watches too much crime TV, and he purposely stabbed downward to make everyone think he was a woman assailant!"

There was no faulting that kind of logic, but it was sure muddying up our suspect list.

"I'm assuming Tom was killed right where he was found, and not brought there and dumped after he was dead," I said.

"Very good, Sylvia." Sheriff Donaldson smiled. "Yes, it's unlikely he was killed in a car, as the driver would have been on his left side."

"So we're assuming that some good Samaritan picked him up hitchhiking home on the afternoon of the 27th, but then pulled off the road to kill him, but not rob him," said Freddy.

"That's what it looks like," said Sheriff D.

"There are only two weather road cams between here and there," said Jimmy. "I don't suppose Tom was standing under one when he was offered a ride?"

"No such luck," said the sheriff.

"Any ideas about the murder weapon?" asked Freddy.

"As a matter of fact," said Sheriff D, "the murder weapon was left at the scene of the crime. It's secured in an evidence locker in the morgue."

I almost snorted coffee out my nose when the sheriff said that. We don't actually have a bona fide morgue in our county, just a designated room for autopsies in the basement of the hospital. And as for being in an evidence locker, most likely the murder weapon is wrapped in plastic and tucked into one of John Stark's medical bags.

"That's a lucky break," said Jimmy. "Do you suppose he just made a mistake not taking it with him? Most perps dispose of the murder weapon elsewhere."

"Actually," I said, "it points more directly to the possibility that this was a crime of passion and not premeditation, so please refrain from referring to the murderer as a 'he'." I looked at the sheriff for confirmation and got an ever-so-slight nod. "So what kind of weapon is it?"

"I hope it goes without saying that everything we discuss here is confidential," said Sheriff D. "We're not releasing any of this to the newspapers for as long as we can keep it quiet."

"Understood," I said, and Jimmy solemnly nodded, using his right index finger to cross his heart.

"The murder weapon is a commemorative oyster shucking knife. One hundred and fifty of them were given out at a festival commemorating 150 years of oyster production on Shallowwater Bay," said Sheriff D.

"Technically, the first oysters commercially exported to San Francisco from Shallowwater Bay were shipped in 1851," said Encyclopedia Jimmy. "But if I recall, the celebration took place in the late 1990s and not in 2001 because for the first several years, oysters were being shipped without any regulations or safeguards by individuals living along the bay and seeing a chance to make a few bucks on the side."

"PLEASE STOP!" I said forcefully to Jimmy. "Let's go back a few steps. The murder weapon was a commemorative oyster shucking knife? Holy Criminitly! That means at least 150 people are now on the suspect list, including Orpha, Goodie, and my mother! In fact, Nadine had one too, but since she's gone, at least we can rule her knife out."

"Maybe we can, and maybe we can't," said Jimmy. "Wouldn't Patrick have access to all Nadine's kitchenware?"

"Patrick only met Tom at Nadine's memorial," I said. "What motive could he possibly have?" I looked at Sheriff Donaldson, but his eyes didn't meet mine.

"Oftentimes," said Freddy, thoughtfully tapping his pen on the pad in front of him, and chuckling softly, "especially on crime TV," he shot a look my direction, "the murderer is the one who points the police in the direction of the body."

Sheriff Donaldson cleared his throat. "The body was discovered when a man allegedly pulled off the highway this morning to find a discreet place to empty his bladder full of coffee. That man was Patrick Paulsen, a.k.a. Patrick O'Leary, a.k.a Paranormal Patrick."

OYSTER SPAT

CHAPTER 16

"*PATRICK?!*" I could barely squeak his name out.

"Way to bury the lead," said Jimmy to Sheriff D.

It took only a couple seconds to regain my voice and gather a big head of steam. "You've got to be kidding me! Patrick can't possibly be a suspect! No! No! No! That's the most ridiculous thing I've ever heard! You cannot be serious! There's no one on this earth more gentle, laid back, and 100% anti-violent than Patrick O'Leary! Killing someone is *not* in his wheelhouse! It would irrevocably harsh his mellow!"

"Now let's not get ahead of ourselves," said the sheriff, first looking at me, and then addressing Jimmy. "And if I had led with the information about Patrick finding the body, it's all at least one of us—" He cleared his throat and looked in my direction. "—would have been focused on from then on."

He had me there. Paranormal Patrick had come into our peninsula lives via a rather untraditional online dating profile, but he had proven himself to be one heckuva upstanding, caring, compassionate, 'I've got your back' kind of guy. But even as I heard myself flying to his defense inside my head, I knew the sheriff was right. The person who reports finding the body goes on the suspect list, no matter who it is, until he or she can be totally ruled out.

"Okay." I took a breath. It wasn't a very big breath, but the oxygen would keep me from passing out after my tirade.

"But what motive could Patrick possibly have to kill someone he hadn't even met until the afternoon of Nadine's memorial?"

"That's what we're here for," said Sheriff D. "You know how this works. First we'll make a list of possible suspects, any possible motives, and who had the opportunity. Then when we start interviewing, we'll start checking out their alibis to eliminate them one by one."

Freddy nodded. "And unless the murder was totally random and from an unknown party, we ought to be able to get this case resolved pretty quickly."

"Don't jinx it!" shouted Sheriff Donaldson, in what would definitely qualify as his "outdoor voice." But the sheriff knew from experience never to think solving a crime is a slam dunk. There are always twists and turns to the circumstances and nothing must ever be assumed.

"But don't you think the oyster knife rules out the random nut job just jonesing to stab somebody?" Jimmy asked. When the sheriff had raised his voice, Priscilla had awakened from her catnap on the couch and now hopped up into Jimmy's lap for some attention.

"It's not a very effective weapon of choice, so premeditation is highly unlikely," said Freddy.

"Let's get going on the suspect list and we'll see," said Sheriff D. He took another donut from the box, this time a cruller, took a big bite and still managed to talk around his very full mouth. "Where does anyone want to start?"

"Lorraine." The other three of us said her name in unison.

"Okay," said the sheriff. "Motive?"

"Spousal abuse." I spoke right up. Three pairs of eyes looked at me, but Sheriff D just wrote it down and said nothing.

"Opportunity?" he then asked.

OYSTER SPAT

"Well, when Tom called her to come get him in South Bend, she refused. That's why he was hitchhiking home," said Freddy.

"She could have changed her mind," said Jimmy. "Women change their minds all the time. Maybe she had second thoughts and felt sorry for him."

"I'm inclined to believe she'd rather let him walk home," I said. "That would give her more time to plan her next move without him around. Maybe she was finally deciding to leave him, or file for divorce, or something like that."

"But thinking he'd be cooling his heels on the long walk home could backfire," said Freddy. "I'd be afraid he was getting madder and madder with every step he took toward the old homestead."

"She reported him missing the day after his release," said Sheriff D, "which would indicate she genuinely cared about him, unless she was just covering her tracks. But when I informed her of his death this morning, she was oddly dispassionate."

"She might have just been relieved she didn't have to kill him herself," I said. "I have first and secondhand suspicions that he's been physically abusing her for a very long time."

Sheriff Donaldson tapped his pencil on his notebook several times, then made another note, but thankfully, he did not comment on my statement. "Next?"

"I guess we need to put Patrick's name down," I said. "Even though I don't want to."

"He said he drives back and forth to South Bend on business several times a week," said Sheriff D. "So that gives him opportunity."

"Yes," I reluctantly agreed. "Patrick has a booming lawn service here on the peninsula, and he helped set some guys up in South Bend to get their own business started." I smiled. "And now that it's legal, he doesn't have to worry about driving back and forth with marijuana in his van."

"So he returned to the scene of the crime the day after it happened," said Jimmy.

I wanted to slap Jimmy. "You're assuming Patrick returned to a crime scene he'd been to before, instead of believing what he reported—that he discovered the crime accidentally when nature called."

Jimmy bobbed his head. "Sorry. You're right."

"What about a motive for Patrick?" asked Freddy.

I sighed. "Unfortunately, I think I might know about one of those, too."

Again, all three men looked my way, but this time Sheriff D quickly encouraged me to continue. When I hesitated to share my theory, the sheriff said, "Now is not a good time to be holding back anything that might help solve this case, whether it condemns or exonerates."

"Well," I began slowly, "everyone knows that Nadine died of Non-Hodgkins lymphoma." My statement was greeted by three solemnly nodding heads. "And maybe some of you have seen the TV commercials suggesting a link between chemical weed-killing products like Roundup and that particular disease?"

"You mean those commercials funded by attorneys looking to get you to sign on to a class-action suit?" asked Jimmy.

"Yes," I replied. "I don't think much of those ambulance-chasers, but it might be possible they're on to something."

The men nodded again.

"Nadine told Patrick she'd had the cancer for some time," I continued. "And she wasn't sure where or how she got it. It could have been from the Agent Orange she came into contact with in Vietnam, or it might have been from the chemicals that helicopters sprayed on Shallowwater Bay back when she was working with Greenpeace. Even in her retirement, Nadine kept fighting for strong legislation for safe and sane Spartina weed control and resolving the burrowing shrimp problem without permanently contaminating the water of the bay."

"Hhmm…" said Jimmy. "So that's why Tom called her 'that little meddling Greenpeace gal' at the memorial."

"And why he and Brent got into it in the first place during the reception," added Freddy.

"Brent and Tom have—had—opposite opinions on how to best control both the weeds and the burrowing shrimp," I said.

"Hhmm," said Jimmy a second time. He scratched Priscilla absentmindedly behind her ears.

"Hhmm indeed," said the sheriff as he made several notes. "So Patrick had both opportunity and motive after all."

"But do you really think he drove around with an oyster shucking knife, looking for his chance to stick it into Tom's neck?" I could feel the veins on my own neck bulging out. There was no way I was ever going to be objective when it came to dear Patrick.

"Who shall we put next on our list?" asked the sheriff.

"Unfortunately, I think we have to add Nautika Henry's name," I said.

"Nautika Henry?" asked Freddy, his eyebrows shooting up to his hairline. "But she's such a sweet little gal. Very bright, helpful, kind. What motive could she possibly have had to kill Tom?"

"Right off the top of my head, I can come up with three reasons."

"Three?!" said Jimmy. "She's only been living in Willoopah since August, and she's got three reasons to murder someone?"

"Let's hear them," said the sheriff. He took his right index finger and thumb and stroked his mustache thoughtfully as he listened.

"They may seem a little far-fetched, but when you add them all up…" I ticked them off on my fingers. "One, that skull found out on the bay belonged to John Henry—her father. But until the skull was found, there'd been no evidence of foul play in his disappearance. Now that his death has been ruled a murder, Tom is definitely a person of interest.

"Two, Nautika's mother Julie also died of Non-Hodgkins lymphoma, and back then Tom was—and maybe continued—spraying with nonregulated toxins.

"And three, Nautika and Lorraine have become pretty good friends out there in the tiny burg of Willoopah, and she knows what abuse Lorraine has suffered at the hands of her husband."

"Wow," said Jimmy. "I never would have pieced all that together."

"That's why I called you all in on this brainstorming session," said Sheriff D. "We all have information that may be important to the investigation. Maybe what we know is not enough by itself, but when you add it up, the whole picture comes into better focus." He scribbled in his notepad for a few minutes while Jimmy silently refilled coffee cups. When he looked up, he simply said, "Next suspect?"

"Well, there's Brent Booi," said Freddy. "It's no secret there's been no love lost between those two for decades. Everyone at the memorial will testify to their hatred of each other."

"True," said Jimmy. "Including me and Sylvia."

"And speaking of Sylvia," said Sheriff D. He turned to look directly at me, and his eyes narrowed. "Any reason your name should be left off the suspect list?"

OYSTER SPAT

"My name?!" I nearly choked on my coffee. "Why in the world—"

The sheriff held up his hand to silence me. "Isn't it true that Tom held you against your will in his gear shed a little over a week ago?"

I glared at Freddy, and my next words were only for him. "I thought I told you it was all just a big misunderstanding, and you wouldn't need to bother the sheriff with it."

"I know," said Freddy, without a hint of remorse. "But I also know you and Tom both lied, and that there were plenty of good reasons to believe you needed to be rescued or you wouldn't have moved heaven and earth to send out an SOS."

"So back to the question," said Sheriff D. "Why shouldn't I put you on the suspect list?"

I swallowed hard. I did have good reason to hate Tom, maybe even two or three good reasons without digging very hard, but I'd never resort to murder—unless it was in self-defense, of course.

"You knew Tom was in lock-up because you were with Freddy when I called him," said Sheriff D. "And you knew he'd be getting out the next day."

"But I didn't know Lorraine wouldn't go get him, or that he'd be hitchhiking!" I said belligerently.

"You could have advised Lorraine to just let him walk home," said Jimmy. "Then you might find him out there walking along the road with his thumb out and—"

"James Noble! You're not helping!" I felt my stomach lurch, even though I knew my alibi was pretty rock solid.

"So with your name added to the list, that gives us three women and two men," continued Jimmy. "And as we've already discussed, the downward strokes of the stabbing could indicate a woman over a man, so…" Jimmy pushed his glasses up with his middle finger. "What do you have to say for yourself now, Sylvia Lee?"

But before I could say another word, Sheriff D held up his hands again for silence. "Sylvia, did you have anything at all to do with Tom Diamond's death?"

I shook my head. "Of course not, Carter. Don't be ridiculous."

He laughed. "Do you really think I'd have invited you here to help brainstorm the suspect list if I thought otherwise?"

I slumped a little in my chair as the wind left my sails. "So I'm *not* on the suspect list?"

"Of course not." Freddy reached over and gave my hand a squeeze. "You couldn't hurt a fly."

Maybe not physically, I thought, but I was pretty sure I could inflict some definite emotional pain if Freddy knew where I'd been, and with whom, the night the hurricane arrived.

"Humor me," said Sheriff D. "To rule out any personal partiality, I'd like to hear your alibi."

"My what?" It was clear my mind had been elsewhere, and I was grateful there were no mind readers among the group.

"Your alibi for the day Tom was released from South Bend," said Freddy.

"Oh. Of course." I squinched up my face and thought hard. "The day Tom was released from jail, I was at the Sandy Bottom Coffee Cup in Tinkerstown all morning going over some senior research papers with Felicity and Mark. Then in the early afternoon I came over here to Jimmy's with burgers from the High Tide. So for corroborators I have at least Bim and Geri, who own the coffee shop, Felicity and Mark, respected teachers in our community, Ray at the High Tide, and this little weasel over here—" I pointed at Jimmy, "to back me up."

OYSTER SPAT

"Oh! That's right," said Jimmy. "I forgot all about that."

Now I glowered at Jimmy. "Next time, you're buying your own lunch!"

"Thank you, Sylvia," said Sheriff D. "I had to ask. I wouldn't want to be accused of playing favorites." He smoothed out his mustache one more time for good measure. "So that leaves two women and two men to interview."

"Three in Willoopah and one in Tinkerstown," offered Jimmy. He lifted Priscilla off his lap and set her on the floor. "Scoot now, Miss Priss, our work here is done," he said to the cat, giving her a little pat on her backside.

The sheriff stood up and put his Stetson on. "Thank you all for your help," he said, "and hospitality," he added, nodding to Jimmy.

"Anytime," said Jimmy, who rather enjoyed being 'in the know' whenever possible.

I nearly jumped to my feet. "Are you headed to Willoopah now?"

"Yes, why?" replied Sheriff D.

"I'd like to go with you," I said, carefully choosing my words, "I think at least the women might be a little more candid and open if I accompanied you."

The sheriff rocked back and forth on his heels, thinking. Finally he said, "They might at that. But you'll need to bring your own car."

I readily agreed, having expected a little more of a fight before the sheriff saw things my way. "Thanks, Carter. And don't worry, I'll let you do all the talking."

"That," said the sheriff, "I'll have to see to believe."

I was hoping when we arrived in Willoopah the sheriff would start his investigation, or rather his interrogation, with Lorraine Diamond. After all, if Lorraine caved in and confessed, the investigation would be over, and we could all go on about our way.

But Sheriff D pulled into the parking lot at the Booi farm, got out and was adjusting his utility vest when I joined him. "About the ground rules," he began.

"I'll be seen and not heard, and I won't speak unless I'm spoken to."

I was more pleased than peeved that the sheriff got such a good laugh out of what I said. It broke a little of the tension, and we amicably entered the small seafood store, which was sporting a flashing neon "Open" sign in the window, in a relaxed and positive frame of mind.

Nautika was at the cash register, ringing up some purchases for a couple who obviously had never been this far north on the North Beach Peninsula before. As she was placing their smoked oysters, canned salmon and crackers into a bag with the Willoopah Oyster Farm logo on it, she gave them directions to a park with picnic tables out on the ocean side of the peninsula. They thanked her profusely and left, leaving the three of us alone in the shop. She did not appear at all surprised to see us.

"Let's go talk in the house," she said. Without waiting for an answer, she reached for the power cord on the Open sign and turned it off. "It will be more comfortable."

Inside the house, Nautika sat on the couch with her hands folded tightly in her lap. "I guess now I'll never know if Tom is the one who killed John." Her eyes welled up with tears. "I was hoping by coming to work in Willoopah I could get some answers—and some real closure—about my mother's time here, and about my past."

The sheriff nodded. "I understand."

"Is it appropriate for me to say I'm sorry for your loss?" I ventured.

Nautika smiled wanly. "Thank you."

OYSTER SPAT

Sheriff Donaldson cleared his throat. "I'm afraid I have to ask where you were the day before yesterday," he said, almost apologetically. "We're just trying to get a handle on everyone's whereabouts the day Tom was killed."

"You mean you want to know if I have an alibi," said Nautika. This time her smile was a little stronger, but not much. "I was out there." She pointed out the window to a dredge working out on the bay. "I was working all day with Pedro and Antonio. Pretty much sun up to sun down."

"Thank you," said the sheriff. He nodded his head toward her in appreciation. "And I'm sure Pedro and Antonio will be able to verify that."

"Of course," said Nautika, without the slightest hesitation. "They are both honest, honorable men. Brent wouldn't keep them working here for long if they weren't."

I was pretty certain the sheriff had already mentally removed Nautika from the suspects list, and it came as a great relief. But who was I kidding? I couldn't just sit there like somebody's gagged ventriloquist dummy. "Is Brent out there working on the bay right now?"

"No." Nautika shook her head. "Brent took the skiff over to Elk Island yesterday afternoon."

"Yesterday afternoon?" I prompted her.

Nautika heard the concern in my voice and smiled a little smile. "Oh, don't worry," she said. "He goes over there regularly. He says cutting himself off from the world for a day or two helps him clear his head."

"So when do you expect him back?" asked Sheriff D.

"Well, he only took supplies for a couple days, so maybe tomorrow." Nautika looked out over the water. "Or the day after tomorrow, for sure."

As we looked out at the ominous silhouette of Elk Island, a Coast Guard helicopter flew over. "Routine maneuvers," we all said at once.

Those of us who've lived on the North Beach Peninsula for any length of time are more than grateful we have two fine Coast Guard stations protecting the waters at the mouth of the Columbia River. But it naturally causes concern when we see the chopper out on days they don't regularly schedule their training sessions. Today, however, we knew all was well.

The three of us observed the chopper in silence for a few more minutes, when the sheriff suddenly got an idea. He used his collar radio to contact the county dispatcher, then instructed him in turn to contact the Coast Guard to ask for a favor.

We watched as the Coast Guard, perhaps looking for something that could add a little more excitement to their day, modified their practice drills. They began a mid-bay tightened grid search, with special attention paid to the western shoreline of Elk Island, then the eastern shore of Shallowwater Bay.

When the sheriff's collar radio started crackling again, we learned that there'd been no sign of Brent's skiff, either in the bay, or along either shore.

"But where else would his skiff be?" asked Nautika.

I saw the concern—or maybe just outright fear—etching itself along her brow. "Perhaps he just pulled the boat up away from the edge of the water and tied it to a tree. The chopper wouldn't be able to see it if it's in the trees."

I hoped my words would console her at the same time I wondered why she was so obviously distraught. "Do you know if he has a favorite camping spot over there?"

Nautika nodded. "He loved to spend time in the old growth cedar stand. He says it helps him put things in perspective."

"Well, there you go," said Sheriff D, with more compassion than I would have given him credit for. "The chopper wouldn't be able to see anything on the ground in that area of the island."

Nautika turned to face us and nodded again, looking over our shoulders at the wall clock in the living room. "If there's nothing else..." she began. "I really must get to the grocery store."

"Got a hot date?" I was teasing her about Cliff, who she'd told me on Christmas worked at the Thriftway in Ocean Crest, but somehow, I managed to hit a nerve.

Nautika's face darkened into a glower for just a brief moment. Then she ignored my remark and said to the sheriff, "Do you have any other questions for me, or may I go now?"

"You're quite free to go," said Sheriff D. Then I assumed he was trying to be funny when he ended with, "We know where to find you."

CHAPTER 17

Pulling out of the Willoopah Oyster Farm parking lot at the same time, Nautika headed south into Ocean Crest, and the sheriff and I both turned north, to continue on to the Diamond farm.

As we walked from the vehicles toward Lorraine's house, Sheriff D confirmed my suspicions that he believed Nautika's alibi and she was no longer considered a person of interest in Tom's murder. "Seems like an odd time for Brent to go camping though, doesn't it?" he asked rhetorically.

I'd been thinking the very same thing, but had kept my mouth shut, not realizing that Sheriff D could, or would, come to the same conclusion without my input.

When the sheriff knocked on the Diamond's front door, we heard Lorraine call out "Come on in!" and so we obediently let ourselves in.

Lorraine looked up over her shoulder and nodded to us as we entered the living room. I noted the room was much, much, cleaner than the last time I'd been here returning the kitchenware and wondered if she'd thrown herself into cleaning as therapy, and if so, was it before or after she learned of Tom's death.

She was sitting in a large overstuffed chair facing the big bay window with a cat curled up on her lap. "Sorry I couldn't come to the door," she said. "I currently have a bad case of COL.'"

OYSTER SPAT

"COL?" asked the sheriff, taking a step backwards. "Is it contagious?"

I chuckled. Having been around Jimmy and his cat Priscilla as much as I have, I knew exactly what Lorraine was talking about. "Cat on Lap disease?" I asked with a smile.

Lorraine nodded. "Sourpuss here just hates it when I interrupt her nap to get up from this chair, so unless I have to, I don't move till she's finished sleeping."

"Your cat's name is Sourpuss?" I asked.

"Tom named her," said Lorraine. She sighed. "Nothing but nothing ever pleased that man, and I had to concede letting him name the cat just so he would let me keep her."

What a way to live, I thought. And what a grumpy old man to be saddled with. No wonder she— I stopped myself from following that thought through, despite the fact, as too much crime TV will teach us, it's usually the spouse that did it. This time I really hoped that wasn't so.

Lorraine waved a hand around and motioned us to "sit anywhere" and told us to make ourselves at home.

I chose to sit on the couch against a perpendicular wall, and the sheriff rearranged the furniture grouping by positioning another wingback chair so he could directly face Lorraine as they talked.

"We're here to ask you a few questions," began Sheriff Donaldson.

Lorraine nodded, absentmindedly stroking Sourpuss. "Yes, I've been expecting you."

The sheriff got straight to the point. "Did you change your mind about picking Tom up when he was released from jail two days ago?"

"I thought about it," said Lorraine. "I even tried to figure out how far he could walk in an hour or two, so I'd know where to look for him along the road. But then, if someone had already picked him up, I'd just be wasting my time and gasoline driving up that way."

"What I'd really like to hear from you is a simple yes or no," said Sheriff D. He had his notepad and pencil out and was all business.

Lorraine sighed. "I think what you'd really like to hear from me is a confession," she said.

It's a good thing I was seated on the couch, and a little out of her line of vision, because I think I might have fallen out of any other type of chair and interrupted her train of thought. As it was, my mouth gaped open several inches.

"Is there something in particular you'd like to confess?" asked Sheriff D in a voice that was neither anxious or excited or in any way leading, or misleading, as the case may be.

Lorraine sighed again. A deep, deep sigh that seemed to take every bit of air from her entire body. She leaned down and set Sourpuss gently on the floor next to her chair. "If you'll excuse me for just a moment, Sheriff, I have some clothes you'll need to put into an evidence bag."

SAY WHAT? This was certainly not a turn I'd expected this interview to take, and I looked quickly to the sheriff to see if he were as flabbergasted as I was, but he maintained a pretty solemn poker face. Neither of us moved a muscle as Lorraine got up and quietly left the living room.

When she returned, she was carrying a small plastic bag, tied closed with a double knot at the top. She set it on the coffee table in front of me, and quietly returned to her chair.

"In that bag is the insurance policy I've saved for the past 25 years."

Neither the sheriff nor I said a single word, and later I'd remind him to give me a lot of credit for keeping still right then.

"It's the flannel shirt Tom was wearing the night he killed John Henry," continued Lorraine. "It's got blood on it that isn't Tom's." She paused and looked out over the water.

OYSTER SPAT

"And you know it's not Tom's blood because?" prompted Sheriff D.

"Because he had no open wounds on him that night. I knew once in a while he'd cut himself on the oyster shells, or ram a screwdriver into his hand, or once he even caught his pants' leg on the chain saw bar and nearly ripped himself open, but not that night. There was not a scratch on him." She sighed again.

"I've known all along he killed John. I'm so sorry, I should have spoken up years—no, decades—ago." She shook her head and wiped her tears on her sweater sleeve. "I suppose that means I'm going to go to jail for withholding evidence."

At this point the sheriff had the presence of mind to ask Lorraine's permission to record her statement, to which she readily agreed. In a flash, Sheriff D was out to his Interceptor and back, carrying both an empty evidence bag and his recorder. He took the plastic bag from the coffee table, allegedly containing Tom's shirt, and placed it directly into the evidence bag, then handed me a pen and a tag to fill out and attach.

He set up the recorder, and began speaking into it, noting the date, time, place, who was present, and who would be making the statement. Then he spoke directly to Lorraine, "Now please state your full name and date of birth for the record."

Lorraine did as she was told.

"And now, Lorraine Elizabeth Diamond, are you making this statement of your own free will, and not under any duress or coercion?"

"I am," she replied.

"Thank you," said Sheriff D. "Now please tell us, in your own words, what you know about the death of John Heikkinen, a.k.a. John Henry. And—if you don't mind, I'd like you to go back to the beginning of what you've already told us and repeat what you've said. This time your statement will be for the official record."

Lorraine was very thorough. She'd obviously given this a great deal of thought over the years. She confirmed that Tom and John had often gambled with dice out in the gear shed and even though she'd begged them not to bet with each other, Tom insisted it wasn't much of a gamble if you didn't risk something. Consequently, John owed Tom a great sum of money, which became larger each day.

"I always suspected Tom was cheating somehow," she said. "John never seemed to have a winning streak, and you'd think once in a while the dice would roll his way."

Both of the men liked to drink alcohol after work, and since John lived in Ocean Crest with his wife Julie, he often chose to walk the couple miles into town rather than take his vehicle, "just to be safe."

On the night John disappeared, Tom had come in from the shed a few hours later than usual. Lorraine had already gone to bed. He turned on the light and waved a piece of paper at her, claiming Tom had signed over his share of the Diamond Oyster Farm to "clear his gambling debt," and that they had dissolved their partnership.

The next day when Lorraine was doing laundry, she saw the blood on the shirt Tom had been wearing, and her gut told her she'd best hang on to it. "So then and there I bundled it up, unwashed, and hid it for "safe keeping" behind the paneling in the back of the utility room cupboard. Nobody but me ever went into that room. I'm the only one who knew how to run the washer and dryer." Her voice had a definite edge to it.

"I'm so sorry I never spoke up," Lorraine said. "I knew I couldn't run the farm alone, I had no other skills with which to support myself, and I panicked. Tom never asked what became of that shirt—he had so many that were just alike, I guess he didn't miss it.

"But when John's skull was positively identified, I told Tom I had proof that he'd been the one who killed him, and I was ready to make damn sure he never hurt another living soul on this planet.

"By the time you came to interview us, he'd begged me not to say anything because I was an accessory to the crime and we'd both go to prison for the rest of our lives. He promised he'd never hit or hurt me again, and I... I wanted so much to believe him."

Lorraine stopped talking as several large sobs escaped her. "But then when he said the rumors of John and I couldn't be true because I was so ugly no other man would want me, well, I... Well that was the very last straw, and I threatened to kill him right then and there in front of God and everybody," said Lorraine. "And that's when you, Sheriff Donaldson, had Deputy Morgan take him to South Bend, and... and I never saw him alive again."

Involuntarily I gasped. "You mean you didn't kill him, Lorraine?"

"No, I did not, Sylvia, although I'd fantasized about killing him for many years. I'm not at all sorry Tom's dead, but I did not leave this house on the day he died, and I had nothing whatsoever to do with his passing." She paused, then said for emphasis, "I did not kill my husband, and I did not hire anyone to kill him either!"

Good grief and gravy! My first thought was "poor Lorraine," and my second thought was Lorraine hadn't needed to ever come forward with the bloody shirt, and I hoped that would weigh in her favor when the prosecutor was trying to straighten this whole mess out.

Sheriff Donaldson thanked Lorraine for her statement, and turned off the digital recorder. "I guess I don't have to tell you not to leave town, do I?"

"No, sir," said Lorraine. "I won't be going anywhere. The burden I have carried for so long has been lifted, and I'm willing to face whatever comes my way."

Sheriff Donaldson and I were just getting into our cars when he got a call that Nautika Henry was "being detained" by the manager of the Thriftway store in Ocean Crest. Even through the crackling static of his collar radio I was able to make out that the store manager was sure she was dealing drugs out in his parking lot.

Sheriff D shot a look at me and forcefully uttered just one word. "No."

I scowled back at him. "Yes, Carter. Yes, I'm coming with you. You can't stop me. I go to that store all the time anyway, and right now I've a feeling Nautika's going to be needing a friend she can trust."

The Thriftway parking lot was pretty full when we arrived, and Sheriff Donaldson took the open spot closest to the entrance, leaving me to park out next to the road and hightail it in there on my own. It wouldn't have killed him to wait for me, I muttered, and quickly turned left to the service department as soon as I flew through the exterior sliding doors.

I could see Nautika through a window between the service department and the manager's interior office. She was hunched forward, sitting on her hands. She stared at the floor, rocking herself back and forth, trying, albeit unsuccessfully, to keep from crying. The store manager was behind his desk, typing frantically on his computer. I tried to get inside to Nautika, but Sheriff D filled the doorway, blocking my path. As I came up behind him, I could neither see around him nor hear what anyone was saying.

I cleared my throat. "Excuse me?"

OYSTER SPAT

No one moved, so I boldly nudged Sheriff D and said with more authority. "Excuse me! I need in here, please!"

Sheriff D begrudgingly stepped to the side, and the moment Nautika saw me relief flooded her face. "Sylvia! Oh my god! I'm so glad you're here!"

The manager was explaining to the sheriff that the guy she was selling the drugs to in the parking lot "got away," but he was now scanning the security camera footage for a description of his car, and if he were lucky enough, he might even be able to provide a license plate number.

"Is Nautika under arrest?" I asked the sheriff.

"Not at this time," he replied. Then he shrugged. "There were no drugs in her possession when the manager grabbed her, and no significant cash. "I'm not sure what he thinks he saw, but as far as I can tell, there's been no crime committed."

"Now hold on just a darn minute," said the manager. "I distinctly saw this woman get out of her car, and without coming into the store, she handed off a package—perhaps it was a brown paper bag—to a man in a dark hoodie, who took it and immediately hopped into his car and left.

"This woman had no intention of coming into the store to shop today. None at all. I caught her still sitting inside her car, using her cell phone, and brought her inside the store."

"Nautika," I said through gritted teeth. "Did the manager leave any bruises on you?"

"Now don't you go trying to take the offensive here!" the manager said. "I'm not the one using the store's parking lot as a drop site for illegal drugs. Somebody has to step up to put a stop to this. Somebody has to keep this town free from the riffraff we don't need infesting our community. Sheriff, I demand you arrest that woman!" He dramatically pointed at Nautika.

"Nautika," said Sheriff D. "You're free to go."

She didn't have to be told twice. Nautika leapt to her feet

and quickly followed me out through the automatic door.

Sheriff D was only a minute or two behind us, and we reconnoitered next to his Interceptor. "So what was really going on out here?" he asked Nautika.

"It wasn't drugs," Nautika replied.

"I figured that much," said the sheriff. "So why don't you just tell us what it was."

I reached over and squeezed her hand. "You can trust him, Nautika. He's one of the good guys." She nodded. Cleared her throat. Then abruptly shook her head. "I don't want to get anyone else into any trouble."

"Was it Cliff you met in the parking lot?" I asked.

Nautika gasped. "How did you know?"

I smiled. "Well, I knew he worked here, I knew you were anxious to get here just about the time the shifts change, and I've never in my life seen any woman who'd been working outside all morning stop to clean up and put on make-up before doing her grocery shopping."

Sheriff D rocked back and forth on his heels. "Nice bit of deduction there, Sylvia." He turned to Nautika. "Now please explain your real connection to this Cliff fellow. I know you two were together when we appropriated the skull on the bay, but I suspect you've known him for some time. Am I right?"

"Cliff and I first met at the University of Washington," she said. She looked at me apologetically. "I'm sorry I lied to you. We weren't planning on letting anyone know we'd met before on campus."

I squeezed her hand again. "You must have had a good reason."

"I… I mean we, do."

"Please start at the beginning," said Sheriff D, "and I'll decide whether your reasoning was good or not."

"Geez, Carter, cut her some slack," I said. It was obvious

my wounded mother bear gene was kicking in. Surprisingly, Sheriff D did give her a little space, and said nothing more to Nautika, allowing her to take a few breaths and think about what she wanted to say.

"Cliff was majoring in Environmental Science and Resource Management, and I majored in Aquatic and Fishing Sciences with a minor in Marine Biology, so we were in a lot of the same classes at the U. In fact, we ended up sitting next to each other in Aquatic Invasion Ecology."

She looked from one to the other of us for comment, but we both stayed silent, so she'd keep talking.

"When I got the job with Brent in Willoopah, Cliff wanted to come with me."

"So he's your boyfriend?" asked the sheriff.

Nautika blushed. "Something like that. But mostly, we're just passionate about saving the Shallowwater Bay ecosystem, which includes everything from the native oyster fishery to the indigenous plants along the shoreline. Unfortunately, those kinds of jobs are hard to come by, so for now, he's working at Thriftway to pay his rent."

Sheriff D and I both totally understood peninsula economics. "So what was in the package?" asked the sheriff.

"Just my research." She nodded. "Research on the damage the burrowing ghost shrimp are doing to the bottom of the bay." Her lips pursed tightly. "Hundreds of acres of oyster beds are being lost every year due to those nasty inedible crustaceans."

"If it was just research, then why the clandestine hand off of the paperwork in the parking lot?" asked Sheriff D.

"Well…" Nautika looked at me with her big brown eyes. "First off, I think I owe you a second apology, Sylvia."

"Another apology? Whatever for?"

"It's all my fault Tom locked you in his gear shed last week," Nautika began.

"But how— How did you—" I sputtered.

"Lorraine told me about it, and I'm so very sorry."

"Why would that have been your fault?" asked Sheriff D. He pushed his hat up a little higher on his forehead with his index finger, and stared intently at Nautika.

"Because I was the one who'd been snooping around his farm," said Nautika. "But Lorraine doesn't know anything about that, and I'd like to keep it that way, please. She just said Tom had caught some woman snooping around the farm and, and… Well, it turned out it was Sylvia, and I'm just so very sorry…" Her voice trailed off and ended in a whimper.

"But why do you think you need to keep your research hidden?" I asked.

"Cliff and I were trying to gather enough solid evidence that Tom's been breaking the laws governing the spraying of the burrowing shrimp so that the EPA could get a search warrant for the Diamond Farm."

"I see," I said, although I didn't really.

"Were you actually inside the gear shed over there?" asked Nautika.

"I'm afraid so," I admitted.

"I don't think even Lorraine has been in there for many years," said Nautika. "The door is always padlocked. Tom just tells her that end of the operation is none of her business." Then she brightened. "Did you happen to see anything in there that might help our cause?"

I scratched my head. "Maybe." Closing my eyes, I tried to remember what had been in there with me. Tractor, forklift, totes, HAM equipment, dark 55-gallon drums of something that didn't smell so keen, and of course, those space suits.

I opened my eyes and looked at Nautika. "So how are your Spanish lessons coming?" I asked.

OYSTER SPAT

Nautika frowned. "Okay, I guess. Why?

"There were some large barrels in the Diamond's gear shed. I'm not 100% sure, but I think they were labeled in Spanish. There were words stenciled on the barrels, and over and over there was one word next to a skull and crossbones."

I closed my eyes again. "V-E-N-E-N-O. Veneno?"

Nautika drew in a quick, sharp breath. "Oh my god, Sylvia. If you'll sign an affidavit as to what you saw in that gear shed, I'm almost 100% sure we could get the search warrant right away. Veneno is the Spanish word for poison."

CHAPTER 18

Nautika was plenty rattled about her brush with being arrested on top of not knowing exactly when Brent was returning, and she asked if I'd come back to the Booi farm and keep her company for a little while.

The sheriff was in favor of that, perhaps so somebody would be there to let him know immediately upon Brent's return. On the other hand, he could have just been looking for a way to keep me from trailing him to his next interview—with Patrick.

It only took a few minutes to arrive at the Booi Farm, and the first thing Nautika did was to go out to the main dock and check for the skiff. I hadn't yet had time to bone up on any boat identification, and I still wasn't sure I'd know a skiff if I saw one, but I could tell by the look on her face Brent had not yet returned.

"I need to call Lorraine," said Nautika as we entered the house. She reached for the landline phone in the kitchen. "I hope you don't mind."

"Of course not," I answered automatically. Then I walked to the front windows to give her a little privacy. Once again, I was struck by the beautiful view. What a magnificent, unobstructed wilderness view. I gazed at the uncluttered land and seascape. A person could get lost in their thoughts forever looking out at such an unspoiled pastoral expanse of nature. Whew. I suddenly realized I hadn't taken a deep breath in some time.

"Sylvia?"

I must have jumped a foot when Nautika touched me on the shoulder. "Oh, I'm so sorry," she said. "I didn't mean to startle you."

"No worries," I told her. "I was just enjoying the scenery." I sighed. "Do you ever get tired of it?"

"Not so far," she laughed softly. "But then, I've only been here a couple of months." She walked closer to the window. "It looks so quiet out there today. I hope that..."

I waited, but she didn't finish the sentence. Instead she turned abruptly. "When I told Lorraine what happened in town, she was insistent upon coming over."

I nodded. "How much did you tell her?"

"Only that I was nearly arrested for drug trafficking. She doesn't know I've been gathering information for the EPA, or spying on her husband's business practices concerning the spraying of the burrowing shrimp, and I'd like to keep it that way."

"Do you think Lorraine supports whatever Tom's been up to out there?" I asked.

"No, not at all. In fact, I think she'd be appalled to learn how he's disregarded the environmental safeguards that have been put in place. For 50 years, the shrimp were controlled fairly well by spraying Carbaryl on a rotating schedule every three to five years. But that chemical was phased out a few years ago. Recently, it looked like Imidacloprid would successfully replace it. But then an article came out in the Seattle Times that said our Shallowwater oysters were being filled with residual nerve gas, and warned the city restaurants against using them."

"Nerve gas? That can't be right—can it?"

"Well, technically, the spray paralyzes the nervous systems of the burrowing shrimp, and they sink down in their own mucky mess and suffocate, which is ironic, because the oysters have been unable to survive in an area where the shrimp have been burrowing for exactly the same reason. They can't breathe in all the goo."

"So what's the answer?" I asked.

Nautika smiled. "That's precisely what we're looking for."

We both turned toward the front door as we heard a car drive up.

"But I know one thing for sure," said Nautika. "The answer is not in those barrels Tom's been spraying out there when he thinks nobody's looking. I'll bet you anything the stuff he's using is not even registered for use in the United States."

A knock on the door put an end to our conversation. "Please," said Nautika, "not a word about this in front of Gem."

"But now that Tom's gone, perhaps Lorraine will willingly allow you access to the gear shed."

"Oh! I hadn't thought of that." Nautika hesitated. "Okay, then let's just play it by ear."

Lorraine came laden with two pasta casseroles, a rhubarb pie, a container of leftover Christmas sugar cookies and three bottles of wine. "Since word of Tom's death was made public, I'm being overrun with casseroles," she said. "I figured you gals wouldn't mind us having a little dinner together. You know what good cooks those Catholic women are!"

I was almost taken aback by her rather jolly demeanor until I realized she'd gotten a head start on that wine.

After a surprisingly wonderful dinner, we settled down with our beverages of choice. Lorraine and Nautika were on their second bottle of wine, and I was having a nice, hot cup of tea. The wine had loosened their tongues a little, and I was content to do a lot more listening than talking. It's surprising what a person can learn that way.

"We should toast!" said Lorraine, holding her glass up high. "To the Oyster Women of Willoopah."

"The Oyster Women of Willoopah?" said Nautika. She laughed. "Does that make us the OW OW?"

Lorraine's laughter joined Nautika's. "Let us drink to the Ow-Ow having a Pow-Wow!"

Okay, that was pretty funny, and I started laughing right along with them.

But before things got too out of hand, Lorraine announced she was calling it a night. She stood up, looked out at the mess in the kitchen, and said, "Would you mind if I came back tomorrow morning and helped you clean up?" And before Nautika could respond, she toddled on out the door, singing, "We are the Oyster women, and a-oystering we go…" to a tune I'm sure she was making up as she went along.

After the door closed, Nautika and I looked at each other and busted up again.

"Oh my!" said Nautika, wiping her eyes. "She's a real hoot when she gets a snoot full."

I agreed. "Here. Let me help you get all this stuff put away."

By the time we finished in the kitchen, Nautika's happy buzz had been replaced by one much more somber. Or sober. Whichever the case may be.

"Sylvia," she said, "would you mind spending the night here? It's not that I'm afraid to be alone or anything, that would be silly, but it's just when I'm here by myself, I get too much into my own head and imagine all kinds of horrible things."

I gave her a hug, and she melted against my shoulder. "I totally understand."

"No, I don't think you do," she said softly. "Nobody does. Yet."

I held her at arm's length so I could look into her eyes. "Nautika? Is there something you'd like to tell me?"

She squirmed beneath my hands on her shoulders. "About what? The chemicals? It's not illegal to have them, but I wanted to find proof that Tom had been spraying his oyster beds. You know, my mother died of Non-Hodgkins lymphoma, and I've always wondered if there's a connection to the chemicals they were using on the oyster beds back before I was born." She sighed. "I think I might be barking up the wrong tree, though. The connection just isn't there. Lorraine is fine. Tom is… was… fine…"

Nautika had run out of steam on that topic, so I gently steered her back to the one I really wanted an answer to. "Is there anything *else* you want to tell me? Maybe about Brent? Maybe about Brent and you?" Her big brown eyes got even bigger when they dilated in surprise.

"How did you find out?" asked Nautika.

"I've known something wasn't quite right around here for some time," I told her. "Call it a hunch born of years in the field of Child Protective Services. Now tell me the truth. Have you and Brent been intimate?"

"Brent and me?" She looked truly horrified. "Oh, no… Oh ewwwww!" She shivered. "No, it's nothing like that. It's…" And she abruptly clammed up.

"Go on," I urged her.

"You promise not to tell anyone?"

"If it's breaking the law or endangers anyone's life or liberty, then I cannot promise."

Nautika considered that for a moment. "Okay. But only under those circumstances."

"Agreed."

As prepared as I was to hear of how a man more than

twice her age had taken advantage of her, perhaps maybe providing room and board for certain "favors," I was as unprepared as the only fly on the surface of a pond filled with hungry fish when she dropped the bombshell on me.

"Brent has to come home safely, Sylvia." Her eyes overflowed with tears. "I lost my mother earlier this year; I cannot lose him now, too." She sniffled, and rubbed her nose on her sleeve. "Brent is my biological father."

Bright and early, Sheriff Donaldson arrived at Willoopah Oysters with "no news is good news" concerning Brent's whereabouts. Since Nautika was still sleeping, I took that opportunity to inform him how both Nadine Larsen and Julie Henry had died from the same kind of cancer.

"What are the odds?" asked Sheriff D.

I was ready for his question. "Last year in the US, over 11,000 men and 8,000 women died from Non-Hodgkins Lymphoma," I told him. "So it could just be a coincidence."

"You know I'm not inclined to believe in coincidences," said the sheriff.

"Then what are you inclined to believe?" I asked.

"Nadine and Julie were both exposed to the same chemicals being sprayed on the bay for many years," said Sheriff D. "And chemicals that kill insects and weeds may increase your risk for this type of cancer."

"Yes, but Nadine was also exposed to Agent Orange in Vietnam." I shook my head. "My money's still on Agent Orange for causing Nadine's disease, Carter."

"I suppose you could be right," Sheriff D begrudgingly agreed.

I poured the sheriff a cup of coffee. "This is where Kanji would interject the idea of Occam's Razor," I said. "But since he's not here, I guess I'll just do it myself."

"Refresh my memory," said the sheriff.

"The simplest explanation for something is typically the most likely," I replied. "Which means, in this case, that Nadine and Julie dying from the same type of cancer does not necessarily mean they both got it from being exposed to a burrowing shrimp toxin."

"I'm ready to concede that point," said Sheriff D.

Nautika chose that moment to enter the kitchen, still in her bathrobe. "Oh good! You made coffee." She poured herself a cup and sat down at the kitchen table with us, looking warily at the sheriff. "I take it there's been no news?"

As if on cue, Freddy arrived, rapped twice on the door, and barreled on into the house. "I figured with all the cars out there, I could just let myself in," he said. Then to the sheriff, he added, "I'd like your permission to head over to the wildlife refuge and launch a boat across the channel there to Elk Island to search for signs of Brent."

"What makes you think you can find him if he doesn't want to be found?" asked Nautika, crossing her arms tightly across her chest.

"I'm also part Native American, remember?" said Freddy.

"Tracking is not genetic," I reminded him.

"The island is not that big," Freddy retorted. "Besides, if it's okay with the sheriff, I'd like to take Doobie along with me."

Doobie was Sheriff Donaldson's K-9 drug dog, but since the legalization of marijuana in Washington, Doobie'd been officially retired and living out his senior dog years with Sheriff D.

"Unless Brent's got pot on him," said the sheriff, "I don't know what good Doobie will do."

"I was hoping that Nautika could provide me with a few articles of Brent's clothing so that Doobie can track the scent. Maybe a pillowcase or an unwashed t-shirt?"

OYSTER SPAT

Nautika excused herself and went into Brent's bedroom. When she returned a few minutes later, she was considerably paler than when she'd gone in, but she carried several articles of Brent's clothing and handed them to Freddy. "Will these do?"

"Sure thing, Thank you." Freddy tucked the clothes into an evidence bag, then turned to face me. "You know the cell service on the island is nonexistent, so don't worry when you don't hear from me as soon as you think you should."

Then he leaned over and gave me a quick kiss on the lips. "Don't worry. Got it?"

I nodded, hoping I could control my blush. "Just be careful."

The sheriff and Freddy left at the same time, and I managed to regain my composure. "So Nautika," I said, "you want to tell me what else you found in Brent's bedroom?"

"How do you do that?" asked Nautika.

"Do what?"

"How do you know what I'm thinking almost before I do?"

"Chalk it up to 30 years of watching people under stress," I replied. "Now about whatever it is that took the color right out of your face…"

"Well, for one," Nautika disappeared again into Brent's bedroom and returned holding up a pair of sealed envelopes, "I found these on Brent's dresser. One is addressed to the sheriff, and one is addressed to you, Sylvia Avery, to be opened "only upon my death," and he wrote his signature across each of the envelope flaps like a wax seal or something." Nautika sighed. "I'm not sure about the first one, but I'm guessing the second one is his will."

"That would make sense," I said. "Brent and I go back a long way, and I know he trusts me. So what's for two?"

"For two," said Nautika, "Brent took his pistol with

him."

"Is that unusual?"

"Not necessarily, but it could also mean he's got no intention of ever coming back."

"That's quite a leap, dear one," I said. "You've got yourself a pretty vivid imagination." I took a breath. "So let's take this one step at a time. Right now, there's no question as to what we should do."

I went over and took the envelope addressed to me and stuck it into my back pocket. "I'm hoping we don't need this one for a very long time to come, but the sheriff needs to see the one written to him right away."

Nautika flinched, then nodded. "I was hoping you wouldn't say that."

Fortunately, the sheriff hadn't gone far. The dispatcher informed me that he was signed out over at "Ms. Mercedes" for lunch, "or maybe he said it was for breakfast or coffee..." And after she informed him there was a letter from Mr. Booi addressed to him back at the farm, he instructed the dispatcher to tell me not to open it—he's on his way.

While we waited for the sheriff to return, Lorraine drove by. She honked her horn and motioned for us, so we went out on the front porch to see what she wanted.

She made no motion to get out of the pick-up, and the motor was still running. "I'm sorry to stick you two with last night's clean-up," she said a bit too cheerily. "I'm on my way to the mortician's."

"No problem," said Nautika. "Do you— Do you want someone to go with you to make the arrangements?"

"Thanks, but not necessary," said Lorraine. "Nobody liked him much, so there's no point in having any kind of a service. That man is going straight to hell. He abused me throughout our marriage, and he killed your—your, uh, father. So I just want to get him buried and out of both our lives."

"It's okay," said Nautika, "I told Sylvia last night that John wasn't my dad." She involuntarily looked out across the water towards Elk Island. "And she knows who is."

Lorraine nodded approvingly. "That's good, Nautika. One less secret to worry about keeping." Then she spoke directly to me. "I think we both realize you're good people, Sylvia."

But before I could reply, Sheriff Carter Donaldson, with lights flashing but no siren, appeared on the far end of the street, and Lorraine waved and moved on.

Sheriff D slid his Interceptor into the gravel driveway and bounded up onto the porch.

"Chill out, Carter," I teased him. 'The letter isn't going anywhere. Come on in; have a seat. Have a cup of coffee—I mean if you aren't all coffeed out already this morning."

With a grunt, Sheriff D lowered himself into a chair at the kitchen table while Nautika retrieved another coffee cup. Although he was wearing the same uniform he'd been wearing less than an hour ago, he looked a bit disheveled. And he was definitely short of breath.

"Fine," he said. "I'm pleading the fifth." He shot me a look. "Mercedes sends her regards, by the way."

I smiled. It wasn't often I got the upper hand with Sheriff D, and I chose to relish the moment.

After filling our coffee cups, Nautika handed him the still-sealed envelope, and we sat in painful silence while he read the multi-paged letter. By the varied expressions flitting across his face, and the random mutterings of "I'll be damned" and "Sonuvabitch," punctuating his reading, I could surmise he was surprised, relieved, angry, pleased, and downright flabbergasted. But I couldn't tell exactly what evoked those expressions.

At last, he set the lengthy letter down, took a big gulp of

coffee, and said, "Nautika, do you have any idea what Brent's written in this letter?"

She shook her head. "Not a clue."

Sheriff D nodded. "I thought not." He picked up the pages and shuffled through them. "It's a confession."

"Confession?! For what?! What would he have to confess to?" Nautika tried to snatch the letter out of the sheriff's hands. "There must be some mistake!"

"Afraid not," said Sheriff D. "It's handwritten, dated, and signed, and it appears he wrote it of his own free will, therefore fully admissible according to US legal code, section 3501."

Nautika sat frozen in time, unable to form the obvious next question, so I asked it for her. "What, exactly, did Brent confess to?"

"He confessed to killing Tom."

"NO!" Nautika and I both rose halfway up out of our chairs and shouted the word.

Sheriff D held up his hand for silence. "Now hold on there, ladies, and I'll share the pertinent details with you." He narrowed his eyes at me. "Just let me finish without interruption."

I made a show of zipping my lip, then scooted my chair over closer to Nautika. She was visibly shaken, trembling head to toe, and I gave her shoulder a squeeze of reassurance, before taking her hand for moral support.

"It says here that Brent picked Tom up on the way back from South Bend where he was consulting with another oyster farmer on the burrowing shrimp problem. Apparently, Tom was berating Lorraine, his..." Sheriff D consulted the letter, "his 'ungrateful wife,' for not coming to pick him up. He said he should have gotten rid of her way back when he got rid of John."

Both Nautika and I gasped, but the sheriff gave us a

warning look and we refrained from saying anything.

"After Tom's admission, Brent just snapped. He slammed on the brakes and pulled his truck off at the next logging road. He planned to…" Again, Sheriff D consulted the notes. "…punch Tom's lights out. He came around the front of the cab and threw the first punch. Tom fell, and Brent spit on him. He realized beating him up wasn't going to be at all satisfying, and started back for the truck, telling Tom to get his own ride home."

The sheriff looked up, but Nautika and I remained silent. "But Tom lunged at him, and caught him from behind. Tom was choking Brent, and Brent knew he was about to lose consciousness. He flailed around trying to grab a rock, or maybe there was something in his pocket he could use for a weapon.

"And he found Nautika's oyster shucking knife in his pocket."

Nautika let out a little whimper and buried her face in my shoulder.

"Shall I go on?" asked Sheriff D.

"Yes, please," I answered for both of us.

"He flailed up and over the top of his right shoulder, thrusting blindly, again and again until Tom released his grip. Brent pulled away and immediately saw the wounds he'd inflicted on Tom's neck were fatal. He threw the oyster knife down, disgusted with himself.

"Then he came home, wrote this letter, and one to Sylvia—" Sheriff D glowered at me. "We'll talk about the second letter a little later," he said. "Then Brent said he was going out to Elk Island to spend a last night under the stars before turning himself in. He says his biggest regret is he'll undoubtedly spend the rest of his life in prison instead of on the bay with his daughter."

Sheriff Donaldson paused. "Is that true, Nautika? Are

you his daughter?"

Nautika sat up and wiped her eyes on her sleeve. "Yes, it's true, Sheriff. I was conceived a few months after John disappeared, and my mother moved to Olympia to hide that fact." She took a deep breath. "Is it true that Brent will spend the rest of his life in prison?"

"Maybe," said Sheriff D, drawing his index finger and thumb apart to smooth his mustache while he mulled things over. "But it's also possible that he'd get off on self-defense."

CHAPTER 19

We were still sitting at the kitchen table when the Booi landline phone rang. Nautika picked it up on the second ring. "Hello?"

I could tell there was a lot of static coming over the line, and she was having difficulty making out what was being said. My sixth sense instantly told me two things. First, that the caller was Freddy, trying to contact us despite his apparent lack of cell service. It could be he was still over on Elk Island, but more likely he was on his way back and wanted to check in as soon as possible. Secondly, it was clear the news he shared with Nautika was not good news.

"Thank you... for calling," was all Nautika could choke out before she set the phone back on its cradle. "That was Deputy Morgan," she began. She started to say more, but just shook her head, put her face into her hands, and burst into tears.

I moved to her side and put a protective arm around her shoulders. "Take your time, honey."

She nodded, and fought to regain her composure. "With Doobie's help... they found Brent," she managed to say. "He was sitting by a cold campfire, slumped over and unresponsive. Deputy Morgan thinks it was a massive coronary."

"A heart attack?" said Sheriff D. "Did Brent have a history of heart problems?"

Nautika stood up and motioned for us to follow. "I knew he was dealing with a little heart problem," she began. "But we'd never really talked about it."

In the bathroom off Brent's bedroom, she hesitated, as if afraid she was violating his privacy, then took a deep breath and opened the mirrored medicine cabinet. The shelves were lined with dozens of prescription bottles, and most of them were heart meds. Some were for blood pressure, some for cholesterol, some for water retention—

"Maybe it wasn't such a little problem after all," said Sheriff Donaldson.

"Oh dear." As we returned to our chairs at the kitchen table, I pulled the second envelope out of my back pocket and stared at the instructions to not open it unless it became absolutely necessary. I guess that meant now.

When the sheriff saw what I had in my hands, I swear the top of his head almost exploded. "Sylvia! Just how long have you been withholding evidence in an ongoing investigation?"

"It's a letter to me, Carter. Me! A personally addressed letter. And I haven't opened it. See?" I waved it in front of his face, but he wasn't quick enough to snatch it from me. "So how could either of us know right this moment if this is 'evidence' or not?"

I was nearly in tears myself as I tore open the envelope. I glanced briefly at the multi-paged legal document, then said, "It probably comes as no surprise that this letter contains a handwritten copy of Brent's Last Will and Testament."

Nautika openly sobbed again while I read Brent's words aloud. Naturally, Brent first acknowledged Nautika as his daughter and only heir. So naturally, she would inherit the oyster farm, as he knew she loved the ecosystem there as much as he did, and would fight to protect it. He apologized to her that the community would find out about their relationship this way, and said if he had it to do over, he'd have one heck of a party to welcome her publicly and with very open arms.

At this point, I skimmed the rest of the letter and said, "Nautika, I think most of the rest of this is meant for you." I looked at the sheriff for confirmation, and he nodded. "It's obvious that Brent was one proud Daddy."

Nautika took the letter, and held it to her chest. "I barely got to know him, and now he's gone forever."

"You barely got to know who?" asked Freddy, coming through the front door without even bothering to knock this time.

"My dad," said Nautika without hesitation.

"I thought John Henry died before you were born," said Freddy.

"You've missed a lot," I said, then scowled. "How did you get here so fast?"

"I was already on Sandspit Road coming north," Freddy explained. "But let's back the truck up for a minute... Let's go back to the part about Nautika barely getting to know her father."

"As it turns out," I said softly, "Brent was Nautika's biological father."

"Oh," said Freddy. "OH!" he said again as the light dawned on him. "Oh Nautika, I'm so very sorry..." He looked around the table at all our sad faces.

"Whoa now. Let's just back up another step," Freddy said. "You must not have been able to hear my whole message. When I called, I was coming up from the hospital in Unity." He paused. "From the hospital, not the morgue.

"Nautika, you misunderstood me. Brent—your father—isn't dead. I'm so sorry I gave you that impression. He was transported to the hospital in Unity and the doctor expects a full recovery, but with some permanent limitations on his physical activities." Freddy nodded. "He'll probably have to retire from the day-to-day operation of the farm, but he's going to be fine, Nautika. Just fine."

The speed at which the energy in that room changed 180 degrees literally took my breath away. I dissolved into a heartfelt puddle of tears myself, while Nautika bounced off the ceiling with joy, and Sheriff Donaldson quickly filled Freddy in on Brent's confession.

And just when we were about to get our emotional feet back beneath us, Lorraine returned, saw the two police vehicles parked outside, and decided to come in and find out what was going on. Sheriff Donaldson took this as a sign that it was high time for the sheriff's department to leave us to our own devices, and I knew Mercedes would be more than happy to have him stop by again.

"Can I see you later?" Freddy asked me as I walked him to his car.

"Later? You mean today?" I shook my head. "I'm meeting with your Hospitality Specialist this afternoon to put the finishing touches on the New Year's Eve party at your casino. Or have you forgotten I was helping Kanji with that?"

Freddy scowled. "I was hoping we could squeeze in some quality time together," he said. "December has been such a helluva month."

I agreed. "Between Nadine's memorial, the hurricane and 4-day power outage, the discovery of John's skull along the bay, Tom's... uh... passing, and Brent's near-fatal heart attack, the month needs to end on a high note. Perhaps the New Year's Eve Party can put a positive end on this miserable month."

"And my first New Year's Resolution is going to be to spend more quality time with you, my Sylleegirl," said Freddy. He reached out and squeezed both my hands, and

OYSTER SPAT

looked adoringly into my eyes. Then his kiss, which was happily expected, totally curled my toes, and set my head to spinning, which was kind of unexpected.

"I'm..." I swallowed hard. "I'm really looking forward to that." And I smiled and waved good-bye as he drove away.

Back inside, Nautika and Lorraine had their heads together and were brainstorming in a way that only besties can do. When Nautika looked up, she was grinning ear to ear.

"Sylvia! Lorraine and I are going to be the only two female oyster entrepreneurs on Shallowwater Bay, and we're thinking of consolidating our farms back into just one piece of tideland property. What do you think of the name "Diamond Booi Seafarms?"

"Wow!" I said. "You two certainly move fast!"

"Or maybe you like the name Oyster Women of Willoopah better?" asked Lorraine.

We all dissolved into a fit of giggles, and I gotta say, laughter is certainly far better for the soul than tears any day of the week.

"We're thinking about a new logo, too," said Lorraine. She handed me a sheet of paper with some sketches on it. "It's a large moored buoy channel marker designed with the metal crossbars forming diamond shapes."

I squirmed a little. "You're going to run this all by Brent first, aren't you?"

"Of course!" said Nautika. "And we plan to keep all the symbolic colors of the Willoopah Oyster Farm. The buoy will be gold and black, floating on pristine sea green water with the darker green foliage of Elk Island in the background."

"Black for constancy as well as grief," added Lorraine, nodding emphatically. "Gold for generosity and elevation of mind, and green for hope, joy, and—" she smiled at Nautika, "especially in this case, loyalty in love."

That afternoon at the Clamshell, Jimmy and Kanji were already doing their own rendition of "the battle of the bands" when I arrived.

Jimmy stood next to the refrigerator, shaking his head. His lower lip stuck out about a mile, his hands were akimbo, and he appeared poised at any moment to stomp his foot and throw a major, as in category five, temper tantrum.

Kanji seemed oblivious to the storm brewing, and was holding his phone in one hand, playing a snippet from a 1940s jazz ensemble, and waving his other arm around as if playing the part of a manic maestro.

"Hey guys! What's up?" I said, stepping around Jimmy and retrieving a soda from the fridge.

"Kanji thinks the casino attracts nothing but ancient, toddling, fuddy duddies, and he wants the band to play nothing but oldie-moldy music for New Year's Eve. I, on the other hand, still belong to the hip, slick and cool generation, and those kinds of tunes would put me, and all my young, party-animal friends, to sleep in half a heartbeat."

I scowled. "Kanji, I was under the distinct impression you hired a band for New Year's Eve several months ago."

"That is quite true, Miss Sylvia," said Kanji. "But the drummer—I believe you know him—has graciously allowed some leeway in creating the set lists he will play. He's quite willing to include many tunes from different eras to satisfy everyone's musical taste on the celebratory eve of a new year."

"So Jimmy," I turned and raised my eyebrows at the pouting boy still standing at the end of the table, "what is stopping you from making your pitches for the songs you like to be added to the playlist?"

Jimmy pushed his glasses up with his middle finger.

"Nothing, I guess." He begrudgingly sat down and started making a list he thought "his people" would most enjoy.

"How's everything else shaping up for tomorrow night?" I asked Kanji.

He set down his phone and gave me his full attention. "I believe, my dear Sylleegirl, that you will be most pleased with the way we are ready to usher in a fresh year with a clean slate." His smile was warm and genuine, and it took me back a couple weeks—to the evening of the Crab Pot Tree Lighting—and the things that transpired later that night.

I shot a quick glance at Jimmy, but he was so absorbed in making his tune list he'd missed Kanji affectionately calling me by my pet name—a name I sported on my mustang's vanity license plate, but reserved for only those who were, shall we say, intimately close.

I returned Kanji's smile. "Let's take a look at your party plan, Mr. Kumera."

"I like the way you take charge," said Kanji. "Business before pleasure, then." And as he started to hand me his folder of preparations, he caught my hand and pulled it to his lips.

But before I could follow up on the rush of warmth suddenly flowing to all parts of my body, I heard the unmistakable sound of a Harley 883 pulling around the motel office and into the back parking lot.

"Freddy's here," said Jimmy, without looking up.

Yes, Freddy had indeed arrived. Unexpected, uninvited, and with unbelievably poor timing. Or maybe it was good timing, depending on your point of view. I hadn't told him where I'd be meeting with Kanji today, but it didn't take a brain surgeon to narrow down the options. Either he'd successfully deduced our meeting location, or he'd put a tracker in my purse, and I was hoping it wasn't the latter.

"Hello, hello, hello!" said Freddy, coming through the

interior door.

I had to admit, the guy looked like a young Marlon Brando and an older James Dean, all rolled into one. He set his motorcycle helmet on the counter and unzipped his leather jacket about halfway down his chest before he opened the fridge and retrieved a soda. "Okay if I take the last root beer?" he asked Jimmy.

"Thanks for asking," said Jimmy, "I actually saved that one for you."

Freddy popped the top, took a long swig, and joined us at the table. "I've got some great news," he said. "We've got another thing to celebrate." He stopped talking, like he thought one of us should have to prompt him into giving up what he knew, but none of us fell for the bait.

"Okay, fine. Nobody cares." He pretended to be offended.

When we still didn't beg him to spill it, he finally started talking all of his own volition. "The kids who tried to break into the slot machines during the hurricane have been apprehended."

"Oh my gosh! How did that come about?" I asked.

"Well, we had some welcomed help from two mothers who are doing everything they can to keep their teenage boys out of serious trouble," said Freddy. "God bless moms with integrity!" He lifted his root beer and took another large swig.

"Am I to understand that these mothers turned in their own sons?" asked Kanji.

"Yes indeedy," said Freddy. "One of them overheard the boys talking about not scoring any money for Christmas presents while they were at the casino during the hurricane.

"The mothers had heard us announce a $100 reward for information regarding an attempted break-in in the gaming room. They put their heads together, decided to let them

OYSTER SPAT

enjoy their Christmas at home, but then they needed to teach the boys that they need to be 100% accountable for their actions. So the mothers had the boys both write letters of apology, and they marched them into my casino office a few hours ago."

"Wow!" said Jimmy. "Those mothers should get some kind of medal or something."

Freddy laughed. "As a matter of fact, I had them split the reward money."

"It is very fortuitous that you weren't seriously injured," said Kanji. "Those young men could be facing murder charges on top of everything else."

"What *are* they going to be charged with?" I asked. "Attempted robbery? Assault and battery? Attempted murder?"

Freddy's eyes met mine. "They're not going to be charged with anything."

"*WHAT?!*" I knew my eyes were about to pop out of my head, but Freddy held up his hand to stop me from saying anything more.

"A very long time ago," he said, "I could have been one of those kids. I did some dumb stuff I'm not very proud of, but I was lucky. A mentor came on the scene and intervened and helped me get a second chance to grow up right. Now I'm getting an opportunity to pass that good deed on. The boys, Tim and Jack, are juniors in high school this year. They will be doing 100 hours each of community service, which I will personally oversee, and they will not miss any school from now until they graduate in 18 months.

"And on the off-chance they don't adhere to the terms of our agreement, I can always change my mind and press charges then," concluded Freddy.

While Kanji slowly nodded his understanding, I was still opening and closing my mouth like a fish out of water, and

Jimmy was wiping his tears away with his sleeve, pretending he'd gotten something in his eye.

I swallowed the lump in my throat and very softly said, "And when all is said and done, you're going to pay them for the work they do, aren't you?"

Freddy grinned. "What good is having money if you don't use it to do good?" Then he abruptly set down his soda can and turned to Kanji. "Everything set for tomorrow night?"

Kanji nodded. "Yessir. Miss Sylvia was just double checking our preparations. I believe we are in very good shape for the end of year festivities."

Freddy smiled. "That's terrific. What band did you get to play?"

"It's a local blues band," said Kanji. "They're called the North Beach Blues. They are quite a crowd pleaser here on the North Beach Peninsula."

"A *blues* band?" Freddy looked surprised. "You hired a band to play the blues on New Year's Eve?"

"Don't jump to conclusions," I said. "This is Cliff Evert's band—you remember Cliff? Nautika's potential new boyfriend?"

"Yeah, so?"

"So they don't just play the blues. They're very versatile. They play rock, and country, and songs from the big band swing era, along with the popular top 40 from the radio. In fact, I don't think there are too many songs they don't know. I'm sure they'll be perfect for the diverse crowd that will be celebrating at the casino."

Freddy chewed on that information for a few minutes, then looked at Kanji and smiled. "Forgive me for trying to micromanage. I should trust you've got it covered, from the music to the meal and back again."

Kanji bowed his head, pleased by the praise. "I

OYSTER SPAT

appreciate your vote of confidence, Boss."

Jimmy snorted when Kanji called Freddy "Boss." Freddy and Jimmy are roughly the same age, but Kanji is 5 years older than I am, which makes him 20 years older than his "Boss."

"Miss Mercedes will be the warm-up act in the main dining room," said Kanji. "She'll be playing appropriate dinner music until the boys come on at 9. The band members and their significant others will be treated to a free prime rib dinner before they go onstage."

"Oh," I interjected. "I so hope that Cliff has invited Nautika." I clasped my hands together. "They seem like just the perfect couple."

"Yes," said Freddy. "Those two really hit it off during the Christmas Community Dinner. I think they might have enough in common to sustain a lasting relationship."

I smiled as I thought about the young couple, just starting out. And when I smiled, I was sure Freddy thought I was thinking of my relationship with him, and Kanji thought I was thinking of my relationship with him, but in reality I was thinking only of Nautika and Cliff, who had known each other in college, and had many similar passions in common. Of course, neither Freddy or Kanji knew this, and since I had promised to keep the young lovers' secret safe with me, I did just that, and said not another word.

Jimmy, though, had plenty to say. "Julio is my date for tomorrow night. It's the first time we're actually acknowledging our couple status." He grinned from ear to ear. "So I want to make sure the music includes some of our favorite dance tunes. He handed his list to Kanji.

"I promise to give them this list, along with my own," said Kanji. "I have a few favorite songs I'm fond of dancing to as well."

I dared not look at him at that moment, and circled the

conversation back around. "So Mercedes has the first shift, and when the little old ladies and gents toddle off to an early bedtime, she'll hand over the musical reins so the party can really get started."

"Yes," said Kanji. "That is the plan."

"And speaking of plans," said Freddy, speaking to all three of us. "Did you know that the Spartina Point Casino and Resort has plans to become a major investor with the Willoopah Oyster Farm? I was talking to Brent about drawing up some paperwork last week."

"Better get with the times," I said. "It looks like the Willoopah and Diamond farms are merging into the Diamond Booi Seafarms. Nautika and Lorraine will be calling most of the shots pretty much from now on."

"I'm not worried," said Freddy. "I'm sure they'll recognize a solid business plan when they see it. It's a plan to raise local oyster seed, larvae, and spat for use in Shallowwater Bay, creating dozens of jobs, not only raising the mollusks, but also growing their own algae. Eventually, we'll be looking to export some of our live products to other growers, but right now the focus is on bringing back Olympia Oysters!"

"Olympia Oysters?" I asked. "That's our state oyster, right Jimmy?"

"You betcha!" said Jimmy. "They're the best tasting oysters anywhere. But after the Olympia Oyster became our state oyster, it's been getting a lot of attention all along the west coast and even in Asia." He turned to Freddy. "Oops, I hope I didn't steal your thunder."

Freddy laughed. "No harm done—I ought to hire you to work on our publicity team."

"I think from now on you'll have to have the Willoopah women's seal of approval on those kinds of decisions." I laughed. "They just might have a few ideas of their own."

OYSTER SPAT

"Ooo! Ooo!" said Jimmy, bouncing up and down on his chair. "I could help them bedazzle their oyster boots! We could do Gem's in sparkly clear stones, you know, like diamonds, and Nautika's could be jewels in all the colors of the rainbow."

"I think she'd really like that," I replied.

"Then Lorraine and Nautika will become the true Gems and Jewels of the recovering oyster industry," said Kanji.

Jimmy, Freddy and I turned and looked at Kanji in surprise. Although he had said it with a straight face, I could tell he was quite pleased with his little word play, which had hit the nail right on the proverbial head.

"Good one, Kanj," I said, just to break our shocked silence. Good one, indeed.

CHAPTER 20

"Hail! Hail! The gang's all here," played Mercedes on the keyboard as friends and family gathered in the casino's main hall to ring in the new year. Right from the start, I knew it was going to be a heckuva lot more fun than the last time we were all together, which had been for Nadine's memorial service, a few short weeks ago.

Bim and Geri set the wardrobe bar pretty high when both of them arrived in floor-length sequined ball gowns this year. Felicity's coral evening gown perfectly matched the shirt Mark wore with his smartly tailored suit. Nova and Rich, with Orpha hitching a ride with them from Unity, were only staying for the dinner and would be leaving early, but it was sure good to see them, and they looked sincerely happy.

Even Patrick and Goodie showed up. Patrick wore what he needed to stop calling his "funeral suit," and Goodie wore a full-length taffeta gown. She had Stella with her, Nadine's special needs dog with separation anxiety, with permission to bring her from Freddy as long as she stayed on a leash. Stella wore a little sequined rainbow tie to glam her up.

I was standing with Kanji and Jimmy when Meredith showed up with Lester. Mom had truly outdone herself, literally head to toe in red sequins and feathers, and I wondered if Les had known what he was truly getting into when he proposed to her a week ago.

"Hey Jimmy," I said, with a nod of my head in

Meredith's direction, "I can see who the poster child is for the expression, but do you have any idea where 'dressed to the nines' comes from?"

But before Jimmy could open his mouth to respond, Kanji spoke up. "'To the nines' is an English idiom meaning 'to perfection' or 'to the highest degree,' or to dress 'buoyantly and high class.' In modern English usage, the phrase most commonly appears as either 'dressed to the nines,' or 'dressed up to the nines.'"

"Another theory," Jimmy added, "is that it comes from the name of the 99th Wiltshire Regiment, known as The Nines, which was renowned for its smart appearance."

He glowered at Kanji for stealing his thunder, and Kanji clapped him on the shoulder. "Now, now, Jimmy, don't be upset. I can't let Sylvia think you're the only smart one around here."

I had a hard time keeping from laughing out loud. Men and their egos! "No one will ever match your encyclopedic brain," I quickly said to Jimmy, "but it is nice to know there's more than one educated man on the North Beach Peninsula." And, so help me, I actually batted my eyelashes at Kanji.

Kanji smiled, and nodded his head, acknowledging my compliment with that adorable little bow he does. "Now if you'll excuse me," he said, "I must fulfill my employment responsibilities by making sure all our guests are as happy as you look right now." Then he took my hand and kissed it before disappearing into the crowd.

"He makes it really hard to hold a grudge," said Jimmy. His smile deepened as he saw Julio entering the ballroom. "Gotta run, Syl. Happy New Year." And he, too, left me standing there, all alone, dressed in a shimmering burgundy gown I'd borrowed from Bim and Geri's closet.

Fortunately, I wasn't alone for more than a few seconds

before Nautika found me and greeted me with a tight hug that threatened to break me right in half. Goodness! That gal has some serious strength in her arms!

"Sylvia! Isn't this amazing?" she asked, indicating the champagne-colored balloons and streamers decorating the hall. She glowed with excitement. "I wasn't going to come, but Brent's resting just fine at home now, and he insisted I get out and have some fun tonight."

"Are you here with Cliff?" I asked.

Nautika nodded. "How'd you guess?"

"I figured it wasn't seeing me that was putting such a spring in your step." We both laughed, and I reached over and squeezed her hand. "So tell me, how's Lorraine? How are your plans coming to consolidate the oyster farms? What did Brent think of all your ideas? Did you know that he and Freddy had been talking about the farm's expansion and the casino's financial backing for months?"

"Whoa!" said Nautika. "Let's not talk business—well, not too much—" she laughed. "Let me just say that everything is coming up roses these days out in Willoopah. And yes, Brent has shared with me the idea of Freddy's financial backing so we can raise our own seed, spat, and algae, and I think it's a wonderful idea! Lorraine's totally on board with everything too, and next week we're going to the lawyers and create the Diamond Booi Seafarms corporation, all legal and official."

She grinned ear to ear. "So maybe you'll have more quality time to spend with Freddy when he's not always running out to the bay side to settle any oyster squabbles."

"Oyster squabbles?" I asked.

"I thought it might sound too cheesy to refer to the former disagreements between the farmers as *oyster spats*," said Nautika. She winked at me and we both laughed heartily.

OYSTER SPAT

Nautika went to find Cliff and their reserved dinner table as Freddy appeared at my side for the first time since I'd arrived.

"Hello gorgeous," he said, kissing me on the cheek. "Nice dress."

It had been an inside joke since last March that I owned scant few dresses of my own, so he knew good and well this was another borrowed outfit. I loved the fact we had such an easy relationship—despite our age difference. And I hated myself for always thinking about those dozen or so years between us, since it never seemed to bother him.

"Remember our first date?" asked Freddy. Apparently, he'd been thinking about our relationship history as well.

"I wouldn't exactly call that a date," I said.

"It began right here in this room." He motioned with the hand that wasn't holding mine.

"And it ended with me covered in chocolate from the dessert fountain, literally head to toe, and you putting towels down in your car so I wouldn't damage your upholstery on the ride back to Jimmy's so I could shower."

"Yeah," said Freddy. "Good times."

We chuckled amicably, then Freddy squeezed my hand. "A casino owner's job is never done," he reminded me, as if I could forget. "But promise me you'll save me a dance or two."

I looked into his dark brown eyes and smiled. "Three, if you're lucky."

"That's my Sylleegirl," he said, almost with a sigh. He kissed me on the cheek, then he, too, left me standing there, surrounded by love from every direction, but still feeling a bit abandoned.

Les came to my rescue. "Your mother requests the pleasure of your company at our dinner table," he said. "And she's not one to take no for an answer."

I laughed. "No argument from me on that!" Les offered me his elbow to escort me to dinner. "Les? May I ask you something?"

"Yes, Baby Girl, you may ask me anything you want," said Lester.

When he called me Baby Girl, my eyes threatened to overflow. I'd lived the majority of my life not knowing this man—the man who'd created me with my mother over a half century ago—and now I could not imagine any of our lives without him.

"Les, how did you know Mom was the one?"

Les pulled his elbow in tight to his chest, taking my hand along with it like a one-armed hug. "There's never just one person we could love forever," he said. "A lot of it has to do with timing, and location, and how the stars align at that moment. I loved your mother 'back in the day,' and I love her today, and in between there were others, but I always hoped someday our paths would cross again." He paused. "Why do you ask?"

I shrugged. "Just curious as to how you'd answer. I guess everyone is different."

"When it's time, you'll know," said Les. Then he settled me into the seat next to Meredith and took the chair on the other side.

Dinner was delicious and delightful, as slow-roasted prime rib with creamed horseradish often is. And after strawberries dipped in chocolate for dessert, I was sure I'd be too full to get out on the dance floor for maybe a week.

"Have you set a date yet?" I asked Meredith when I caught her looking at her engagement ring for maybe the 20th time inside an hour.

"Not yet," she replied. Then she smiled. "I was thinking that maybe my daughter and I would like to have a double wedding ceremony this spring…"

OYSTER SPAT

"*WHAT?!*" Every hair follicle on my head stood up at attention. "Mother! Do you know something I don't know?"

"Well," said Meredith, "I'm not supposed to know, but Les never could keep a secret, and I understand that a certain young man has asked your father's permission for your hand."

"No! When? Mom!" My panic button was fully pressed. "Please tell me you're kidding. Please tell me you're just pulling my leg! *MOM!* You can't be serious!" I leaped to my feet.

Orpha, who never misses a thing, bless her heart, turned to Nova and told her she'd decided to stay for the dancing after all, and that she'd catch a ride home with Felicity and Mark.

"If Syl's finally going to get a proposal tonight," Orpha explained, "I'll for sure want to be here for that."

The table starting buzzing with speculation. As for me, I was on my feet, fervently looking this way and that, wondering how I could manage to avoid both Freddy and Kanji for the rest of the evening. Good grief and gravy! I didn't know my heart could pound this fast.

"Where do you think you're going?" asked Meredith.

"I… I… I'm not feeling well," I said, which was, to some extent, the god's truth. "I think I'll call it a night and head home a little early."

"You'll do no such thing," said Meredith. "Now sit your butt back down here young lady, and try to act surprised when it happens."

No! The room started a slow spin, and I edged my way through the crowded tables, hanging onto the backs of chairs for balance, working toward the exit.

Suddenly, Freddy appeared at the very door I was moving toward, blocking that escape route. I took a righthand turn and ducked into the ladies' restroom.

Whew! After splashing a few handfuls of cold water on my face, I felt much better, and my heartrate had slowed considerably. Maybe Mom had just been messing with me. I knew I had not given either Kanji or Freddy any indication I was interested in marriage, which I'm not, so why would they want to press the issue by popping the question? Especially not here, not tonight, and not in front of every single person I'd ever known.

Several women came and went from the restroom while I stared into the mirror and self-talked my way back down from the fight-or-flight adrenalin rush. And as my heartrate returned to a more normal speed, I got a little of my gumption back. I realized there was no way there'd be a proposal tonight, and it really irked me that I'd fallen victim to Mom's practical joke.

Jutting my chin out, I left the restroom and headed back into the ballroom. Mercedes was playing what she called her generic "I'm on a break tape" while the extra dinner tables were being folded up and put away to provide an area to dance. Merc looked my way with a thumbs up and a big smile, and I smiled back. Surely, if anyone had their finger on the pulse of the gossip gals, it would be Mercedes, and she would have told me already if something important was brewing.

Returning to the seat I'd so quickly vacated, Meredith reached over and patted my hand. "I'm glad you've decided to stay and enjoy the rest of the evening."

I decided that was her way of apologizing, and gave her a nod and a little smile. "I just needed a little air. I'm fine now."

Up on the bandstand, Mercedes moved her keyboard to the back of the platform while four young men quickly set up their own gear. The only one I recognized was Cliff, settling in back behind the drum set.

"Now that dinner's over," said Cliff into his mic, "it's time to get this party started!"

His announcement met with raucous cheering from the younger set. I managed to see where Nautika was sitting, and she was bouncing up and down in her chair, clapping excitedly. Good for her, I thought, and I was glad to see her so genuinely happy.

Cliff introduced his three other band members, "plus that little guy sitting on the front edge of the stage," he said. "That's Phillip. Phillip the tip jar."

His corny joke was met with a large number of groans as well as much applause as they launched into their first song, "Blues is My Business, and Business is Good."

By the end of their first set, a nice mix of old and new, fast and slow, I was over my earlier panic attack and really enjoying myself. I'd danced a few times with Les, and with Patrick, and even with a frolicking threesome which included Jimmy and Julio.

During the second set, the evening was running along well enough that both Kanji and Freddy managed to stop at our table for a moment, saying hello again to everyone, and Kanji took Orpah out on the dance floor for the last half of "Love is a Many Splendored Thing." His gesture brought such a tender fullness to my heart that tears welled up in my eyes. What a gentleman he was! How could anyone not love that man?

That sudden thought was immediately intercepted by Freddy coming around with a box of special "New Year's Chocolates," placing one on a napkin in front of each of us with kitchen tongs. When he got around to my chair, he leaned down and whispered, "There's a lot more where these come from," which made me both giggle and feel a flush of heat pass through every part of my body. There was an awful lot to love about this guy, too.

During the break between the second and final third set, Les tucked several bills into "Phillip the tip jar," and spoke briefly to the lead guitar player, no doubt making a song request. The musician looked over at Meredith, smiling and nodding, and she and Les took the dance floor as the third set began.

The song was a familiar 1970's tune by Dr. Hook and the Medicine Show. But when they started the first verse of "Sylvia's Mother," I realized the original words had been changed.

"Sylvia's Mother says, Sylvia's single, so why won't she just tie the knot? Sylvia's Mother says, "Syl, be a grown up, and see what a fine catch you've got. Sylvia's Mother says, don't be so silly, you're not getting younger you know…"

I was a shiny salmon on dry land, my mouth opening and closing and opening and closing, and yet I wasn't getting any air into my lungs, and I thought I might faint at any minute.

Fortunately, the band only played the first few lines before switching into "Jeremiah was a bullfrog, was a good friend of mine…" and the audience erupted into laughter and cheers and refilled the dance floor.

Mercedes, who was now sitting next to me, hoping Sheriff Donaldson might make an appearance around midnight, put her arm through mine and pulled me closer to her. "They wanted *me* to sing that, but I refused."

"Of course you did. You've got more class than that."

"Well, I don't know about class," said Merc, "but I was smart enough to know you wouldn't be amused." Then she excused herself to go get ready for the countdown to Auld Lang Syne. "The guys asked me to join them onstage to welcome the New Year. Wasn't that sweet of them?"

She didn't wait for an answer, and I wouldn't have had time to give her one anyway. Kanji swooped in, took my hand, and pulled me onto the dance floor before I could resist. I must admit that being in his arms felt wonderful, but when our slow and slinky song ended and the band switched to "Beyoncé's "Single Ladies," my stomach started tightening up again.

Naturally, the younger set loved it, and all the single women out there were singing along with the chorus "If you like it then you shoulda put a ring on it… If you like it than you shoulda put a ring on it…" And yes, the tune was catchy, and the alcohol had been flowing, so I just relaxed and went with the flow… Until the band suddenly stopped.

How had I gotten myself into the middle of an unwitting, and definitely unorganized flash mob? When the music stopped, the dancers all pulled back, leaving Kanji and me alone in the middle of the dance floor. He took a step back, reached in his jacket pocket, pulled out a velvet-covered ring box and dropped to one knee in front of me.

Mercedes, back on the bandstand behind her electronic keyboard began hitting the keys in Morse Code: "dit-dit-dit, dah-dah-dah, dit-dit-dit." In English that was an SOS, the international signal of distress, loud and as clear as day, and Freddy came running at top speed.

Before Kanji had had a chance to say a word, Freddy arrived inside the spotlighted circle, and did a rough imitation of Tom Cruise in Risky Business. He dramatically slid on his knees, all the way across the circle, and arrived in front of me with a ring box of his own clenched in his left hand.

"Two men on their knees!" exclaimed Orpha, clapping her hands excitedly. "And both come bearing rings! Oh, this is so much better than staying home and watching the ball drop on TV!"

Neither of the men had said a thing to me yet, no questions had officially been asked, and the clock was ticking. In the nanosecond of uncomfortable silence, Mercedes grabbed a microphone and started counting down to the New Year: "10—9—8—"

The crowd, not wanting to miss out saying good-bye to the old year, chanted with her, "7—6—5—"

Somehow, above the noise of the countdown, I could hear Jimmy yelling, "Eenie, meenie, miney, mo…" While my mother's voice loudly declared, "Just kiss one of them already!"

"4—3—2—"

"I just hope she'll pass her leftovers my way," said Orpha to Goodie, but of course I couldn't hear that, because the room had begun to spin uncontrollably.

"HAPPY NEW YEAR!" yelled most everyone in the room.

The room was instantly filled with the sound of toy horns and confetti and balloons were falling everywhere. The band started playing "Auld Lange Syne," and I knew this Cinderella only had a few scant seconds in the middle of the chaos to make her decision—or make her escape.

I kicked off my shoes, hiked my dress up thigh high, and bolted for the door.

Jimmy and Julio intercepted me in the parking lot. Jimmy handed me my car keys, which I had earlier given to him for "safe keeping" in case I decided to have some New Year's Eve champagne.

"Holy Mother of all oyster spats," he said, shaking his head. "You sure know how to make an exit!"

ABOUT THE AUTHOR

Hook, Line, and Sinker is Jan Bono's fourth book of a proposed six-book Sylvia Avery Mystery Series set on the southwest Washington coast. She's also written five collections of humorous personal experience stories, one self-help weight loss book, two poetry chapbooks, and one book of short romance. In addition, she's penned nine one-act plays, and a full-length dinner theater play. Jan has written for numerous magazines ranging from Guidepost to Star to Woman's World and has had more than 40 stories included in the Chicken Soup for the Soul series.

See more of Jan's work: www.JanBonoBooks.com

JAN BONO